THE
RICHMOND
PAPERS

SAM SIMPSON

SPL

For Nicole

CHAPTER ONE

The Executive Mansion
Richmond
Virginia
2 April 1865

Davis read the affidavit again - astonished the author had recorded his crimes in writing. The testimony was written on yellowing parchment, but the ink, although faded, was still perfectly clear. This affidavit signalled hope. President Jefferson Davis could start again. The South would be reborn, and a new, more powerful Confederacy would be created.

Davis turned to the window. The sound of Federal artillery signalled that eleven states, just hadn't been enough to defend the Confederacy. But he wasn't finished yet, he would meet General Lee in Danville and regroup.

The affidavit was fragile, so he took pains to fold it carefully - gently sliding it, and the letter, into an envelope. Next, Davis picked up the great seal of the Confederate States, holding it firmly between his thumb and index finger - noting the tiny image of George Washington, surrounded by a wreath, made of wheat, corn, tobacco and cotton. The scene was taken from a statue a short walk from where he now sat. It was the place he'd been inaugurated, on Washington's Birthday, only three short years ago - happier times.

Despite the weak sunshine, a lit candle stood on the table by the window. Davis got up from his desk, walked towards the light, and peered out onto Clay Street. Drawing back the lace drapes, he spotted two men approaching the grey neoclassical mansion. The sentry on the door saluted the man in uniform and they entered the building. Davis quickly tilted the candle, dripped red wax onto the envelope, then affixed his seal.

There was a knock at the door. Harrison, his personal secretary, entered without waiting for an invitation. Davis was irritated by the lack of protocol, but more muffled artillery fire necessitated urgency, so he remained silent, as Harrison approached.

'Colonel Le Jeune and Mr Steele are here, Mr President.'

'Show them in.'

'Yes, sir.'

The men entered the room. Le Jeune lazily saluted his Commander-in-Chief. The officer seemed relaxed, bemused, and expectant.

The other man was James Steele - the British envoy. Steele advanced with a look of warmth and offered his hand, which Davis took.

A cursory glance around the empty room had told Steele the order had been given. 'I wish we could be meeting under happier circumstances, Mr President,' said the diplomat with apparent sincerity, 'I take it the city is to be evacuated?'

'Yes,' said Davis. 'I met the heads of department this morning, and relayed the message from General Lee that Richmond can't be defended. I leave with my Ministers for Danville tonight.'

'You intend to fight on then?' said Steele, with mild surprise.

'Naturally,' barked Davis, looking incredulous. 'Lee and Johnston will regroup in Carolina, for a combined attack on Sherman.'

Davis spoke these words with such conviction that the visitors realised he believed them. Surprised, Le Jeune glanced at Harrison who looked away guiltily. Le Jeune studied Davis, and saw the only man in Richmond who denied that the war was lost.

'I must concede though,' continued the President, 'that evacuating the government carries risk - looting, thievery, desertion, that sort of thing. Despite my best efforts, there will be some disorder.'

On his way to the Executive Mansion, Steele had witnessed mobs of drunken rioters and looters. As the city garrison pulled out, Richmond would quickly descend into anarchy.

Davis picked up military orders from his desk. Turning back to Colonel Le Jeune, he drew himself up to his full height, and with an elegant sweep of his arm, handed them to the expectant officer. With a continued sense of ceremony, he reached inside his grey frock suit and pulled out a folded slip of paper. The paper was also handed to Le Jeune.

3

'Gentlemen,' proclaimed the President formally, 'I wish you to make haste and travel to England.' Davis pointed to the paper in Le Jeune's hand. 'That paper empowers you, Colonel, to act with my full authority to that end.'

Le Jeune unfolded the paper and read it.

JEFFERSON DAVIS, PRESIDENT OF THE CONFEDERATE STATES OF AMERICA

To whom it may concern.

All civilian and military personnel, of whatever rank, are to give the bearer of this letter, Colonel Pierre Le Jeune, their total and unconditional cooperation. Colonel Le Jeune, in order to perform the duties with which I have tasked him, has my full authority to direct any and all civilian and military personnel, of whatever rank, as he sees fit.

Given under my hand this second day of April in the year of our Lord, one thousand eight hundred and sixty five.

Signed,

Jefferson Davis

Le Jeune eyed Davis quizzically, 'and with which duties *have* I been tasked, Mr President?'

'Whilst I've no doubt we'll ultimately prevail in this war,' replied Davis, stoically, 'the proximity of Federal troops, leaves open the chance that some of my Ministers, or even myself, may be apprehended when we try to leave Richmond.'

Davis paused, and looked at Steele, but addressed Le Jeune. 'It's vitally important to the future of the Confederacy, that this sealed envelope is taken to London, and deposited in our bank there. Under no circumstances are you to break the seal and open the envelope. You're not to give the envelope to anyone other than myself. Is that clear?'

4

'Yes, sir.'

'When you leave here, I want you to go to the Treasury and present yourself to Secretary Trenholm. He's expecting you, and will issue you with bullion and acceptances up to the amount I've agreed with him. You will deposit the bullion in our bank in London, along with this sealed envelope.' Le Jeune's amused expression increased Davis's irritation. 'Do you understand the gravity of this mission, Colonel?'

'I do, Mr President,' confirmed Le Jeune, forcing seriousness as the envelope was handed to him.

'If you have to make a choice between the bullion and the sealed envelope, the sealed envelope comes first - save that at all costs.'

Davis now turned to Steele. 'I am of course, grateful to your government for the document now in Colonel Le Jeune's possession, but it would've been useful if I'd received it a year ago. To publish it now, will have little or no effect on the war effort!'

'I can only apologise once again, your Excellency,' replied Steele. 'I was despatched earlier, as you know, but unfortunately the Spanish authorities detained me illegally in Havana. Then securing passage on a blockade runner wasn't easy. It was bad luck that after twenty successful runs, the ship I was on was captured by the Union navy. It took some time to convince the Federal authorities of my status, and restore my liberty.'

Davis snorted and gave Steele a separate letter. 'That is for your Prime Minister Palmerston.'

Steele had hesitated before accepting it. 'I've already disclosed to your Excellency, that I'm here in an unofficial capacity. You chose to revoke the exequatur of Consul Moore two years ago, and I reiterate that Her Majesty's Government, doesn't recognise you or this republic. I am, however, willing to convey this letter to the Prime Minister in a private capacity.'

'Very well,' snapped Davis. He continued in a sarcastic tone, 'in a private capacity, British firms have done very well supplying us with the guns and ammunition we need. Now, tell me, in a private capacity, that is, why did your Prime Minister give you the document which Colonel Le Jeune now has in his possession.'

Steele lied. 'I'm not privy to Lord Palmerston's reasoning, nor do I share his counsel.'

The President's expression was fierce, but he restrained himself. 'I would like to speak to the Colonel privately,' he said, with feigned politeness.

Steele nodded and left the room. Davis relaxed slightly when he spoke, 'our London agent tells me he's Palmerston's enforcer, and a trusted advisor.'

'Why do we need him then?' asked the soldier.

For a moment the façade dropped, and a look of despondency crossed Davis's face. The famed belligerency was gone, and he looked spent, hollow, ill. 'Most of our ports have been overrun, our ships seized, and our desertions mount daily. Finding passage to England won't be easy, but if you can get to Nassau, or any of the British West Indies, then he'll have some influence there.'

'But why should he help us?' asked Le Jeune innocently.

Davis flared up again and turned a hostile eye on the officer. 'I've ensured he will. No more questions now, Colonel. Go and do your duty. Collect the bullion and get to the station, whilst the line south remains open. Whatever you do, get that sealed envelope and the documents inside to London.'

The bemusement in Le Jeune's face still hadn't faded, but before Davis could react the soldier saluted and left the room.

Outside Steele was waiting. 'Quite an inspirational leader you've got there,' he said mischievously.

Le Jeune laughed, 'well he's no Lincoln, that's for sure.'

CHAPTER TWO

Norlands House
South West Scotland
Present Day

He'd often toyed with moving his writing desk out of the bay window. When the sun shone from the South - as it did now - it almost blinded him. He didn't care, he loved the view, and knew the brightness would fade when the sun dipped below the tree line. Besides, if he tried to move the desk by himself, it would probably kill him, he was far too old and it was far too heavy.

Although his view across the dale was uninterrupted, panoramic almost, any vehicle driving along the old drovers' road towards Annan couldn't see the house. He knew this, because Victorian landscapers had created an optical illusion, by planting five trees in a diagonal line from the south easterly corner of Norlands. Consequently, the men in the red car parked at the end of the long drive, wouldn't know he could see them.

The old man watched the car edge up the road, as if it *was* looking for the house. Other than the occasional tractor, there was rarely traffic in this part of rural Dumfriesshire, so the car could take its time, stopping frequently, starting again, looking for gaps in the tree line which would reveal Norlands in all its splendour.

Along with everything else, his eyesight was failing, so he was tempted to grab the binoculars which were on the table at the far end of the library. It took a tremendous effort to get up from his seat, but he could see the red car had stopped again, so curiosity got the better of him. Placing one wrinkled palm face down on the leather inlay of the desk, he reached for his walking stick, and pulled himself up out of the green upholstered chair. His vision blurred briefly as he stood - there was little power left in his arms, and even less in his legs, so he swayed unsteadily from side to side as he fought to gain his balance.

'Time I was in the knackers' yard,' he thought, as his head cleared and he staggered away from his desk. He picked up the binoculars and returned to the bay window, resting them on the sash. It took a minute to find the car because it had moved past the driveway, and there was further delay as his stiff fingers toiled with the dials to bring the image into focus.

The car was one of those big, old style Jaguars, and in it were two men. Although the distance was too great to see them clearly, one of the men appeared to be pointing to where he thought Norlands should be. From where they were parked, the old man knew all they could see were trees, but they must have had directions, because he saw the car stop, then reverse slowly back up the road. The old man lost sight of it behind a dry stone wall, but the vehicle reappeared at the bottom of the long drive, then picked up speed as it headed towards the house.

Leaving the library, the old man hobbled slowly to the front porch. He opened the glass inner door, then stopped for breath, before shuffling a few steps to the oak door. The hinges were recently oiled, so the door swung open noiselessly to reveal the Jaguar, crunching to a halt on the gravel.

A man in a blue suit got out of the passenger side. He was in his mid-Forties, had lanky black hair, pale brown eyes, and a fixed sneer. There was a large gold ring on one of his long thin fingers - there was a motif on the ring.

The visitor looked up at the porch and saw, framed by the door, an old man shielding the sun from his eyes. The old man was dressed in a tweed jacket, blue shirt, and red corduroy trousers. The old man's thick white moustache matched his thick white hair, which was combed neatly to the side, and held in place with a touch of Brylcreem. The old man was very elderly, but even from that short distance; his pale blue eyes pierced the visitor with a sharp, ferocious intensity.

Switching off the engine, the driver clambered out. He was huge, six foot tall, barrel-chested - wearing jeans, a t-shirt, some heavy-looking boots and black gloves. He had a shaved head, a stud in one ear and a string of tattoos running up both arms. The old man saw one tattoo was a flag which he recognised. The driver slammed the car door and started walking towards the house.

The old man was worried – he would talk to them from behind the chained door. He stumbled backwards and pushed the door with all his strength. He saw through the narrowing gap, the thug was running, and he pounced at the closing door with cat-like speed. The old man smiled to himself, as he heard the lock click and the thug shout, 'you motherfucker,' through three inches of solid oak.

The intruder had an American accent, which reminded the old man that he'd seen the flag on a car, in some 1980s TV show - the sound of gravel crunching under foot, meant the men were trying to get in, so the flag, was for now, forgotten.

The old man's heart was thumping as he turned and shuffled back through the porch. Defensively he knew his options were limited. The house was isolated, and his best hope of getting help was the phone, but that was in the kitchen. Could he make it?

The kitchen was at the far end of the house, and as he trundled along the tiled hall, he realised the back door would be unlocked - every day, when the housekeeper left, she never locked it. As he opened the kitchen door, he saw a shaved head appear at the pantry window, then the back door was open, and they were in the house.

The old man retreated along the hall, and felt in his pocket for his keys. He quickly found the smallest, and slotted it first time into the lock of his mahogany gun cabinet. He heard the kitchen door opening behind him, but he'd already let his walking stick fall to the floor and snapped shut his Purdey. He nestled the Turkish walnut stock into his armpit, leant against the cabinet for support, and swivelled towards the men. The sound of the barrel snapping shut, stopped the intruders barely eight yards away.

After a few seconds of silence, the man in the blue suit moved slowly out from behind the thug, to stand at his side.

'Stay where you are,' barked the old man, swinging the gun to cover both men, and flicking off the safety catch. There was a further short silence.

'I thought you Brits weren't allowed guns,' said the blue suited man sarcastically, in an educated southern drawl.

'Who are you and what do you want?' the old man asked. There was no reply this time; the men just looked at him, as the gun trembled in his hands. His arms were already weakening, and the end of the barrel began to dip - he couldn't hold the Purdey for much longer. The intruders began to inch forward.

'Stay where you are,' the old man said again, jerking the barrel upwards, and making them pause once more. The old man scanned the hall, and saw the red burglar alarm sensor, blinking at him. The control panel was to his right - if he activated it, a police car would be at Norlands in twenty minutes.

The old man looked at the panel again, and took a few steps towards it. The thug saw his chance and darted forward. The old man half turned, but he was too slow, and the thug's gloved hand was on the barrel. The loud click of the hammer on an empty chamber, signalled the end of the encounter. The thug used the gun to push the exhausted old man into a chair, before yanking the weapon from his grip, and dropping it on the floor.

'Well, I must say that wasn't very welcoming, Mr Steele,' said the blue suited man with a lazy smile. He walked over to the chair, and placed his hands on the shoulders of his tweed jacket.

The old man looked up at the face of his attacker and didn't see anything he liked. 'You seem to know my name young man, what's yours?'

The man in the blue suit ignored him and looked at the thug. 'Take a look around, Travis.'

Travis disappeared into the library and returned immediately. 'Looks like his office is in here.'

'Let's move him in there' said the suited man, lifting his hands from Steele's shoulders, and walking into the library.

Travis half carried, half pushed, the old man into the library, and dumped him in the desk chair.

The suited man walked into the bay, and stood looking out of the window. He had his back to the room when he spoke. 'A lovely view - I bet you've spent hours watching the world go by from here.' The man turned to face Steele. 'It's a long time to keep a secret. Time I unburdened you. My cousin has passed the torch to me, and you must do the same. I must have everything which relates to this sorry saga. He paused, 'please,

please, be sensible, I urge you....' The suited man looked over to the thug, '... as you can imagine, Travis here, can be very persuasive.'

'If I said I hadn't a clue what you're talking about, would it make much difference?'

'Come come now, Steele - a grand house like this, lavishly furnished. Where did the money come from?'

'This isn't my house. It's my great grandson's. He was given it. He's the one with money, if that's what you're after.'

The suited man smiled cruelly and drawled, 'is that right?' He nodded at Travis.

The old man's head dipped, then righted again, as he looked at the Americans. A resigned smile broke across his thin lips. But the old man wasn't finished yet. For years, he'd infuriated the housekeeper, by refusing to wear his panic button around his neck. The device now hung from his umbrella, a mere two feet away, its huge red button enticing him to lunge.

'Yes, I can see your dilemma,' said the old man, as he gripped the desk and pulled himself onto his feet. 'I'll tell you what I would do if I was in your position.'

'What's that?' answered the suited man, shifting on the carpet.

'Go to hell.'

The old man reached across the chair, grabbed his umbrella, and swung it round with all his strength. He caught the suited man on the jaw with the sharp metal point, lacerating the skin. The American's head jerked back sharply, as the umbrella flew out of the old man's hand and onto a table, sending a full decanter and a board game crashing to the floor. Instinctively,the intruder's hand flew up to his face, and clamped down on the bleeding flesh.

'You stupid old bastard,' he screamed, his hair now hanging untidily across his forehead.

The old man ignored him, and bent forwards towards the panic button on the floor. As he moved, Travis stepped forward and lashed out with a clenched fist, landing a ferocious punch above the old man's right ear, driving his head against the corner of the desk. The head bounced off with a soft thud, and Steele crumpled to the ground, lying with his head twisted at an awkward angle, facing the window.

A defence lawyer would have called it manslaughter; a crown prosecutor would have called it murder. Either way, John Steele, didn't care, because he was dead.

CHAPTER THREE

Clinton Street
Washington Square West
Philadelphia
Present Day

The Good Karma café was empty, so Mackay bought coffee, and was back on Clinton Street within five minutes. Glancing up, he appraised his house as he approached. Two storeys of red brick, with enormous windows flanked by green shutters, looked Dutch - the street could be in old Amsterdam. The house dated from 1850, and although he knew the Dutch had been swept away by the British, long before then, it was clear their influence still lingered.

He skipped up the four steps to the front door, juggling coffee, pastries and keys. The sound of CNN from the kitchen implied Sally was up. She was dressed and watching the monitor. She turned to face him as he proffered the pain au chocolat and latte. She was petite, curvaceous, and very, very attractive. Her hair was discreetly highlighted and loosely bobbed - her huge blue eyes simply drew him in.

'Thanks,' she said flatly, indicating with a tilt of her head that he should look at the screen.

Mackay glanced at the crawling text. 'How many dead?'

'Twenty, they think, and as many again injured.'

'Where?'

'Somewhere in Texas - on a campus.'

Another mass shooting, thought Mackay. Since he'd moved to America to be with Sally, he'd been astonished how often these incidents happened. The worst atrocities had, of course, been reported in the British press, but the gun crimes with fewer casualties, stayed under the international radar.

'I really don't understand why you people don't get a grip on this. That there needs to be more gun control is stating the obvious.'

Her expression softened as she took him in her arms. 'We can't, and it's all your fault.'

'My fault?' he exclaimed.

'Yes, you, the British,' she said mischievously. 'The Second Amendment to the Constitution - it gives us the right to bear arms. This is because you, the British that is, tried to disarm us prior to the Revolution. It's a safeguard against Government tyranny.'

She was really sharp, thought Mackay. No surprise given she was the daughter of a Supreme Court Judge.

'Ok, fair enough,' he said, 'but that was over two hundred years ago. We aren't going to try and disarm you now. Countless murders must surely mean it has to be repealed.'

She smiled sweetly at him, as if he was the village idiot. 'Doesn't quite work like that here. The Founding Fathers made it difficult to change the Constitution, and its Amendments.'

'A simple act of Parliament is all it'll take,' said Mackay, 'followed by Royal assent.... or Presidential assent I should say.'

She laughed at him and kissed him lovingly on the lips. 'You really are no lawyer, are you? First, you need two thirds of Congress, that's the Senate and the House of Representatives - bit like your Houses of Commons and Lords - to approve a reform. Then, three quarters of the States need to ratify any changes approved by Congress. To get Congress, the States, and the President to align behind an issue is tricky at the best of times - impossible over something like gun control.'

'I see the difficulty,' pondered Mackay, 'is there really no other way?'

A look of intense concentration was flowering on her face, 'there is one other way.'

'Oh,' replied Mackay, transfixed by her brains and beauty.

'A constitutional convention.'

'A what?'

'A constitutional convention,' she repeated, 'it could delete the Second Amendment.'

'How often do these happen?'

14

'Not very often,' she grinned, 'the last one was in 1787, just round the block from here, in Independence Hall.'

'Maybe you could ask your boss whether it's something she might be interested in?'

'I will,' said Sally, picking up her bag and heading to the door. 'Whether it would derail her campaign is another question.'

'Or it might galvanise support. I thought Democrats would welcome more gun control.'

Sally turned to face him, 'moderates do. But there's a big leap between that, and a Democratic President promoting abolition of the Second Amendment.'

She opened the door and as it swung back he could hear, 'let's get her elected first,' echoing back at him.

Then she was gone.

A few years ago, Mackay had acquired independent means. That was why he was now, in Philadelphia – sitting in his two million dollar house - supporting his girlfriend's campaign to get Ruth Callaghan elected as President. He was happy, content - in their own way they were trying to change the world for the better.

His cell rang and he picked it up. He could see the call was from his father and knew instantly something was wrong - it was the middle of the night, UK time.

'Tom.'

'Yes, Dad.'

'Bad news!'

'Go on.'

'Your great grandfather is dead. You need to come home.'

CHAPTER FOUR

Perrier Street
New Orleans
Louisiana
Present Day

The land and estates may have long gone, but the Le Jeune family home in uptown New Orleans, was still an impressive building. Painted lilac, with small Doric pillars, it was a century old French inspired plantation house, in miniature.

The Congressman knocked at the door and waited. Meeting constituents in their homes was rare, but the Le Jeunes were an old Louisiana family, and Miss Le Jeune was friendly with his mother. He knocked again and hoped for silence. After a decent pause, he began to retreat to the road, but a loud click signalled the door was opening.

He spun round and saw the face of his mother's friend. 'Rebecca, good to see you again. I should have reached out to you earlier, but it's been busy, what with the election and all.'

'I understand,' the old lady replied warmly, 'come in David, come in.'

The Congressman followed her through the foyer into the panelled salon, and took the seat she indicated. Scanning the room, he saw it was unchanged from his last visit. It was crammed full of three centuries of the Le Jeunes. Dusty paintings of French colonists and fading photos of Confederate Officers, fought for space with sepia images of Notre Dame and the River Seine.

She took the seat opposite and clasped her hands together, appraising him rigorously, every bit the elderly school mistress about to interrogate an errant pupil.

He shifted his weight nervously in the chair. Did she know something? He'd been very discreet.

'Your mother well, David?'

'Very well, thank you,' he paused, 'she's still frightening the members with some of her tee shots off the first.'

She smiled warmly at his weak humour. Was the blow about to fall he thought? Nothing went on in New Orleans society without her knowledge. He remembered she'd always been direct, and this occasion was no different.

'I have a favour to ask you,' she began, 'it relates to some instructions given to me by my late father.'

'Oh,' he said, relieved.

'On his death bed he gave me this.'

She delicately handed him an aged envelope, blank on the front, but fixed at the back with a wax seal. He glanced at the image but couldn't place it.

'It's Jeff Davis's mark,' she declared, answering his thoughts. 'He gave it to my grandfather the day he left Richmond in 1865. It's an important document.'

'What is it?' He was curious now. 'Let's open it?'

'No,' she said sharply, retrieving the envelope from his hand. 'Only the President can read it. You must contact the President and I must give it to him.'

He sat back in his chair and examined her more closely. She could be ninety he thought, but she wasn't frail, and her mind was quick. 'Why must you give it to the President?' he asked, with an effort at sincerity.

'Jeff Davis gave this envelope to my grandfather for safekeeping. My grandfather was to hold onto it and keep it sealed until Davis or his successor asked for it. The information in the envelope was to be used to rebuild the South, after the Civil War. Of course, Davis never came and my grandfather gave it to my father with the same instructions. Now I'm the last of the Le Jeunes, and I have cancer.'

The Congressman smarted at this. He looked at her closely; she seemed to be in rude health. 'I'm very sorry to hear that, Rebecca.' After an awkward moment, he continued. 'I'll do my best to get you to see the President.'

'But David, I must see him,' she said vehemently, 'this is a very important document.'

17

'How long have you got?' he asked.

'Only a few months.'

The politician sighed. 'I really will do my best, but getting to see the President isn't easy, even for a Congressman.' He reached forward and clasped her hands. She felt vital, alive, vibrant. 'I promise.'

She looked into his eyes and believed him.

The Congressman was used to making promises he didn't keep, but this felt different. He released his grip. 'Now, is there anything else I can do for you?'

In his office the next day, the Congressman regretted his promise - he was wasting his time - it was humiliating. Asking the President to meet one of his constituents, so an old envelope sealed by Jeff Davis could be opened, was ridiculous. The Congressman was going to look foolish.

Rather than embarrass his secretary, the Congressman made the call to the White House himself, and explained to an aide as best he could the purpose of his call. When the awkward conversation ended, a sense of virtuousness swept over him. A promise to an old family friend discharged, case closed.

Later that afternoon, the Congressman's personal cell rang, caller unknown.

'Yes,' he said, a little apprehensively.

'Congressman, this is FBI Director, Wade Andrews.'

Instantly he knew the purpose of the call - he was astonished. 'What can I do for you, Director?'

'Your call to the White House this morning - I'm afraid it won't be possible to schedule a meeting for your constituent.'

'I thought not,' replied the Congressman, half relieved. 'I'll let Miss Le Jeune know.'

There was silence for a moment, before the Director, authoritatively, began again. 'If you could tell me all you know about Miss Le Jeune and this sealed envelope, I'd be grateful.'

'Of course, Director,' replied the Congressman submissively.

The Congressman relayed the details of his meeting, stating all he knew about the Le Jeune family history - he gave Andrews the provenance he was looking for.

'That is helpful, Congressman,' concluded Andrews. 'No need for you to contact Miss Le Jeune again over this, or for you to concern yourself any further with this matter. I'll deal with this myself.'

Andrews's request sounded like an order. 'If you think that's best, Director.'

'I do Congressman. Thank you for your service.'

Director Andrews hung up. He opened the fat dossier on his desk marked, 'The Richmond Papers'. The file had been assembled by J Edgar Hoover, but some of the papers were earlier than 1924, predating when Hoover himself took office. Only FBI Directors had access to this file, fewer than a dozen men had ever known its contents; Andrews doubted whether many Presidents, had even known of its existence.

Andrews thought for a moment about his FBI predecessors, six still lived. One of them, a centenarian, was succumbing to dementia, which was a risk. He looked at Hoover's looping handwriting and read his last entry, dated 1 May 1972, just a day or so before his death. Hoover had spent fifty years hunting for the Richmond Papers, could they really have landed in Andrews's lap so easily?

CHAPTER FIVE

Norlands
South West Scotland
Present Day

The view from Norlands took in all of Annandale's luscious green beauty. To the south, Mackay could see across the Solway Firth to the Lake District. The flat, table top hill to the east, he knew to be the site of Burnswark Roman Fort, and to the west, across the cattle filled fields, and partially obscured by a wood, was the old drovers' road to Annan.

Mackay's sister was late for her train and he saw his parents' Volvo speed down Norlands's long drive. As the Volvo joined the main road, it passed a parked red car, before picking up speed on its way to the station. Mackay was relieved when his parents had agreed to live in Norlands. With his great grandfather gone, there was no one else to look after the place.

The funeral had been a low key affair. At his advanced age, most of John Steele's friends were already dead, and Mackay's family was small. The wake was over, and with his parents' departure, Mackay was left alone in the house. He regretted that Sally had decided to stay in Philadelphia, to focus on the campaign, but as she barely knew his great grandfather, he understood.

Mackay looked around the library and imagined the old man's last moments. An accident the police had said. 'The elderly fall and knock their heads all the time, sir,' the sergeant had asserted, a little too flippantly, but Mackay was uneasy. He'd visited the house only a few months ago, and sensed that whilst things appeared to be in the right place, they weren't, quite. The room felt disturbed. The whisky decanter, which sat on the table by the old board game, was missing. And the game itself, a Christmas favourite designed by a relative, wasn't set up right. All the pieces were in the wrong starting positions, and the card decks faced the wrong way - only a Steele or a Mackay would know the correct configuration. Why would anyone bother to put them back at all, he thought, as the board had been upended by his falling grandfather?

Somehow the library felt wrong. The corner of the desk, where blood had been found, was some way from the table where the game was, and where the decanter had been - the old man needed to be a contortionist, to knock the table then bang his head the other side of the desk. Mackay had dealt with unusual deaths before, and he sensed this could be another. He took some photos with his phone, and resolved to contact the police again.

The sound of high revs and a grating change of gear, caused him to glance at the window. An old Ford Escort had turned into the drive and was screeching towards the house. The racket had disturbed the parked red car, which pulled out onto the road and hurried away. The Escort accelerated towards the house, its screaming engine alarming the pheasants, rabbits and cattle, in equal measure.

Fearing for a moment that the car was going to hit the porch, Mackay started up, but the driver applied the brakes and sent a shower of gravel rattling against the brickwork like grapeshot.

The door flew open with a loud crank, and an uncoordinated blend of tweeds, oranges and denim bundled out. The woman's flowing scarf was far too long, and almost garrotted her as she launched towards Mackay. She unhooked it from the steering wheel and smiled at him foolishly.

'Tom Mackay?'

He nodded.

'I'm very sorry to hear about your grandfather.' She paused. 'Did he mention me at all?'

Mackay appraised her. She could have been anywhere between forty and sixty. Her mass of curly long hair was silvery, her cheeks ruddy, and her round glasses, scholarly. She didn't seem like his grandfather's type.

'Mary Coggins,' she continued, 'from the family history society.'

Mackay vaguely recalled his great grandfather working with someone on a family history project, so he showed Coggins into the library. 'Can I get you anything?' he asked, 'tea, coffee, a dram?'

She shook her head.

'Plenty of food in the kitchen - the buffet was largely untouched.'

She nodded, and he returned a minute later with a plate of egg sandwiches.

'I'm very sorry to intrude, but I have to speak to you before you go to America,' she said quickly.

Mackay could see she was emotional - she would have spent a lot of time with the old man - she had been John Steele's friend. 'We should've asked you to the funeral,' Mackay said kindly.

'Your mother did invite me, but I didn't want to intrude.' Coggins looked at the desk. 'I'm surprised he fell like that, he always seemed so sprightly.'

Mackay glanced at the board game suspiciously. 'Yes, it's a shock.' She waited for him to continue. 'Now, what is it you wanted to see me about? The history project you were both working on?'

'That's right.. Absolutely fascinating. John and I had such fun. We discovered that, James Steele, he'll be your...now, let me see...your... great...great...great grandfather, was widely travelled. He was a diplomat of sorts, at the height of the Empire. A sort of trouble-shooter for Lord Palmerston.'

Mackay thought back to his school history lessons. He recalled that Palmerston, was the Prime Minister most noted for furthering British interests via liberal use of the Royal Navy, a policy known as 'gunboat diplomacy.' Mackay wasn't surprised that Palmerston was out of fashion with modern historians.

'James Steele left extensive diaries and journals,' continued Coggins, 'he documented most of his travels, but there are gaps. The biggest void is his time spent in America, during their Civil War.'

'What was he doing there?' asked Mackay, his interest piqued.

'Up to no good for Palmerston most likely. We know he was in Richmond the day before it fell to Union forces. From there he travelled south with a Confederate officer, on a train heaving with gold bullion.'

Mackay raised his eyebrows, 'gold bullion?'

'Gold bullion,' she repeated excitedly. She could see he was hooked, the way his great grandfather had been. 'We traced their route through Virginia, the Carolinas and Georgia, then onto Florida.'

He was impressed. 'How did you do that from here?'

'Meticulous research,' she replied, beaming from ear to ear. 'Local newspapers, online libraries, lengthy correspondence with American history societies, that sort of thing.'

Mackay imagined the two of them seated in Norlands's library, peering at computer screens, opening letters, fist pumping the air when some elusive piece of the jigsaw fell into place.

'Your ancestor and this officer made fairly good progress south, not without some mishaps mind you.'

'What sort of mishaps?' quizzed Mackay.

'Run-ins with Union cavalry, encounters with Confederate deserters, desertions from their own escort, blocked rail lines, broken trains…I could go on,' she paused, 'it was a miracle they made it unscathed.'

'And that was fairly good progress?' said Mackay, bemused.

She finished her sandwich and continued. 'Things began to unravel, when news of Jeff Davis's arrest reached them. By then, they weren't that far from Florida's Atlantic coast, a place called Gainesville.'

'Remind me, who was Jeff Davis?'

'He was the Confederate President.'

Mackay was enthralled, 'then what happened?'

'Unfortunately the trail goes cold. No mention of the train in any Florida newspapers. We drew a blank with the local history societies. No one seems to have recorded anything.'

Mackay took a sandwich from the plate and nibbled at the crust.

Coggins opened the drawer of the desk and took out a map of the US. 'Since you live in America, your great grandfather was going to ask you to visit Gainesville, to see if you could find out what happened next.'

Mackay had never been to Florida and was intrigued. He didn't hesitate. 'I'll do it.'

She smiled at him warmly.

'Now, Mary, you'll need to show me your research. I want to understand everything.'

It was beginning to get dark outside and cold in the library. Mackay went to close the curtains and noticed the red car he'd seen earlier. With the light fading, he saw the flash of a lighter followed by the dull glow of a cigarette - he felt a little uneasy.

CHAPTER SIX

Perrier Street
New Orleans
Louisiana
Present Day

A nosey neighbour, on the south side of Perrier Street saw three black SUVs with darkened windows, pull up outside the lilac painted house, which belonged to Rebecca Le Jeune. Two suited men got out of the leading vehicle. The taller of the two men, whom the neighbour vaguely recognized by virtue of his striking white hair, knocked at the door. 'What has Rebecca been up to?' thought the neighbour, 'those men look like the FBI.'

Rebecca Le Jeune opened the door.

'Miss Le Jeune,' said the man warmly, 'please don't be alarmed. My name is FBI Director, Wade Andrews. Your local congressman asked me to look at a sealed envelope you have. May we come in?'

'But....but, I wanted to see the President,' she protested, feebly.

'The President has asked me to look into this matter,' lied Andrews, effortlessly. He took her gently by the arm and guided her to a chair. 'Now, if you could show me where this envelope is, I'd be most grateful.'

She scrutinized him. Something wasn't quite right - she felt like a criminal. 'No,' she said, regaining her courage. 'I must give the envelope to the President. Now, please leave my house.'

Andrews frowned. 'I'm afraid I don't need your permission, Miss Le Jeune. I have a Federal warrant here.' He showed her the warrant and she sat back in her chair. Andrews's expression softened. 'Why don't you let Agent Morris here make you some coffee? My men won't be long.'

Andrews went out onto the veranda, and beckoned to his men in the cars. Soon a dozen FBI agents were searching the house.

Rebecca Le Jeune watched them. Agent Morris brought her a coffee. She spoke fiercely. 'My God! What is this? A police state?'

Andrews's trip back to Washington, seemed to take an eternity. He sat alone, at the front of the FBI plane, reading a variety of briefing notes, but couldn't concentrate on any of them.

In an unlocked drawer of a Louis XVI style bureau, in Rebecca Le Jeune's salon, inside a soft leather journal, a sealed envelope - bearing Jeff Davis's cipher - had been found.

The search had been over quickly, but Andrews had watched his men like a hawk, in case the finder of the envelope ignored his orders, and broke the seal - he knew the envelope *had* to contain the Richmond Papers.

Andrews knew his men must be curious; an FBI Director's participation in a search, was almost unique. When an agent handed him the envelope, Andrews had checked the seal wasn't broken, and put it in his briefcase. He wasn't going to break the seal at Rebecca Le Jeune's, in his car, or on his plane, it would have to wait until he was at his desk, in the safety of the Hoover Building.

It occurred to Andrews, that although his predecessors, all the way back to Hoover, and Hoover's own predecessors, back to Attorney General Bonaparte, would have known about the Richmond Papers and their explosive content, none of them would have examined them. No official had read the documents since the Federal Government lost control of them in the nineteenth century.

The pitch of the Gulfstream 550's engines dropped, as the pilot eased back the throttle. Andrews glanced out of the window and saw the twinkling lights of the capital below.

Within the hour, he was back in his wood panelled office, but a phone call from the President, further delayed and exasperated him. It was a long conversation. Ostensibly it was a regular update but - with a slender lead in the polls - the President was fishing for any news of misdemeanours, or better still, criminality, which Andrews had gathered on Ruth Callaghan's campaign. The President couldn't hide the disappointment in his voice, when Andrews told him he'd found nothing.

After the President abruptly hung up, Andrews considered his own position. He'd been one of the FBI's longest serving directors, but would he keep his job after the election, if the President won?

At last, he opened his briefcase and snatched at the envelope. With a silver paper knife - emblazoned with the FBI seal - he gently prized open Jeff Davis's wax. It really was astonishing, thought Andrews, that the wax had remained unbroken, since Davis sealed it himself on his last day in Richmond, in 1865.

It reminded Andrews that the public service rendered by the Le Jeune family to the American people - by not breaking the seal and revealing the contents of the envelope - should be recognized at the appropriate time. But as he read the documents he found inside, and re-read them, open mouthed, he realised there would never be, an appropriate time.

CHAPTER SEVEN

The White House
Washington DC
24 August 1814

B
eing the first sitting President on a battlefield was one thing, but being the first sitting President evicted from the White House, by an invader, was quite another. The British were weak, they'd told him, and Canada was lightly defended. A swift strike north would send a message to the British, that they couldn't impress Anglo-American sailors or impede trade with France.

An invasion of Canada, they'd said, would also pacify the Indians - supported by the British - who'd been causing trouble south of the Great Lakes. And once annexed, Madison himself had thought Canada would be hard to give up, and could easily be added to the Union.

But all that was two summers ago, and before Napoleon's abdication - which released Wellington's veterans from Europe, and brought them to Bladensburg. Now, with the battle at Bladensburg lost, those veterans were only a few miles from Washington.

Madison thought back to the incident at Bladensburg Bridge, earlier that day. Unaware the British had advanced so far, he and his escort had galloped through the American positions, and were crossing the bridge, when they'd met William Simmons - a War Department accountant he'd fired last month - going the other way.

'Where are you going, Mr President?' shouted Simmons. 'There's nobody behind me but the British.'

Madison knew that if Simmons had crossed the bridge a few seconds earlier, and he'd missed him, Madison would now be a dinner guest of General Ross and his redcoat officers. But that was hours ago, and the President still had his liberty.

With nothing barring Ross's troops from Pennsylvania Avenue, Madison had instructed Secretary Monroe to secure the Revolutionary Nation's most precious documents. Madison was confident there was enough time for Monroe's clerks to spirit away the Declaration of Independence and the Constitution, but there was one more document, Monroe didn't know anything about. Perhaps in time - if Monroe one day became President himself - he would learn of the document's existence, but until then, only Madison, and two others, would know about it. So despite the danger, that was why the President and a small bodyguard, galloped back to the White House.

It hadn't rained for three weeks, so Madison choked on a fine dust, which had also stuck to his sweat soaked coat. Entering by the side of the White House, he saw the guard had already gone.

The President walked swiftly through the dining room, passing the table laden with food and wine, which had been prepared for his cabinet and military guests to celebrate their victory. He knew this meal would now be enjoyed by the British.

Madison was sixty three, but he bounded up the stairs like a gundog and burst into his study. The room was empty. The President opened the glass doors of a mahogany bookcase, and gently placed his thumb on the spine of volume four of Edward Gibbons 'Decline and Fall of the Roman Empire'. The false book clicked open to reveal a small wooden compartment. The hidden chamber had been installed by President Adams, and shown to Madison - on his first day in office - by the outgoing President Jefferson.

Horrified, Madison saw the chamber was empty. It was futile, but he ran his hand around the compartment, hoping the document had somehow defied the laws of physics. But it hadn't, and it was gone.

Madison exhaled loudly. No one, but no one, knew of this chamber's existence. As far as he knew, only Adams and Jefferson were aware of the document. Anticipating the disaster at Bladensburg, had they or their agents somehow slipped into the city, and taken it for safekeeping? Madison rejected the idea. Both were on their plantations, Adams at Peacefield, and Jefferson at Monticello. Madison was perplexed. Other than the two former Presidents, not a soul could have known what was hidden. But someone else did know. And that person was still in the White House.

CHAPTER EIGHT

J Edgar Hoover Building
Washington DC
Present Day

It was getting late and darkening outside. The rain pelted, against the FBI Director's floor to ceiling windows. Andrews checked again the document was secure at the bottom of the safe. It was there, but what to do with it? He wasn't sure the American people could handle the truth. But who was he, an unelected official, to decide what they could, and couldn't know?

The document would provide succour to America's enemies, he was of no doubt. But this was a secondary problem that could be ridden out. The difficulty was this document went to the heart of America's DNA - Andrews worried that that heart, couldn't take the strain.

He toyed with the idea of approaching his most trusted predecessor for advice, but concerns about leaks and possible disagreements about strategy, persuaded him otherwise. There was no question of filing the document in the FBI's archives, even that was a risk. No. In the FBI Director's personal safe it would stay, at least while Andrews remained in office. He alone would carry the secret, until his successor unburdened him of it.

He picked up the soft leather bound journal - marked 'PLJ' - from the same shelf as the Richmond Papers, and closed the door to the safe. The electronic locking mechanism whirred for a few seconds before clicking into place. He took the journal to his desk.

Official FBI business hours had ended, so he took off his tie, loosened his collar, and sat back in his generous leather chair. Not satisfied, he got up from his desk, poured himself a large tumbler of scotch, then lay back on his chestnut coloured sofa.

He flicked through the pages until he found what he was looking for. In Le Jeune's elegant handwriting, the top of the page was marked, April 2nd, 1865.

On leaving President Davis, the British diplomat and I separated. He went to the Exchange Hotel to collect his things. I went to the Treasury where I met Secretary Trenholm. The sense of panic in the building was palpable. Trenholm hurriedly told me that over ten million dollars worth of bullion had been loaded onto a train. As well as bars, there were silver and gold coins, chests of jewellery, Spanish doubloons, and English acceptances drawable on the Bank of England.

How I was going to get all this safely out of Virginia, to a friendly port, onto a ship, through the blockade, across the Atlantic, then deposit it at the Bank of England in the Confederacy's account, wasn't yet clear to me.

I walked swiftly to the Exchange Hotel, where I was directed to the Briton's room. I knocked at the door.

'Who is it?'

'Le Jeune.'

'Come in.'

I entered and saw him lowering his pistol. He smiled warmly as the gun clunked down on the desk where he was sitting. 'My apologies, but the city is descending into anarchy.'

'I understand.'

He sat back in his chair, and scanned the room with a bemused expression. 'They tell me your President Tyler died in this room. I understand he was never elected, rather he inherited the Presidency. Sounds a bit like, how my Queen got her job,' he paused, allowing the sound of artillery to subside. 'You sure you colonials have done the right thing, getting rid of us I mean? This war seems a mess to me.'

I laughed. 'First of all, I'm French-American, as you've probably guessed. We French know how to deal with inherited heads of state as you call them. We guillotine them.' Steele nodded, accepting the point. 'And secondly, President Tyler didn't inherit the presidency. He was elected Vice President, and succeeded when President Harrison died in office.'

Steele closed the carpet bag on his desk and stood up. 'Oh, I see,' he said, with fake enthusiasm, 'sounds like a superb method of government. So if your President Lincoln dies, Vice President Johnson inherits?'

I shook my head and grinned. 'Yes, not a difficult concept to understand, even for a Briton. But you won't provoke me. Jefferson Davis is the President here.'

'At least until this evening,' replied Steele sarcastically. 'Shall we go?'

In the short time I'd been in the hotel, the situation in Richmond had deteriorated considerably. On Franklin Street, a number of fires had broken out, lit by one of the many drunken gangs of thieves and deserters, who now roamed unchallenged throughout the city. The previous day my uniform would have afforded protection against such mobs, but now, after months of deprivation and hardship, the uniform was a symbol of misery, and a target for retribution.

Food, clothing and liquor, which had been hidden by speculators whilst Richmond's women, children and soldiers starved and froze, was now seized by the mob. The whiskey, which the Provost Guard had tried to pour away to deny it to the invaders, was now being scooped out of gutters and drunk. The disorder was akin to a battlefield.

We skirted around mobs and chose quieter back streets, but a few blocks from the station, a dozen thugs barred our way. They were sprawled on a broken cart, some lying on it comatosed, some using it for support as they stood, and others pivoting around it as if in some demented war dance. We hugged the buildings as best we could, but as we passed, one of the dancing men lost his balance, spun away from the cart, and staggered into me.

'Look, an officer', he slurred. This caused a ripple of movement from some of the other men. Three of them peeled off from the back of the cart and obstructed us. Others stirred and reinforced the leading three in a loose formation. I could see the mob's leader was a deserter with faded sergeants' stripes on his arm. He was drunk, but his bloodshot violent eyes were focused.

'Your wallet, sir' he said sarcastically, emphasizing the sir. I smiled broadly at him. 'The wallet,' he repeated, taking a step towards me.

'Please stand aside, sergeant,' I ordered soothingly, 'we don't want any trouble!'

'The wallet then,' he drawled, taking a further step towards me and pulling his pistol. The men behind him did the same, but their reactions were slowed with whiskey. I cocked and levelled my pistol in an instant. Befuddled with drink, they were impervious to the danger and tried to cock their pistols. I fired three times in quick succession. Five men went down instantly and the rest scattered as best they could. I turned to see Steele re-holstering his smoking gun.

He was grimacing. 'Richmond's close to anarchy. Let's get to the train.'

'Follow me!' I said.

As we crossed the canal and approached the station, I could see the building was encircled by troops of the 25th Virginia Infantry, Richmond's city battalion. A crowd of wealthy citizens were pressed against the soldiers, but for civilians, the station was sealed off. I showed our military passes to an officer and went in. Compared to where we'd just been, there was a semblance of order, but it was still a chaotic scene.

Two trains sat puffing on the tracks. One had a dozen cars and was ready for departure. I recognized Davis's ministers sitting at the windows of the passenger cars; this was the government fleeing the city. Civilians who'd managed to gain admittance to the station, clung to the train like bees on a honeycomb. People were stuck to the top of the passenger cars, the freight cars, the box cars and even the locomotive. Others gripped the sides of the train, one hand holding on, the other hand grasping overflowing carpet bags stuffed with valuables.

The second train was further down the track. As I approached it, I was surprised to see boys scuttling about as if on some school trip. An officer sidled up to me and saluted. 'Commander Clark, sir. You're Colonel Le Jeune?'

I nodded and gestured to Steele. 'This man is a British diplomat and will be travelling with us.' I scanned the train slowly from one end to the other. 'Is all the bullion on board?'

'Yes. All boxed up and secured.'

A boy of thirteen or fourteen, in a uniform I didn't recognise, edged up to Clark and saluted. 'The President has arrived, sir.'

We glanced at the other train and saw Davis and his aides pushing through the throng. He alighted one of the carriages as a huge puff of smoke emanated from the engine. The train began to ease forward, inching south, taking with it the full machinery of the Confederate government. Better to have surrendered in a dignified way to Grant at the Executive Mansion, than this debacle, I thought.

I turned to Clark, 'well, we'd better get going ourselves. If our train is as slow as that one, we'll be caught by Grant's cavalry.' I looked at the boy with a growing sense of unease, 'when does the guard arrive?'

For a brief moment, Clark appeared to be affronted. He paused, 'this is the guard, sir, sixty of us.'

The boy grinned at me. Clark was stony faced. Steele raised an eyebrow. I was incredulous. 'What, these boys?'

Clark remained expressionless. 'Yes, naval academy midshipmen, aged fourteen to eighteen. I'm the Superintendent of the Academy. We're all that could be spared.'

So it had come to this. The Treasury of the Confederate States of America, transported South, at a snail's pace, and guarded by five dozen adolescent boys. I couldn't help laughing. The boy giggled. Clark looked perplexed.

'And since when ,Commander,' I said, my laughter subsiding. 'and since when, Commander,' I repeated.'

'Yes, sir.'

'And since when Commander,' I tried for the third time, 'does the navy sail trains?'

Andrews gulped down the remainder of his Scotch. It was very late now - his wife would be expecting him. Deciding that Le Jeune's journal wasn't classified material, he flung it into his briefcase. He grasped the door handle as the phone rang. Andrews turned back towards his desk, took several paces, and then hesitated - it could wait. The caller rang off. Andrews retraced his steps and opened the door, but this time his cell rang - he sighed, and then answered, 'yes.'

'Director Andrews?'

'Yes!'

'It's Special Agent Ross, in the Phoenix office.'

Andrews's sense of foreboding intensified.

'We've had a mass shooting on another campus.'

'Casualties?'

Ross paused, 'looks like dozens.'

CHAPTER NINE

Clinton Street
Washington Square West
Philadelphia
Present Day

Mackay rarely got jet lagged flying to the States from the UK, and this time was no different. He breezed airily into Clinton Street at Friday lunch time, unaware of the sombre mood developing. He found Sally in the kitchen and planted a kiss on her lips, but she was unresponsive. 'What's up?' he said, the concern clear in his voice.

She looked at him fondly. 'Another shooting, Arizona this time, another campus.'

'Bloody hell.'

He pulled Sally towards him and hugged her. She always felt these things personally. She gently pushed him away and looked into his eyes. 'I'm sorry. I'm forgetting. How was the funeral?'

'Subdued. Low key. Typical for a man of his age I guess.' Mackay wondered whether to air his suspicions. 'Somethings not right though. The way he fell. The way the room was arranged afterwards.'

'Oh please, not again Inspector,' she teased.

'Seriously though Sal, something was amiss.'

She sensed it wasn't the time to joke. 'And you voiced your concerns to the police?'

'They're convinced it was an accident. In that part of the world they're sleepy, and under-resourced. Without a smoking gun or blood-stained dagger, they won't investigate further, they'd rather focus on speeding offences and drunk drivers.'

The hall toilet flushed and he looked at her quizzically. She grinned, 'prepare yourself. Take a deep breath.'

'Oh, no. When did he arrive?' asked Mackay.

'Yesterday.' She lunged forward and kissed him full on the lips as the door began to open, 'and he's staying for about a week,' she whispered.

Justice Anthony Purcell, longest serving Associate Justice of the United States Supreme Court, walked in. Appointed by a Republican President, he'd been the archetypal, dry, conservative, interpreter of the law ever since.

That Sally took after her easy going, carefree mother, there was no doubt. She loved her father, but with her mother now dead, that part of him which she and her mother admired - his keen sense of fairness and equity - had all but been submerged, under the weight of inflexible precedent and prohibition. She knew with her mother's passing, that he'd lost his key reference point. Purcell viewed Sally's job on the Democratic campaign as a direct affront to him and his deteriorating value system.

On entering the kitchen, Purcell glanced coldly at Mackay, and directed himself at Sally. 'I see your playboy Brit accountant is back then.'

Sally snapped back at him, 'yes, back from his great grandfather's funeral.'

Purcell's expression softened a little, 'Oh. I'm sorry. I forgot.'

There was an awkward silence. Mackay spoke first. 'Campaign going well, Sal?'

It wasn't the best of ice breakers. Purcell grunted and opened the fridge. 'No,' she replied, 'the President stubbornly remains two or three points ahead. We've tried all sorts, just can't shift the dial.'

'Your woman's too left wing for most Americans,' came Purcell's voice from behind the fridge door. 'Universal health care, climate change, higher taxes, a review of the Second Amendment.'

'After this morning's events, I would say a review of the Second Amendment is long overdue,' she retorted.

Purcell closed the fridge and was now brandishing a cold pie. 'You, me, the President, Congress,' said Purcell. 'None of us have the right to change what the Founding Fathers wrote. None of us.'

She was exasperated and looked at him severely, 'even if eighteenth century laws have no place in the twenty first century?'

He nodded at her, and then began looking for a plate.

Sally turned to Mackay, 'there you have it, Tom, from the horse's mouth, from the very highest echelons of the justiciary.'

Purcell began opening doors, rattling cutlery drawers and clanking plates. Her irritation subsided. 'What the hell are you doing father?'

He looked at her with a lost smile. 'I'd thought I'd make some lunch.'

She stepped forward and seized the plate from his hand and gave it to Mackay. 'You're not making lunch, Dad. Why do you think I keep Tom hanging around here?'

Mackay laughed and reached for his apron. 'Your wish is my command, my love,' he paused, 'but there's one thing I ask in return.'

'Name it,' she replied, with a dirty look hidden from her father.

'Come with me on a weekend trip to Florida, where we'll follow in the footsteps of my great grandfather and seek out Confederate gold.'

'Sounds intriguing,' she said. 'I'm in.'

CHAPTER TEN

T he family meal was a sombre affair. Andrews tried to field his young son's questions about the Phoenix shootings, as best as he could, but like any small boy, he was only interested in the gory details. His daughter was also playing up, refusing to eat her vegetables. Andrews retreated to his study before he lost his temper.

The Director went to bed from his study and found his wife was still reading. He reached into his briefcase and brought out Le Jeune's journal. He hoped the next instalment, would help him put the horrors of the Phoenix murders, out of his mind.

Andrews's wife was intrigued by the leather tome, 'is that work?' He grunted a response. 'If it's work, should you have it out of the office?' He remained silent. 'Well, what is it?'

He turned away from her and lay on his side. 'If you must know, it's a Civil War diary. It's not classified. Now, please stop pestering me, I've had a bad day!'

She sighed and turned away from him so they lay back to back. The FBI Director opened the journal.

We arrived at Danville the following day, and pulled into a siding by President Davis's train. It soon became apparent that the town was now the seat of the Confederate government.

During that afternoon, Treasury officials frequently boarded my train, and I made the disbursements they requested without question. By the evening, I was conscious of my orders to get to England and fearful that a restless Consul Steele, who I needed to smooth my passage through the British West Indies, would abandon me.

I showed my travel authority to Secretary Mallory, who seemed to be in charge of logistics. He returned an hour later, presumably having checked with

Davis himself, and we were ordered to proceed to Greensboro, where I was to give $39000 to General Johnstone, so he could pay his troops.

The hour before I left, I was visited by several high ranking cabinet ministers, including Secretary of State Benjamin, who each personally withdrew thousands of dollars of hard currency. If Davis was still delusional about the war's outcome, it was clear his cabinet were not.

I reached Charlotte, North Carolina, two days later, having made the disbursements to Johnstone in Greensboro. There was a rumour in the town that General Lee had surrendered at Appomattox, but I disregarded this as Federal propaganda and proceeded onto South Carolina. The rail line ended at Chester, so at gunpoint I commandeered wagons from furious residents, and proceeded to the next station at Newbury.

The twelve hour forced march was arduous, with insufficient horses even for the officers. At every village we passed, we were told Federal cavalry were ten miles away, or five miles away, or even over the next rise, so I left guards at every bridge we crossed, with orders to burn them if General Stoneman should be sighted.

The fifty young midshipmen who marched into Newbury, hungry, sore footed and ragged, were a credit to Commander Clark and his academy.

When the Abbeville train at last arrived, I again commandeered it and put the bullion on board. It was a long train, and with our additional weight, the locomotive was underpowered and couldn't move. I ordered four carriages to be uncoupled, and left them and their incensed passengers at the station. Remarkably, some of the passengers on the train knew the boxes contained bullion, which was a concern.

On reaching Abbeville, a paroled officer told me a group of deserters planned to attack the train that night. An attempted robbery did take place, but we were prepared, and a couple of disciplined volleys from the midshipmen saw off the threat.

The next day, I proceeded into Georgia, where I learned to my dismay that both Generals Lee and Johnstone had surrendered. I halted the train at Washington, to try to find out if the war was over, but with the rail line behind us now cut south of Charlotte, and the telegraph down, the whereabouts of Davis and his entourage was unknown.

Whilst preparing the train to continue onto Augusta, my scouts saw a large body of men on the outskirts of the town. General Breckenridge, Secretary of War, arrived at the station with a large cavalry escort shortly afterwards. He hailed me from his horse as soon as he saw me. I knew him well.

His expression was sombre, his face haggard, his moustache drooped almost at right angles. His uniform was caked with mud. He forced a smile. 'Le Jeune. You've done well to make it this far.'

Clarke and most of his midshipmen were within earshot, they deserved praise. 'It's these boys, sir,' I replied, indicating the midshipmen with a sweep of my arm, heroes every one. Breckenridge scanned the exhausted adolescents, then saluted them. Clarke and his sailors returned the salute.

The General got off his horse and edged closer to me. He spoke in a low voice, 'I won't tell them it's all been in vain.'

'It's over then?'

The General nodded. 'Yes. Davis has probably dissolved the Government by now. He's gonna try to make it to Florida.'

Breckenridge, who was the former Federal Vice-President, sat down on the carriage step and signalled me to join him. The General looked out across the railway track at his escort, many of whom were still trotting in and dismounting. 'I have 4000 men here,' he said. 'I'll pay them from your bullion and then discharge most of them. I also have other requisitions which I'll deposit in some banks here.'

Steele appeared from the other side of the carriage and stood off my shoulder. 'Ah. The British Consul,' said Breckenridge, with a hint of distaste. 'No need for your Government to choose a side now.'

Steele was pleased. 'Thank God it's finished. What now?'

Breckenridge looked at Le Jeune. 'If you're willing, the President would like you to continue your mission. You're to take the remaining bullion to Florida, where you'll seek passage to England. If you make it, you're to deposit the gold in the Confederacy's account in London as planned.'

Breckenridge paused and stared at Steele, before switching his gaze to Le Jeune, 'I understand you also have in your possession some sensitive documents. When I was Vice-President, President Buchanan thought it prudent to inform me of their existence, in case he died and I succeeded him. Buchanan had never read them himself, nor was I told any more about them. Apparently each new President is informed about these documents by his predecessor. And each new President *then tells his Vice-President of their existence. I understand that for fifty years, no one has known where they were located, or whether they had been destroyed.'*

I was suddenly uneasy, conscious that Breckenridge was intrigued and wanted to read them. I was astonished the Federal President knew of the documents, and put in place contingency plans for their safety. I feared Breckenridge would order me to hand them to him. That would put me in an awkward position. Davis had commanded me to take the sealed letter and the documents inside to the Bank of England, or give them directly to him. But did it really matter? The war was over. Did I really care?

I looked at Breckenridge closely. He was waiting for me to offer them to him. That would save him the problem of countermanding an order from Davis, who was still, in theory, his Commander-in-Chief. I said nothing. He remained silent. The moment passed. 'Of course, we'll continue to Florida,' I declared. 'What will you do?'

His face hardened. 'A disgraceful outrage has occurred in Washington. President Lincoln has been assassinated in the theatre by one of our sympathisers.'

I gasped. Steele shook his head. The General let the news sink in, then continued. 'Even before this murder, I was loathed in the North. Many there think I'm a traitor. There's a real risk of the noose for me. With a small escort, I intend to create a diversion in Georgia to allow Davis to escape. Then I'll try and make it to Europe myself.'

A loud whistle from the locomotive brought Breckenridge and I to our feet. 'Very good, General,' I said, 'let's get some of this bullion unloaded so you can pay your men.'

41

CHAPTER ELEVEN

Florida
Present Day

Mackay had toyed with the idea of giving the Morgan a run to Florida. He'd bought the V6 Roadster when he'd arrived in the States, but since then had hardly driven her. The romance of a night drive with the roof down, Sally at his side, did appeal, but US speed limits, meant he'd have little chance to open her up, and so to avoid a fourteen hour drive, they flew to Orlando instead.

The C-Class Mercedes, was the best open top for hire at the airport. It was warm and sunny, and they headed north on Interstate 95 with the wind in their hair, and the azure Atlantic on their right. Because Mackay had discovered it was the oldest town in America, they decided to stay in St Augustine, where they checked into a suite at the Casa Monica Hotel. The hotel itself - themed like a Moorish palace - evoked faded old world splendour.

In their suite, Mackay turned away from the window, where he'd been watching a yacht tack, and then nose towards the harbour. He saw Sally was already dressed for the beach - in his favourite polka dot bikini. She filled it perfectly, and he reached for her. She was too quick and wriggled away from him, threw on a gown, and was out of the door before he could react. 'Catch me if you can,' floated down the corridor, 'I'm going for a swim.'

After lunch - in the Spanish inspired dining room - they jumped into the convertible and headed inland. The directions to Gainesville given to Mackay by Mary Coggins, were detailed and clear.

Arriving at the city, they found the former train station easily, despite the line itself being long gone. The two amateur history buffs, were delighted to discover that the old wooden building had recently been restored, complete with wooden platform, passenger waiting room, and freight shed.

Mackay took a picture of the station with his phone, and Whatsapped it to Mary Coggins in Scotland. Mackay's phone immediately pinged back a 'thumbs up' emoji, with 'now go to the library' written underneath it.

'Amazing to think, my ancestor got off a train on this very spot 150 years ago, Sal.'

'Yes,' she replied, whilst trying to pump the metal handle of a historic water butt that stood on the platform. The handle had seized and she gave up. 'Where next then?' she said.

'The library?'

CHAPTER TWELVE

FBI Director Andrews's Home
Washington DC
Present Day

Daylight edging the drapes pulled Andrews out of a light sleep. He realised his wife was already up, and she soon appeared with a mug of tea - a habit they'd picked up in the London embassy, earlier in his career.

High pitched shouting, followed by doors banging, implied the children were also awake, and having a fight. His wife looked at him affectionately, 'I'll deal with the kids,' she said, 'you enjoy your tea.'

She left the room and Andrews reached for Le Jeune's journal.

Breckenridge had replaced my exhausted midshipmen with 50 regulars under the command of a Captain Watson. As our train trundled south, and as the Confederacy continued to wither, I began to suspect their loyalty.

At Swainsboro, we were intercepted by outriders from President Davis's entourage. With them was John Reagan, the new Treasury Secretary. By his order I dispersed $55,000 in gold sovereigns for Davis and his escort. I also noted that Reagan put $3,500, in his own saddle bags.

The meeting with Reagan steadied Watson and his men for a while, but as the weeks passed, and as we travelled further into Florida, their enthusiasm for our mission waned. At Gainesville, we learned of Davis's arrest, and with it all semblance of my military authority disappeared.

My entreaties to Watson and his men proved futile. There was no interest in using the funds to re-establish the Confederacy at a later date, and it was clear Watson and his men would use force to take the gold. With my command reduced to Steele, and three others who'd travelled with me from Richmond, I was in no position to negotiate.

By this stage the Treasury was much depleted, and as it lay on the station platform, it amounted to only fifteen boxes; eleven boxes of CSA stamped gold bars, and four boxes of silver coins. Prompted either by a realization that the bars were not easy to transport in saddle bags, or by a late surge of nationalism,

Watson relented, and took only the coins, amounting to a tidy $200 per man. The bars, and the English acceptances, he agreed were to be taken to London and held there for Davis, as the President would need funds for a legal team to fight the treason charges against him.

I watched Watson and his men, disappear north along the rail track in a cloud of dust of their own making. I suspected the stragglers on foot would soon be caught by Federal cavalry. We'd heard from the Gainesville townsfolk, that Union soldiers swarmed in all directions, and that Federal detectives hunted the Treasury and the Confederate State records. It was clear to me, we had to abandon the train, and find another route to the coast.

I turned at the sound of a match being struck behind me. Steele was sitting on one of the bullion boxes lighting a cigar. He offered one to me, which I took. I sat next to him on a second bullion box and lit it.

'I picked them up in Havana,' he said, exhaling a cloud of smoke, 'during my enforced stay there.'

'They're good.' After a further puff I continued, 'you told Davis in Richmond you got stuck in Cuba. I never asked why.'

He grinned at me. 'For some reason the Spanish thought I was a spy.'

I sucked on the cigar and blew out, 'are you a spy?'

His eyes flickered neutrally, 'of sorts.'

Like Captain Watson, my passion for the Confederate cause was on the wane. Although a sizeable amount, the bullion which we sat on, would make no difference to the war effort. Divided by five, however, it would make a huge difference to our lives.

'Can't see us making England now,' I ventured, hoping he would agree. 'This bullion would have more value here. Would do more good.'

He looked at me closely, taking the hint. 'Your call, of course,' he said evenly, 'but that sealed letter in your pocket from Davis. That has more value than all of this.'

I was surprised he knew its contents. 'You've read it?'

'No', but Palmerston gave me the gist when he briefed me in London.' He flicked away some ash, 'it has more value as a weapon, later I mean, no point in exploiting it now, it would be futile.'

I'd been curious before, now I was intrigued. With Davis arrested and the Confederacy gone, who would know if I broke the seal? On the other hand, I'd *given my word to Davis I would deposit it in the Bank of England, unread. I was in a quandary.*

Steele saw my dilemma. 'I can open it without breaking the seal. If you want to read it, that is.'

I looked at him, puzzled. 'How?'

He smirked, 'I am a spy after all.' He waited for my response. I didn't give one. 'Very well,' he said, getting to his feet and extinguishing his cigar. 'Heat a pan of water on the locomotive. I'll need some steam.'

Ten minutes later, I'd read and reread the document. I was flabbergasted by what it said.

Steele had read it too. 'Well, well, well,' he chuckled, 'who would have thought it!'

I turned to him sharply, suddenly pricked by a sense of acute national pride. 'You must promise me not to reveal this to anyone.' He looked at me blankly. I'd felt we'd bonded over the last two months, but sometimes Steele was impossible to read. 'Swear it.'

I sensed Steele did respect me and making promises came easily to men of his profession. 'I swear it,' he declared, in a formal tone.

Satisfied, I reached again into the envelope. 'In case we get separated, I think you should have this for safe keeping.' I handed him the copy which was the same as the original in every way. Written in the author's own hand, and signed by him.

Andrews sat bolt upright in bed. He reread the last sentence. A copy. Of course! In those days, the days before photocopiers and scanners, hand written copies were often made by the authors of important documents. He vaguely recalled, there was even an original copy of the Declaration of Independence.

But where was this copy of the Richmond Papers now? The envelope in his safe in the Hoover Building, must contain Le Jeune's original. Had this Brit Steele, disappeared with the copy? Did Steele give it back to Prime Minister Palmerston, and it now lay hidden in the British state archives, ticking away like a time bomb, until some dull academic came across it and made the discovery of a lifetime? Or was it hidden in the attic of Steele's descendents, ready to be revealed during a school ancestry project?

Andrews flicked through the last few pages of the journal. They revealed nothing more. Was there another volume they'd missed at the Le Jeune home in New Orleans? He'd have to send a team back to check.

He leapt out of bed and reached for his cell. The Hoover Building duty officer was surprised to hear Andrews's voice so early on a Saturday. 'Good morning. Now, this is gonna sound strange. I want you to find out all you can about a dead Brit named James Steele. When he died? Where he lived? Who his living relatives are? I want it all in a nice big file.'

'Can you give me anything else, Director?'

'Not much, no. Except he was a sort of Ambassador, to Jefferson Davis's Confederacy in Richmond, in 1865. He'd have been born in the 1820s or 30s I guess.' There was a long silence at the other end of the line.' Did you get that?' pressed Andrews.

'Er, yes Director. We'll see what we can find out'.

It must have been a slow morning in the office, because Andrews was called back just as he was finishing breakfast.

'This guy Steele didn't have much family, Director. He has one direct descendent living in Scotland, a woman named Elspeth Mackay. Her son lives in Philadelphia.'

Andrews was impressed with the duty officer. 'What's he doing in Philadelphia?'

'Not a lot. Seems to be independently wealthy. Moved Stateside to be with his girlfriend.'

'What does she do?' asked Andrews quickly.

'A lawyer by training. Sally Purcell is her name. She's working on the Callaghan campaign team.'

Andrews began to have a sinking feeling. A smart lawyer working for Ruth Callaghan, would instantly realise the impact the document would have. And Callaghan herself, was known to favour scraping the Second Amendment as part of wider constitutional reform. This couldn't get much worse. Could it?

'One more thing, Director.' Andrews held his breath with a sense of dread. 'This Sally Purcell, is the daughter of Justice Purcell, the Supreme Court judge'.

'For Christ's sake,' muttered Andrews. Justice Purcell was no liberal, but some of his judgements had been quirky to say the least. Politically, Purcell wasn't on the same team as Andrews, and that was another risk.

This was turning into a nightmare, thought the Director. It was obvious where this Brit's money have come from. Steele had set his family up for generations with Confederate bullion. But where was the copy of the Richmond Papers? If it was lying in the dusty attic of Steele's family home, it would be easy to get at. Obtaining it from the British state archives, would be trickier.

'Looks like this Sally Purcell and her boyfriend are taking in some sun, Director,' continued the duty officer, 'they just checked in on a flight to Orlando. They've a rental car booked for the weekend.'

Surely a coincidence, thought Andrews. But was it? He'd never been a subscriber to Carl Jung's synchronicity concept, but this coincidence seemed to be meaningful. Were they going to Gainesville? If they were going to Gainesville, then why? There might be clues in the Florida city, but who could he send to deal with something as sensitive as this? It was difficult to brief an agent without giving too much away. There was no alternative; he'd have to go himself.

'Have a plane ready to fly me to Orlando.'

'Yes, Director.'

CHAPTER THIRTEEN

The White House
Washington DC
24 August 1814

'Read it again, Gabriel'. The slave picked up the pamphlet and pointed his finger at the first word. Samuel watched in wonder, as his friend spoke the words written on the page. Gabriel couldn't read well, but to read at all was a marvel. Gabriel pronounced the words slowly and carefully, with little fluency in his diction.

'A Proclamation.

Whereas it has been represented to me, that many persons now resident in the United States have experienced a desire to withdraw there from with a view to entering into His Majesty's service, or of being received as free settlers into some of His Majesty's colonies. This is therefore to give notice that all persons who may be disposed to migrate from the United States, will, with their families be received on board of His Majesty's ships or vessels of war, or at the military posts that may be established upon or near the coast of the United States, where they will have their choice of entering into His Majesty's sea or land forces, or of being sent as free settlers to British possessions in North America or the West Indies where they will meet with due encouragement.

Given under my hand at Bermuda, this second day of April 1814, by my command.

Alex Cochrane, Vice-Admiral.'

Gabriel put down the pamphlet and looked at Samuel, 'you see, there is no mention of slaves.'

'No,' reflected Samuel, 'but this Cochrane is encouraging us to join him. I know of many, some from the city, who have already fled to Tangier Island. Soon they will be in Canada.'

Gabriel wasn't convinced, 'who's to say we'll be treated any better by the British?'

Gabriel had a wife and children - he was much older than Samuel - and his family had plenty to eat every day, and lived in a comfortable house. He knew his lot was better than a good many free men. Gabriel was envious of Samuel's bid for freedom, but mostly, he didn't want to lose his young friend.

But Samuel had already made up his mind. 'Maybe so, but at least we'll be free. We may not get another chance.'

Gabriel lacked Samuel's spirit. His friend was young, smart and energetic. He'd already been earmarked for schooling by the Madisons, and would soon be able to read himself. Gabriel made a final attempt to dissuade him. 'But the Master is fair to us, and Mrs. Madison treats us kindly.'

'I know but I'm still going. I'll get my things,' said Samuel, the excitement clear in his voice.

Gabriel shrugged his shoulders. 'You'd better be quick. I think the President's already gone, and Mrs. Madison will want us to go with her.'

Samuel went to the sleeping quarters to gather the food and clothing he'd been storing. On his way, he passed French John, the cook, and another slave, Paul Jennings, who were removing the portrait of George Washington which hung in the East Room. When he returned they'd gone, leaving faded wallpaper where the picture had been.

He heard the under-butler, Brown, calling for him, so he remained motionless for a moment, until the voice drifted away to nothing.

Gabriel was right. President Madison was a fair man and Dolly Madison was a kindly woman, but they still owned Gabriel and his family. That wasn't right. No man should own another. Gabriel was also right, that life as a freed black man in Canada, would be harder than life as a White House slave, but at least in Canada, Samuel would have an opportunity to better himself. He knew in his heart, that the British were only liberating thousands of American slaves because they wanted to win a war, but they *had* abolished the slave trade, and slavery was gone in Britain itself.

50

Samuel knew a way to help the British. He didn't know what it was, he couldn't read, but he would help himself and other slaves, if he gave them a gift.

Samuel had been little more than a boy, when President Madison had succeeded President Jefferson. Small boys, especially small slave boys, don't get noticed. They blend in, go about unseen, and are almost invisible. When President Jefferson, had shown President Madison the secret compartment behind the old book about Rome, Samuel had been hidden in a recess. He'd heard Jefferson, tell Madison that the papers in the compartment contained a great secret. Samuel had seen Madison read the documents. He'd seen him shaking his head as he read. The two men then had a heated discussion, using words he didn't understand. They'd talked about giving the papers to Congress, they'd talked about burning the papers, but in the end, they'd put them back into the secret compartment, and President Jefferson had left.

After Jefferson had gone, Samuel saw President Madison staring blankly at the bookcase. Samuel watched him stagger to his desk and crumple down. There Madison sat, with his head in his hands, crying and whimpering in a most heart wrenching way.

Samuel realized the documents contained a great secret. That is why, when he knew the British were on the outskirts of the city, he sneaked into the study and took them. He understood why the President had risked danger to return to the White House after the battle. He'd heard the President frantically searching the study. He'd felt sorry for him, and contemplated somehow returning the documents. But those feelings of guilt soon passed, and the documents were now in his coat pocket, as he exited the building.

Outside, the first thing that struck him was the intense dry heat that immediately enveloped him; the second thing was Brown's fist.

'I know what you're up to boy,' seethed the under-butler vehemently.

Samuel stepped back, his ears ringing. Brown stood between him and a cart. The cart was loaded with valuables, which he could see included Washington's portrait. French John and Paul Jennings waited by its side.

51

'Get on the cart,' ordered Brown fiercely.

Samuel quickly assessed the situation. Brown was middle aged and puny, he could be overpowered easily. But, if he was joined by French John and Jennings, there could be a problem. Sensing Samuel's determination, Brown turned to the two men at the cart.

'Help me,' he commanded. Jennings remained motionless, but French John started towards them, then stopped and listened. The distant sound of fifes and drums wafted through the hot air.

'The British are coming,' shouted the Frenchman, turning back to jump on the cart.

Samuel took a couple of steps forward, and threw a punch at Brown with all his strength. The under-butler staggered backwards, a look of astonishment and pain on his face.

Samuel turned and was on Pennsylvania Avenue - racing towards the sound of the drums - before the others could react. He ran until he reached Constitution Avenue, where he halted for breath. He wiped the sweat off his brow and looked behind him. He wasn't being followed.

Around him there was chaos. Slaves darted in all directions, warning residents to escape whilst they still could. Those Washingtonians who remained, fled into their grand residences and barred the doors. Speeding carts loaded with furniture and other worldly goods, lurched dangerously as they headed for the Potomac River and safety.

Samuel passed one portly gentleman - red faced, puffing and sweating in the unrelenting heat - who grabbed his arm, and pointed towards the White House. 'You're going the wrong way, boy.'

Samuel shook his arm free and smiled at the man, who shrugged his shoulders and ran on. The sound of drums was loud now, and between the beats Samuel could hear the crunch of marching boots. At the junction with Constitution Avenue, he looked up the road and saw, sandwiched between a double row of elegant Lombardy trees, two neat columns, perfectly parallel to the trees, advancing towards him.

The irony wasn't lost on Samuel. The redcoats, for so long the oppressors of the Founding Fathers, now offered him a gateway to liberty.

At the west end of the Avenue, the stately houses were well spaced out, and afforded views of the road from all angles. As Samuel approached the column, he noticed the windows of one large neo-classical property were open, which struck him as odd - although it was a hot day, all the other windows in the street, were locked to prevent easy access by the invaders.

He walked on towards the small group which led the two columns. Out of the corner of his eye, he caught the tip of a rifle barrel poking out of a window to his left. Samuel craned his neck and saw more guns trained on the leading horsemen.

'Ambush,' he roared, waving his hands frantically as the volley crashed out. The leading horseman had seen Samuel, and pulled back on his reins, adjusting his position just enough for the bullets to miss him, and hit his horse. Two infantry men went down to the horseman's right. The officer's horse buckled slowly under him, and he leapt off. A sergeant barked an order, and a dozen redcoats ran towards the mansion where the belligerents hid.

Samuel spotted blood pouring through the fingers of one of the soldiers, as he clasped his throat. The other fallen infantry man was groaning. Samuel saw a bullet had hit his white duck trousers, which were rapidly turning red. The officer who'd narrowly avoided a similar fate, checked his men, then bounded up to Samuel, with the energy of a man given a reprieve.

Samuel observed he wore a silk cord across his right shoulder, which was fastened to a button on the front of his red tunic. He looked to be a senior officer.

'I'm in your debt, sir,' declared the officer, pumping Samuel's hand vigorously. 'Cochrane said you people would be useful, but I never for one moment thought you'd be as useful as this.' The man looked more closely at Samuel, noting the fierce intelligence in his eyes, 'you *are* a slave, I take it?'

'Yes, sir,' replied Samuel, a little overwhelmed.

'Were a slave,' corrected the man.

A sense of elation swept through Samuel's body, and he grinned wildly.

'What is your name?'

'Samuel, my name is Samuel.'

'I am Robert Ross,' said the soldier, 'and I command here.'

Samuel reached into his pocket and pulled out the documents. 'Then I have this for you, sir, I took it from President Madison's study.' Samuel handed him the papers. 'President Madison, is... was my master, sir. I worked at the White House.'

Ross roared with laughter. 'Well, this is something. First you save my life, then you bring me intelligence directly from Madison's study.' He paused, a look of triumph glinting in his eyes. 'A study I'll soon be visiting.'

Ross glanced over to the mansion, and saw his men appear at the windows where the shots had come from. He looked again at Samuel. 'Where is Madison? We nearly had him at Bladensburg Bridge today, when the idiot galloped into our lines.'

'He's gone across the river, sir,' said Samuel.

'Mmm. Escaped then.' Ross unfolded the documents. 'What is it?'

'I don't know, sir. I can't read. All I know, is that it's a great secret. It was very important to the President and President Jefferson before him.'

Ross read the paper, then carefully folded it. 'And what's this other document, and this letter?'

'It's the same as far as I can see, sir, a copy. I didn't realise there was a letter as well.'

Ross glanced at the letter and nodded. 'Well, well, I can see why they want to cover this up. No bearing on my endeavours in Washington today though, but I can see how it might be of use to our officials in Whitehall.' Ross turned to an aide and handed him the papers. 'See these go in the dispatches to Lord Palmerston, the Secretary at War.'

Another officer approached from the house where the snipers had been concealed, and saluted, 'I'm sorry, General, they've escaped.'

Ross frowned. 'Very well, major, form up, and prepare to advance.'

Ross turned to Samuel and his expression softened, 'now, what can I do for you. You've been of great service to your King today.' Ross paused for thought. 'We could use a resourceful chap like you in our Colonial Marines. They're at the back of the column somewhere. I'll make you a sergeant.'

Samuel didn't hesitate. 'I'm grateful, sir, but I'd like to get out of America, quickly.'

Ross couldn't hide his disappointment but recovered quickly, 'I quite understand. Being Madison's former slave won't make you too popular if anything should go wrong for us. Where then, Canada, Trinidad, Bermuda, where?'

Again Samuel didn't hesitate. 'Canada, sir. I know people who've already gone there.'

'Canada it is then.' Ross looked at his aide again. 'Give this citizen twenty pounds out of our funds, and detail a couple of men to see him safely to Tangier Island.'

The aide left on his errand.

Samuel beamed. 'Thank you, sir.'

'Think nothing of it young man,' said the General, 'it's the least I can do.'

Samuel looked round, shielding his eyes from the sun, as the column lurched forward to the sound of drums, whistles and marching boots.

Ross clapped him on the shoulder. 'Now, if you'll excuse me, you must begin your journey to Canada, whilst I begin torching the White House and Washington.'

CHAPTER FOURTEEN

Gainesville
Florida
Present Day

At Gainesville library, Sally read all the Civil War editions of the Florida Union paper she could find, but they yielded nothing.

Mackay was also frustrated. 'A dead end.' Sally nodded.

On their way out of the building, Sally accosted the friendly librarian, who'd been so helpful earlier in the day. 'Not much on the Civil War period. Anywhere else we could try?'

The librarian's expression hardened a little, 'you're not treasure hunters, are you?'

'No, researching a family history project,' she replied warmly, flashing him, her most seductive smile.

It did the trick. 'Well, you could try old man Montgomery out at the Montgomery place,' said the librarian. 'There's nothing he doesn't know, about the Battle of Gainesville and the Civil War. But be careful, he doesn't take kindly to treasure hunters.'

Encouraged by the librarian's reference to treasure hunters, they found the extensive Montgomery estate without difficulty. The white building resembled a dolls' house. Five casement windows - framed by green shutters - adorned the upper floor. On the ground floor, two windows flanked a green wooden door, which was painted so well, that it glinted in the early afternoon sun like polished metal. The whole place looked luxurious, but somehow incongruous.

The old man who answered the door was tall, erect, straight. His deep voice and his look reminded Mackay of John Huston - his face was like wrinkled carved stone, and there was clear hostility in it.

'How can I help you?' said Montgomery, who clearly wanted to do anything but help.

Mackay thought it prudent to let Sally lead. 'We're doing some Civil War research,' she said, flicking her hair back with her slender fingers and smiling seductively.

This time it didn't work. The man studied her for a moment, frowned, then began to close the door, 'more damn treasure hunters,' he grunted.

'No,' she said firmly, 'family history.'

The door was now ajar, the gap was small, but it wasn't closed. 'Family history, you say?' his interest piqued. 'Your family at the Battle of Gainesville?'

'No, not mine.' The door began to inch towards closure again. 'His,' she said quickly, 'his great grandfather was in Gainesville during the War.'

'Oh.'

Mackay chipped in, 'yes. He was a British diplomat caught up in it all.'

Mackay's accent added immediate credibility to their story, but Montgomery peered at him closely, requiring more evidence. 'What was his name?'

'James Steele.'

'Well I say,' beamed Montgomery, flinging the door open, 'your grandfather?'

'Great grandfather,' corrected Mackay.

'Then come in, come in,' he said warmly, waving for them to follow. 'I believe your great grandfather and my grandfather were good friends. They went on a perilous adventure together and lived to tell the tale. After the war they also corresponded a little. It was a shame your great grandfather was forbidden from entering the States after the war ended, and they never met again.'

They followed him through the house - to an airy veranda shaded from the sun - then slumped into a Rattan sofa. Montgomery poured lemon water and ice, and with the refreshments deployed, brought up a huge wicker chair next to them.

'James Steele,' mouthed Montgomery, as if the words were exotic confectionary. 'Well, well,' he smiled broadly; the transformation from

57

aggressive gatekeeper to welcoming host, couldn't have been more marked. 'I thought you were looking for the bullion. Dozens of folk come here searching for gold. The gold's gone I tell 'em. Then they come back the next day, asking more tomfool questions.' He shook his head slowly, 'I'm sick of it, I am. Wish that train had never stopped here.'

'Oh really?' thought Sally, who detected concealment in his eyes.

Mackay also had doubts, but didn't pursue it. 'So what can you tell us about my great grandfather?'

'Well, if you're sitting comfortably?' said Montgomery, opening the palms of his hands like some ancient Arabian storyteller, 'I'll tell you what my granddaddy told me.'

Montgomery saw he had their full attention, and continued. 'There was a wooden building here before this brick house. A few acres of land, not much. Certainly not enough to live off. So, during the war, Jeremiah Montgomery made his living blockade running. Cotton for guns. Cotton to Nassau, and from there onto bigger ships, to your mills in Britain. He made some real money for a few years, but towards the end of the war, he was caught in Charleston harbour on a run from Nassau. After his cargo and much besides was impounded by corrupt Federal officers, he was almost broke. He gave his parole and came back here.

Then one day, at the very end of the war, he was on his wagon in Gainesville, loading some supplies, when he heard firing from the rail depot. Although he was still on parole, curiosity got the better of him, and he crept towards the station. There he saw two men - one of them a Confederate officer - besieged by a gang of ruffians intent on stealing wooden boxes. With rumours rife about the whereabouts of Jeff Davis's Treasury, he guessed what might be in the boxes, and decided to intervene.

Jeremiah jumped on his wagon, whipped up his horse, and aimed for a couple of scoundrels at the south side of the platform. Taking the whip and reins in one hand, he fired his pistol at the men as he approached - he winged one, and the other took fright and disappeared.

From a strong position on top of his wagon, Jeremiah held the advantage over the remaining attackers, so he emptied both pistols in their direction and gestured to the defenders, who dragged the boxes towards him under cover of his fire. Before there was time to reload, the two men joined him on the wagon, and were firing at the ruffians themselves. Jeremiah turned the wagon, and they were soon heading safely out of town. But more drama was to follow.'

Montgomery looked at Sally. 'You'll have come off the Jacksonville road a mile from here?' She nodded. Montgomery continued. 'Well, in those days, that junction was in a wood, and just as well. Because a couple of minutes after they'd turned off the road, they heard horses, lots of horses. Jeremiah just had time to hide the wagon in thick trees, before two full companies of the 4th Massachusetts Cavalry, trotted by on their way to Gainesville. After the Yankees had passed, Jeremiah and his new friends retraced their steps, and came back here, exhausted and much relieved.

Jeremiah was much taken by Colonel Le Jeune's tale of their adventures and scrapes, all the way down from Richmond, and being a loyal southerner, he resolved to help them get to the coast. Of course, with Federal troops swarming all over the State, and all the roads blocked, that was no easy job.'

Montgomery sluiced his dry throat with lemon water, then continued. 'By boat they went, down the St John's River, passed Fort Butler, and onto Lake Harvey, where they requisitioned a wagon at gunpoint. The boat was then transported on the wagon, twelve miles overland to Titusville. Back on the river, they found the mosquitoes unbearable, and it was back breaking work, hauling the boat down mudflats and sandbanks, when the water was too shallow for it to float.

But after a week or so of this hell, they sighted the Jupiter Lighthouse, and with relief realised they'd made it to the Atlantic. Their boat was leaking and not fit for the ocean, so they spent time caulking it before they could put to sea. With the repairs done, they hugged the coast, paddling past Palm Beach and onto Miami, where they hid from Federal troops garrisoned at Fort Dallas.

At gunpoint again, they swapped their small craft for a seaworthy sail boat, and headed for Nassau. That is when Jeremiah left them to return here.'

'Quite an adventure,' exclaimed Sally, 'and what did become of the gold?'

'Montgomery chuckled. 'Most of it went to Nassau.'

'Most of it?' she repeated.

Montgomery stood up, and swept his arm in an expansive one hundred and eighty degree arc, gesturing towards the house. 'What do you think paid for all this?'

CHAPTER FIFTEEN

St Augustine
Florida
Present Day

'Well, I'm surprised you've a building as old as this in the States,' teased Mackay, joining Sally at the battlements.

Sally ignored his attempt to provoke her. 'That's a good shot,' she said, putting away her camera phone. 'Across the river and out to the Atlantic. I caught the sunlight on the sea. It glimmered...almost like gold.'

'Very funny.' Mackay put his arms around her and pressed her against the wall, 'of course, British towns have castles five hundred years older.'

'But most are now piles of stone.' She replied, spreading her hands on the warm bastion and scanning the horizon. 'Fascinating, that this spot is America's oldest European settlement.'

Mackay was secretly impressed, that the Castillo de San Marcos, was in such good condition. Situated at the north of the Matanzas River, a short distance from the Atlantic, he could see why the Spanish had chosen this place to settle in the sixteenth century. He noted with satisfaction, that the castle was built in response to a raid by Sir Francis Drake in 1586, it was nice to know the Spanish were kept on their toes.

The trip to Gainesville had filled most of Saturday, so they'd decided to use Sunday to sightsee as much as possible. The St Augustine Lighthouse Museum had been interesting. Then they'd enjoyed shrimp for lunch, at the Floridian restaurant on Spanish Street, but it was now mid afternoon, and with the Castillo explored, the road to the airport beckoned.

'I prefer the name Fort Mark,' said Mackay, consulting the guide book.

'What?'

'This castle was called Fort Mark, during the British East Florida period.'

She deliberately sounded disinterested at his penchant for detail, 'oh, really.'

'Next attraction should be the King's Bakery,' he continued, flicking onto the next page, 'the only surviving structure built by the British. It was constructed in 1763, to supply bread to the troops stationed at the St Francis Barracks.'

She smiled at his childish enthusiasm. 'Next time,' she said, gently. 'We have a plane to catch and I've got a President to elect.'

They motored down to Orlando, regretting they hadn't taken an extra day to explore. Sally was at the wheel of the open top, and she dropped the revs so he could hear her, 'Nassau next weekend then. Let's see what James Steele got up to there with this Le Jeune fella.'

Mackay could barely hear her, so he put up the electric windows and shouted. 'Can't you take a couple of days off? I'm sure Ruth wouldn't mind. Then we could go to Nassau, on say, Thursday.'

She shook her head. 'Can't. With the President three points ahead, I'd never forgive myself. Even taking weekends isn't ideal.'

She accelerated to 70mph, and any further attempt at conversation was futile. Mackay shrugged his shoulders and sat back. They'd made good progress in Gainesville yesterday, he thought. Mary Coggins would be pleased when he told her what they'd discovered. Nassau and the Bahamas, could wait until next weekend.

They dropped the Mercedes off at the rental company, then proceeded to security. The queues were long, but thankfully the use of their priority passes reduced the wait. Mackay always anticipated a problem at US security, and this time was no different.

The official examined Mackay's passport, wearing the default stony faced expression, mandatory for all CBP officers. The official looked at Mackay closely, then contorted his mouth, almost as if he'd eaten something unpleasant. The wait in the queue had already frayed Mackay's temper. 'Look, I've been through this dozens of times before with you people,' he said irritably. 'Yes, my tourist visa has expired, but here's the K1. I'm marrying her. She's my fiancée.'

Sally had postponed the decision on where they would live, until after the election - neither of them was really keen on marriage. If they did decide to stay in the States, and not marry, Mackay knew he would have to invest in a business to obtain a visa. A prospect he didn't relish, given Sterling's Brexit buffeting.

Sally sensed something was wrong. The inspection was taking even longer than usual. Behind them the grunts and snorts from their fellow passengers, were becoming ever more audible. From behind a partition to the left, two Orlando police officers suddenly appeared. One of them addressed Sally, 'nothing to be alarmed about Ms Purcell. We'll see you still make your flight. If you could follow us, please.'

She would never have considered herself any sort of civil rights lawyer, but none the less she remained motionless. 'Are we being arrested?' she innocently asked.

The police officers were as stern faced as the security official. This time the other officer spoke, 'we're asking you to follow us, that's all.' He looked at her severely, 'now please don't be awkward.'

To Mackay the threat was clear - his view of American police officers was largely derived from Mississippi Burning. 'Come on, Sal,' he said, stepping the way they were indicating, 'I'm sure it won't take too long.'

She frowned at his easy acquiescence and followed him. They were led down an over lit corridor, so bright it felt like a hospital, and onto an interview room. Chairs flanked the table in the centre in an adversarial way. One of the chairs was pulled back, and in it lounged FBI Director, Wade Andrews.

Andrews got up, smiling, and shook their hands. 'Sorry to drag you in like that,' said the Director. 'I hope I didn't inconvenienced you too much.'

With his distinctive shock of white hair, Andrews expected to be recognized by most educated Americans, but Mackay was British. 'I'm sorry, who are you?'

Sally answered, 'this is FBI Director, Wade Andrews, Tom.' She maintained a frosty countenance, and tried to hide her astonishment.

'Correct,' confirmed Andrews. 'Can I get you some refreshments? Coffee? Soft drink? Perhaps you'd like some tea, Tom?'

'Nothing for us,' snapped Sally.

Andrews glanced up at the camera which was monitoring the room. Without his own team here, he had to hope the Orlando police had followed his instructions and switched it off - Andrews didn't want his visit to Florida recorded.

Andrews had intended to intercept Sally and Mackay where they'd been staying; he knew the Casa Monica hotel would have been less intimidating than this. He'd patiently waited for Mackay's passport to be flagged when they'd checked into a hotel, but the booking had been in Sally's name. Andrews had only discovered where they were, when Sally had used her credit card to pay for the room, when they'd checked out.

'I understand you're Justice Purcell's daughter,' began Andrews, by way of easy conversation, hoping to break the ice.

'Is this anything to do with my father?' asked Sally, fearing for a moment her father had been caught in some smoky opium den with a hooker on each arm.

'No, no,' reassured Andrews, aware he'd gone off on the wrong track. He pointed his face at Mackay, 'this is to do with him.'

Sally looked more closely at the Director. He embodied everything that was wrong with the current administration. Appointed by the President on taking office, Andrews was a career policeman, who saw the law and civil liberties as things that could be readily dispensed with, all in the name - according to his own definition - of the greater good. With his boss, the President, even more reactionary than him, Sally suspected Andrews wielded a 'Hoover-like' grip on American lives. That was certainly the view from within the Democratic campaign. With Ruth Callaghan in the White House, Andrews's tenure would be over.

She glanced towards Mackay. He looked apprehensive. She knew he thought America was a virtual police state. Like most Brits, he'd been fed a diet of Hollywood conspiracy theories since birth, so who could blame him.

64

'So what does the Director of the FBI want with Tom Mackay?' she said. Andrews was silent. 'I'm surprised such an exalted personage as yourself is investigating visa irregularities.'

Andrews smiled, leaned back in his chair, and clasped his hands together, like some congenial missionary embarking on pastoral care for two wayward parishioners. 'What have you two been doing in Florida?'

Again he looked at Mackay, but Sally answered in a frustrated tone. 'A family history project if you must know. But what on earth has this to do with the Director of the FBI?'

'I'll come to that in a moment. Where did you go?'

Sally was determined to be unhelpful. 'That's none of your business what we....'

Mackay interrupted her, his natural inclination to comply with authority winning out. 'It's okay, Sal. Can't see any harm in telling him.' She fumed, but Mackay continued. 'We were retracing the steps of my great grandfather. He was here during your Civil War. He was a kind of diplomat. He ended up making friends with a Confederate officer and helping him escape Florida.'

Andrews noted Mackay's reluctance to mention the bullion. Perhaps they thought gold was still buried on a deserted Bahamian island, and they saw themselves starring in some 'Treasure Island' type movie. Andrews knew Mackay was already wealthy - he assumed the source of that wealth was the Confederate Treasury. Andrews spoke to Mackay, 'you don't work, do you, Tom. Prime Philadelphia property. Expensive cars. Where does it all come from?'

'My God. You people are unbelievable,' interjected Sally.

Mackay was now irritated that the FBI had snooped on him. He looked at his watch. The plane would be leaving soon. 'If you must know, I inherited my wealth from a family friend. Now, if there's nothing further, we must be going.'

Andrews didn't believe him, but without arresting them for something, he couldn't detain them any longer. He threw his cards on the table. 'Look, I'm not interested in Confederate gold. I don't care if your family fortunes are built on that gold. And if you find more gold, you can keep it as far as I'm concerned; it's not my department that'll want it back.

Andrews hesitated, and prepared to read their reactions. 'It's the Richmond Papers I want.'

They looked at him blankly. They looked at each other, uncomprehending. Andrews sensed they knew nothing. But he'd made a mistake; Sally's interest had been piqued. The daughter of one of the highest judges in the land, now knew what he was after.

She smiled at the Director, 'what Papers?'

Andrews was on the defensive. 'You'd better get going or you'll miss your flight.'

She probed again. 'What Papers?'

She was onto him. The best he could hope for now was an orderly retreat. 'Some Papers I'm trying to locate.' Andrews handed her his card. It was a risk, but one he had to take. 'If you should come across any Confederate State papers during your project, especially anything from Jefferson Davis, I'd be grateful if you could let me know. My direct line is on that card, as is my personal cell number.'

'So it's these Papers you're after,' she thought out loud, 'that's why you're here.' She turned to Mackay. 'Suddenly I'm more interested in your project, Tom.'

'That's good, Sal,' replied Mackay, completely bewildered.

Andrews stiffened and looked at her directly as he stood up. His eyes conveyed a threat, even if his soft words didn't. 'I'd be very grateful for your help here, Sally. In fact, I'd go so far as to say, it's your duty, as an American.'

Andrews's words had an incendiary effect on her but she concealed it well. Appealing to her sense of national loyalty suggested he was trying to hide secrets. She stood up. 'You can rely on us, Director. Come on, Tom.'

'Thank you both,' Andrews replied, with as much sincerity as he could muster.

They left the room. Andrews sank back in his chair and exhaled loudly. She couldn't be trusted. He would have to find the Richmond Papers himself, even if it meant a special trip to London.

CHAPTER SIXTEEN

10 Downing Street
London
31 August 1863

Since Steele had last been in London, there'd been continuous, unrelenting hot weather. As his carriage approached Downing Street, he could see the Thames was at low water. The smell was choking, forcing him to put a silk handkerchief to his nose. He knew the advent of flushing toilets meant that sewage now went straight into the river, so at low tide, the filth stretched fifty feet from each bank and was six foot deep in places.

This part of Westminster was riddled with dark alleys, gin houses and brothels. The Brain of the Empire was a dreadful place, he thought. Since his last visit, Steele saw that number fourteen Downing Street had been demolished, and that numbers ten to twelve, were now the only houses left.

Steele saw a drunk lurch towards his carriage, bounce noisily off the window, then ricochet into a dark doorway, where a couple of prostitutes were competing for the trade of a neat looking punter.

Steele entered through the famous black door and was shown into the private study. The high-ceilinged room was richly decorated with fine Eastern rugs, thick mauve velvet curtains and an array of green leather chairs. On a green baize desk, a red ministerial box spewed out reams of government papers and despatches. A second red box was under the desk, buried beneath piles of documents and official looking books. To a casual eye the room may have looked chaotic, but a more frequent visitor, would have seen the well spaced piles, neat handwriting, and general sense of experienced order.

The Prime Minister was in his seventies, but, with the exception of Cabinet meetings, still conducted government business standing up. He didn't turn when Steele entered the room, but continued writing, and all that could be heard above the gentle fizzing of the fire and the murmuring of the gas lights, was the scratch of a pen.

After a couple of minutes, Steele saw the wrinkled hand put down the pen. Then the hand straightened the despatch, and attached a seal onto the top right hand corner. It was well known that Palmerston had been hated by his Foreign Office clerks for his punctilious record keeping and punishing schedule - Steele assumed the clerks at Downing Street were faring no better.

The Prime Minister spun round and a thin, amused, almost horizontal smile crossed his face. He hadn't changed much since Steele had last seen him. He wore a black frock coat and vest, dark trousers and white shirt. His generous, dyed, carefully brushed whiskers, vibrated more than most men's, and his swept-back hair gave him an Imperial look - which was no surprise – as he was after all, Caesar's heir.

Palmerston's light movements, lack of gravitas, and half mischievous expression, evoked the air of a faded old Regency dandy - which was what he was. Famous for his numerous affairs, close encounters with his creditors, and aristocratic vulgarity, he had somehow endeared himself to working and middle classes alike, an achievement which had delivered one election victory after another.

'Good to see you, Steele,' said the Premier. 'Please take a seat, you know I like to stand.'

'Thank you, my Lord.' Steele took a green leather chair.

'Who do you think represents the biggest threat to British interests, Steele....which country I mean?'

The obvious answer was France, but that was too obvious. Steele toyed between Russia and Prussia, he knew Austria was a power in decline. 'Russia, my Lord.'

'A good answer. Most people would say France. Shrewder observers will have noticed the growing strength of Prussia. France, Prussia, Russia - all in Europe of course, all close to one another, and therein lies the crux of the matter - geography. Geography Steele, it's all about geography.'

Steele looked puzzled, so the Premier continued. 'The United States has no strong neighbours. It rules its own Continent supreme. First they bought Louisiana, then they annexed Texas, and when President

Santa Anna refused to sell them New Mexico, they quickly overran Mexico City, annexing not only New Mexico, but California as well. After that, they acquired another large chunk of Mexico via the Gadsen Purchase.'

Palmerston walked to a large ornate globe in the corner of the room, spun it round, then rested his hand on the North American continent.

'And then there is Canada, Steele. I fear for Canada. The Mexicans did us a favour there. Had President Polk not been distracted by the Mexicans, I suspect he was planning to annex Columbia right up to the Russian border at Alaska - as the majority in his Democratic Party wanted him to do. I couldn't have allowed that to happen. It would have meant war. But because of the Mexican War, I was able to agree the border would be fixed at the 49th parallel. That was nearly fifteen years ago, Steele, and since then Manifest Destiny has caught hold in America. Only last year, we had Lincoln's Homestead Act encouraging settlers to go West by giving them free land.'

'Manifest Destiny, my Lord?'

'It's the belief held by some Americans, that the United States has no natural boundaries. Already the country spans east to west - from the Atlantic to the Pacific Ocean - why not north to south, Canada, Cuba, and Mexico - all are at risk. And when we attempt to check them, as we did with the short-lived Republic of Texas, they cite the Monroe Doctrine at us and back it up with force. We are a maritime power, Steele, a truly great maritime power, indeed perhaps the greatest maritime power the world has ever seen, but ask us to enforce our will ten miles from the coast, and we start to struggle.'

'But surely, my Lord, the country is split in two. The Civil War has weakened them.'

'That is why you're here.'

Palmerston pointed to Richmond on the globe. 'There are those in my Cabinet who wish me to recognise the Confederate States. Last year I was close to doing so. I still haven't completely ruled it out. A divided, frail America is in our interest, and supplying the South has benefited our industries. The problem is the slavery issue. We haven't spent a fortune

69

on the West Africa Squadron, captured 1600 slave ships, and freed 150,000 Africans, to suddenly reverse our policy of fifty years and acknowledge a slave state.'

'I can see your difficulty, my Lord.' Steele began to see where he might fit into the Prime Minister's plans. There was no Private Secretary taking notes. The expedition he would 'volunteer' for would not be sanctioned by the Cabinet. In an official capacity, Palmerston couldn't try to destabilise America, but in an unofficial capacity, through Steele, he could.

'What I'm proposing, Steele,' said the Premier, with a warm, enveloping smile, 'is a mission of nuanced complexity. I need a man of sharp intellect and resourcefulness, who can appreciate the delicacies of the situation and act with the appropriate decorum.'

The rakish charm of the old man was undeniable; against his will, Steele felt himself being drawn in. 'What exactly do you want me to do, my Lord?'

'I have been in government for 55 years now. I was Secretary at War in 1814, when we last fought the Americans, when we burned their White House. A terrible business of which I never approved. During those chaotic days in Washington, thousands of slaves escaped and fled to our colonies.'

Palmerston looked amused, then continued. 'Would you believe one slave, saved the life of our commander, General Ross? Not only that. This slave was from President Madison's household, and came to us directly from the White House.'

'I bet he had some useful intelligence, sir?'

The Premier laughed. 'You could say that. He brought us a document which told of a secret so great, that if it were to become known, it would rock the very foundations of America. After Gettysburg, I doubt it will change the outcome of this war, but it will strengthen Davis's negotiating position. Who knows? It may prolong the life of his odious regime and permanently split America. That would certainly be in the British interest.'

Steele was curious. 'What sort of document is it?'

Palmerston's face hardened. 'Its contents will remain confidential until you deliver it, directly into President Davis's hand in Richmond. He will know best how to deploy the document for maximum effect. He will know that the document comes from me, but you'll give it to him in a private capacity. Then I can deny all knowledge of it later if necessary.'

Steele was irritated he couldn't be trusted; to the Prime Minister he was a mere errand boy. He knew Palmerston only tolerated him, because he'd been good at getting unpleasant things done for him in the past - Steele knew, that like any aristocrat, the Premier despised him and his middle class roots. Steele voiced his frustration. 'So I'm to deliver this document in a private capacity yet not know its contents?'

The Prime Minister bristled, his notorious temper smouldering. 'Do you have a problem with that?'

Steele didn't answer the question. He'd steam open the letter and read the document at the first opportunity, but it wasn't yet clear what his remuneration would be. Could he push the Premier a little further? 'You assume I wish to take up this appointment, my Lord.'

Palmerston's expression hardened. 'Steele, you're a former soldier with few, if any, prospects. I hear your father's business is in severe financial difficulties, and I know you depend on a small East India Company pension. You have served me well in the past. I'm grateful for that. But know this. I am your only patron. If you have received a better opportunity than the one I'm offering you now, please declare it, and we'll say no more of this American venture.'

Palmerston's gaze was so intense it felt corrosive. 'Your Lordship summarises my personal circumstances very succinctly,' replied Steele evenly. 'What is my proposed remuneration for this role?'

Palmerston was known for his parsimony with public funds, and he shifted uneasily before speaking. 'Very well, I'll pay you fifteen hundred pounds plus expenses.' He paused to let the offer sink in. 'Now, enough of this grubby wheeling and dealing, will you accept this appointment or not?' Palmerston fixed his eye on Steele.

Steele didn't trust the Prime Minister - he never had. But as Palmerston had pointed out, he had few options. He nodded in assent.

CHAPTER SEVENTEEN

Four Seasons Hotel
Philadelphia
Present Day

The late evening sun shone through the glazed dining room on the 59th floor with such brilliance, that the guests were silhouetted in gold. Enjoying the stunning views from the Norman Foster designed hotel, were the great and the good of centrist leaning Philadelphia. The occasion was a Ruth Callaghan fundraising event, hosted by the House Speaker, Nancy Poulson.

It had been sometime since Mackay had last worn his dinner suit, months of physical idleness had taken their toll, and his trousers pinched uncomfortably - their next home would have a pool, he thought. Sally looked ravishing. He was pleased she was wearing the Cartier diamond necklace he'd bought her - which plunged brilliantly down her low cut dress like a waterfall.

The dinner promised a good turnout of Democratic bigwigs past and present. Mackay had winced when he'd made out a $40,000 cheque for the tickets, but as they took their seats at an intimate, circular table, he realised it was worth every cent, as sandwiched between himself and Sally, was the aged, but vibrant former President, Alex Freeman.

'Now, you look vaguely familiar,' said Freeman, with a smile, addressing himself to Sally.

She grinned at the man Mackay knew to be one of her heroes. 'Yes, we've met before, Mr President. A White House function I think, I was only a teenager at the time.'

'Remind me.'

'My father was there for some reason, Justice Purcell.'

Freeman laughed. 'I'm surprised he came given I tried to block his nomination. If the election had been a month later, I'd have chosen someone else.'

'Yes. I remember he was quite cross with you at the time. You certainly didn't get his vote.'

Freeman looked around the room at the assembled Democrats. 'Looks like I got yours though. And who's this?'

'My fiancé, Tom Mackay. A displaced Brit. I can't get rid of him.'

Mackay shook Freeman's hand. 'Do I address you as Mr President?'

'I don't think you have to, although some folk do. Alex is fine.'

Mackay studied him more closely. Put on the ticket by a Democratic President only interested in tokenism and the black vote, Freeman had got the top job after a fatal Rose Garden heart attack, and, with his own two terms, had served ten years. In that time he'd changed the American political landscape. As popular as ever, he'd be elected again with a landslide, were it not for the Twenty Second Amendment to the Constitution, which, Sally had told Mackay, limited the Presidency to ten years.

Mackay finished a mouthful of garlic scallops. 'And what do you do with yourself now, Alex?'

'Oh, well there are the grandchildren. And there's my Foundation. Of course, I've spent the last six months trying to get Ruth elected. Keeps me busy.'

Sally had finished her scallops and seemed determined to prevent Freeman from finishing his. 'Tell me, of your time in office, Mr President, what were the highs and lows?'

Freeman didn't hesitate. 'My healthcare programme. I don't think I'd have succeeded without the extra two years which most Presidents don't get. It was a ten year war, with the Republicans battling every stage. Don't forget in those ten years, we only controlled the Senate and House for two of them. That was our window, and thank God we took it.'

Freeman eyed his untouched starter and glanced enviously at Mackay's empty plate, before continuing. 'A low would have to be gun control. Every month we see mass shootings, but there seems little we can do about it with the right to bear arms enshrined in the Constitution. I'm convinced the American people would vote to scrap the Second

73

Amendment if given an opportunity, but the chances of getting any kind of reform through Congress, never mind ratification by enough States, is close to nil.'

Freeman ended his diatribe by forking a scallop into his mouth.

Mackay continued with the topic. 'Across the Pond our system of government isn't perfect by any means, but I remember after the Hungerford massacre in the 1980s, semi automatic weapons were banned by the following year. No constitution, Supreme Court or hostile second chamber to impede reform, no need to put the issue in a manifesto and ask the electorate for its view. Prime Minister Thatcher just went ahead and banned them.'

Freeman gently shook his head. 'The irony is, the reason we have the right to bear arms is because of you British.'

Mackay sat back as the waiters began to clear away the plates. 'Yes, Sally told me.' Mackay smiled. 'Another one to pin on Mad King George.'

Freeman's unfinished plate was the only survivor on the table. Reluctantly he signalled the waiter could take it - he resolved to talk less during the Steak Diane.

'And what do you do, Tom, whilst Sally is out campaigning?'

She chipped in, teasing. 'By profession he's an accountant, but right now he's a man of leisure. I suppose you could say he's a modern day treasure hunter in search of gold. Bit like those early twentieth century Egyptologists seeking the riches of the Pharaohs.'

Mackay's responding smile was watery. 'Don't think the image quite fits, Sal. Anyway, my great grandfather died recently and I, we...' he said, looking at Sally '... are finishing a family history project he started. We were in Florida last weekend and discovered my ancestor had helped a Confederate Officer, a Pierre Le Jeune, escape to the Bahamas at the end of the War with the Confederate Treasury.'

'Pierre Le Jeune,' echoed a voice from across the table. 'That's a name I heard recently. One of my constituents down in New Orleans had some Confederate papers which the FBI were interested in.'

It was difficult to discern whether Sally or Mackay's jaw dropped the furthest. 'Go on Congressman,' she spluttered.

The Congressman was surprised at their reaction. This seemed more than a coincidence. He continued. 'She, Rebecca Le Jeune that is, is the last of her line. She had an envelope from Jeff Davis her family had kept for a hundred and fifty years. Remarkably she hadn't read what was inside. The envelope had remained unopened since the day Davis sealed it, on his last day in Richmond back in 1865.'

The Congressman could see they hung on his every word - even former President Freeman seemed enthralled. The Congressman eyed his untouched steak ravenously, but could see he would have to continue. 'Ms Le Jeune, asked me to give the letter directly to the President. Well, as you know, gaining access to the White House isn't easy. I contacted a White House aide who more or less brushed me off. I was astonished when I was personally contacted by FBI Director Andrews the next day. I gave him Ms Le Jeune's details, then thought nothing more of it. By chance, I saw her the other day at a society function. She told me Andrews himself had turned up at her house with a team of agents, brandishing a warrant. Andrews took the sealed envelope along with Pierre Le Jeune's journal. She was furious.'

Mackay looked at Sally, shocked. Sally looked back at him, then spoke, barely able to keep the excitement from her voice. 'Last Sunday, when we were at Orlando airport on the way back from our research trip, we were more or less arrested by Andrews. He interviewed us about this envelope. He called it the Richmond Papers. He thought we had them.'

Freeman sat upright in his chair, a forkful of steak discarded, his voice calm but concerned, 'what is going on here?'

'Seems these Richmond Papers might contain a big secret,' said Sally, 'something Andrews wants.'

Freeman was deep in thought, his brain processing ten years of meetings and briefings like some military grade computer. 'I wasn't told anything about these Richmond Papers. It's the sort of thing which would stick in my mind.'

Sally saw conspiracies everywhere. 'A cover up I shouldn't wonder. Perhaps Tom and I will discover more in the Bahamas next weekend.'

The waiters appeared again to top up their wine glasses. A round of applause, signalled Nancy Poulson was about to introduce Ruth Callaghan.

Freeman wasn't yet convinced anything was untoward, but he gently placed his hand on Sally's arm and drew closer. 'Keep me in the loop on this,' he said, in a low voice, 'if something was hidden from me, I want to know.'

Sally beamed. She was now on a crusade to find the truth. A truth hidden for ten years from the one elected official who had access to all the secrets. 'Of course, Mr President. You can count on me.'

CHAPTER EIGHTEEN

British Colonial Hilton Hotel
Nassau
Bahamas
Present Day

'You idiot,' she teased, gently cuffing him around the ear, 'you've had nothing to do all week but organize travel. Where's the view?'

'Sorry Sal, I got caught up in the history of the island and didn't check.'

Mackay glanced around the Governor's suite and picked up the hotel guide. 'Like the Casa Monica in St Augustine, I see this hotel was also built by your man Henry Flagler,' he said. 'He built it in the 1920s. This suite in is in honour of Governor Woodes Rogers. He was a character in that historical drama we watched - Black Sails. Remember that guy Rogers put an end to piracy around here – must be why there's a statue of him at the front of the hotel.'

She smiled at him, her irritation softened by his schoolboy enthusiasm. 'The city is gorgeous. The hotel is lovely. I like the colonial décor. This suite is great. It's just the lack of view. When you go to the Caribbean, you need a sea view!'

He didn't reply and looked out over a Nassau shimmering in the early evening warmth.

'Come on then,' she said.

He turned. The polka dot bikini was on, and she had a beach towel in one hand and the Lonely Planet guide to Nassau in the other. Her energy was inexhaustible he thought, as he reached for his swimming shorts.

After their swim, they went to the hotel's Art Deco Bar. Mackay was too lazy to comprehend the hotel's extensive cocktail list and instead, delegated the decision to the attentive waiter.

77

'Two traditional Bahamian cocktails please?'

'Can I suggest a couple of Goombay Smashes, sir? As you'd expect it's rum based, with apricot brandy and pineapple juice.'

'Sounds perfect.' The waiter left.

'You see what this bar is called?' said Sally.

'Yes, I'd noticed that - The Bullion Bar.' Mackay's brain constructed a quick historical timeline. 'Not likely to be Confederate bullion though, more likely to be pieces of eight pinched from Spanish ships taking gold from South America to Spain. Pirates like Sir Henry Morgan were given commissions by the King which legitimized their activities. Made them and the Crown extremely rich,' he paused, his mind locating a parcel of data as efficiently as an Amazon warehouse. 'In fact, I vaguely recall Morgan ended up as Governor of Jamaica.'

Sally nodded, feigning interest as best she could - Mackay's historical blurb washing over her. Thankfully the cocktails arrived. 'That's a great taste,' she said, in between giggles, as Mackay's straw lodged up his left nostril.

'Mmm. Bit too good,' he said, already determined to have a second.

It may have been the tropical heat coupled with the lack of hydration, or the absence of an evening meal in their stomachs, or a hard week working on Ruth Callaghan's campaign, perhaps it was simply the dozen Goombay Smashes, whatever the reason, the pair swayed up to their suite and collapsed into bed even before it was fully dark.

The following morning, Sally got all the sea views she wanted as they ate breakfast in the Aqua restaurant. 'That's better,' she said, pushing away her empty plate.

'Fair to say we overdid the cocktails,' declared Mackay, through a mouthful of toast.

Sally lowered her voice, her eyes flickering with amusement, 'the rum certainly brought out the lusty pirate in you.'

Mackay looked away sheepishly, a drunken memory of boarding Sally without much invitation coming to mind. 'Er, yes....just trying to give you the authentic buccaneer experience, Sal. All included in the tour price.'

His joke was weak, but she laughed to hide his embarrassment. Mackay finished his toast quickly and they left the restaurant.

Exiting the hotel from the rear, they turned east and walked along Bay Street. It was early, but already the temperature was nudging seventy – a pleasant breeze drifted in from the sparkling Caribbean to the north.

After a few minutes, they came to Parliament Square. 'Wow. That *is* quaint,' said Sally, gesturing towards the pink and white mansion which served as the country's legislature.

Further on, at the southern end of the Square, they found the library, an equally charming pink octagonal shaped building ringed with palm trees. They entered and headed upstairs - spending a few minutes enjoying the views from the wrap around veranda - before descending into the reading room.

After an hour or so flicking through endless microfiches, Mackay looked around the room for Sally. He found her partially hidden in a wooden recess, leafing through old newspapers. 'Little wonder we struggled to find anything online. Not a lot of this has been digitalized,' he said.

'These newspapers are useful though, Tom, especially the Nassau Guardian. It seems that blockade running for the Confederacy made this city a boom town. By 1865 it was all over though, and a depression had kicked in.'

Mackay looked at the front page of a yellowing Nassau Guardian. The font was similar to the British Guardian newspaper but the royal coat of arms was more akin to the UK Times.

'The 28th of May is the next one,' said Sally, handing it to Mackay, and taking the 29th of May herself.

After a few minutes, she pointed to a small article at the bottom right hand corner of page 2. 'This seems a bit strange,' she said.

Nassau Guardian

29th May 1865

We are informed that the Confederate States Ship Shenandoah, last night, under the cover of darkness, and without permission, slipped her moorings and put to sea. Last week, following a request from the United States Government, the ship had been impounded by order of the Colonial Secretary. We are also informed that on leaving Nassau, the Shenandoah evaded the Union warships stationed in the harbour and off Hog Island.'

'Sounds a bit too convenient,' agreed Mackay. 'An impounded ship sails out of the harbour, under the guns of Fort Charlotte, without anyone noticing.'

'Le Jeune and James Steele must surely have been on board,' mused Sally, 'why else would the Shenandoah's captain take such a risk?'

Mackay nodded, 'yes, if the captain knew the war was over and he put to sea as a belligerent, he risked being accused of piracy. The sentence for that would have been death.'

Sally agreed. 'I can't believe the captain would take such a chance for a few boxes of bullion. They must have told him about the importance of the Richmond Papers.'

A wrinkled librarian shuffled towards them. 'We're closing for lunch now, dear.'

Mackay smiled at her, 'we're just going.'

Outside the sun was beating down. Mackay regretted not bringing a hat. Sally looped her arm through his and propelled them towards Bay Street. The touch of her arm was cooling on his skin.

'Where next then?' she asked.

'Let's saunter along Woodes Rogers Walk and find somewhere by the harbour for lunch. I know how you like sea views.'

She smiled at him, 'I don't mean lunch. Where next on our quest?'

Mackay couldn't focus properly. Last night's Goombay Smashes had jolted his appetite, he was very hungry, and had a need for bulky carbohydrates.

'Where next?' she repeated, with a touch of impatience.

He halted with their arms still linked. 'Now, you listen to me Ms Purcell,' he said, adopting the tone of an authority figure, a governor perhaps, 'first I'm having lunch and so are you. Then I'm spending the rest of the day sightseeing, a nosey at the Atlantis, Fort Charlotte, Paradise Island tour....and so are you. Then I'm having a romantic meal tonight overlooking the bay....and so are you.'

She tried to look severe.

'Then, next week, whilst you're getting a President elected, I'll research this Shenandoah ship and plan the next stage. Is all that clear?'

She fluttered her eyelashes at him coquettishly and gave him her best Vivian Leigh impression in an affected southern drawl. 'My sir, you British are so masterful.'

CHAPTER NINETEEN

Nassau
Bahamas
28 May 1865

Steele hauled in the sail and let the boat glide towards the quay. He looked at Le Jeune and they laughed hysterically - the sense of relief was overwhelming. Two hundred miles in an open boat from Florida, hadn't been easy.

'And the highlight of your pleasure cruise, sir?' joked Steele, as he threw the painter towards a man on the wharf.

Le Jeune readied the stern line. 'A toss up between the storm and the pirates.'

Steele reflected on their close encounters with death. He had never rated himself as much of a sailor but now he wasn't so sure - the storm had nearly capsized the boat a dozen times.

The encounter with pirates - if you could call them that – had been less hazardous. The small schooner they'd met had been a blockade runner, put out of work by Union warships.

Steele had been glad the pirates' lazy search failed to spot the bullion boxes camouflaged as bulkheads - the pirates had numerical superiority, but were unprepared; Steele knew his rapid fire pistols would have meant a bloodbath. Instead the encounter had ended amicably, with the pirates even giving them much needed water.

A customs official approached and glanced down at their 'empty' boat. 'From Florida?' he asked, noting the remains of Le Jeune's filthy and tattered uniform; Southerners arriving in Nassau was nothing new. The American nodded. It was close to lunch and the official was hungry, 'I see you've nothing to declare,' said the official. He looked at Steele's grimy face and grubby shirt. 'If you want a bath, I can recommend the Royal Victoria Hotel.'

The official turned back to the wharf but then halted, and spun round again, addressing himself to Le Jeune. 'By the way, some of your folk are over there. He gestured towards a full rigged sailing ship across the harbour.

The official left and Le Jeune looked across the water, from the stern of the warship, fluttered the Battle Flag of the Confederacy. 'There's our passage to England, James!' he said excitedly. 'Let's find the Royal Victoria and get this gold in the hotel safe. Then I'll make contact with the captain of that ship.'

'I think we could both do with a set of new clothes,' said Steele, 'have you any pounds to spare? I don't have enough.'

Le Jeune examined his wallet, hoping to find some greenbacks. 'Only greybacks,' he said, tossing the worthless Confederate currency away.

'Well, I guess we'll get credit at the hotel with the bullion in the safe,' said Steele, hailing a man with a handcart.

On their way to the hotel, they passed row upon row of warehouses, all now empty of cotton and war supplies. The port was a mass of idle ropes, pulleys and cranes. Unemployed men hung around in groups, despairing, desperate and hungry.

Le Jeune and Steele headed inland, passing the villas of wealthier inhabitants and - half hidden by fruit trees - a quaint, pink, octagonal library.

Unlike most of wooden Nassau, Le Jeune saw the Royal Victoria Hotel was made of stone. The paved driveway was lined with evenly spaced palm trees, which in turn, were shaded by two dozen stone pillars, three stories high. The pillars supported the long double fronted veranda, which butted up against the main lozenge shaped building. The entrance was through a double arched porch, bordered with pots bursting with brilliantly coloured tropical flowers.

'Man. What a place!' exclaimed Le Jeune, in astonishment.

Steele was also taken aback. 'Certainly a bit roomier than our boat.'

Their appearance didn't suggest they were potential guests, but their bearing, and the boxes in the handcart, persuaded the concierge to give them the benefit of the doubt.

They bathed, ate, and their sleep, aided by mattresses and pillows, was deep. Le Jeune had his uniform cleaned and repaired - he wore it that evening, as he and Steele marched through the fading sunlight and up the gang plank of the CSS Shenandoah.

Steele saw the two hundred foot vessel was an iron-framed sailing ship, but a short funnel by the main mast, also meant steam power. They were met by the officer of the watch, who showed them into a spacious main cabin where Commander James Waddell was seated. The sailor stood to his feet as Le Jeune entered, and saluted.

'Stand easy, Commander,' said Le Jeune, taking one of the seats opposite Waddell's desk and indicating Steele should take the other.

Waddell sat down himself. 'What can I do for you, sir?' he asked, unable to hide the apprehension in his voice.

Le Jeune related the events since Richmond - the meeting with President Davis, the train, the gold, their escape from Florida. He said nothing of the sealed envelope he'd been entrusted with.

Waddell listened attentively, then told of the Shenandoah's own exploits. A year long voyage via Melbourne, twenty union whalers captured in the Pacific, an unsuccessful attempt to enter Charlestown, then onto Nassau.

Le Jeune listened with growing admiration, 'and what's your current status?' he said.

'We were shadowed here by three Union warships,' said Waddell, pointing to a chart, I put in here to recoal, only to find out General Lee had surrendered. The British also said the President had been arrested, but I wasn't sure.'

'That's correct,' confirmed Le Jeune.

Waddell grimaced. 'Then it's over.' He looked at some papers on his desk. 'I've done the right thing then.'

'What's that?' said Le Jeune quickly, alarm in his voice.

'I've all but surrendered the ship to the British. Here are the papers. The colonial authorities are waiting for confirmation from London that she can be handed over to the two Union ships, the far side of the harbour.'

'But you're still flying your Battle Flag,' interrupted Steele.

Waddell felt uncomfortable. He sensed these two men were hardened professionals. Le Jeune was his superior officer and there was no hint of surrender in his eyes. This could be awkward. 'Technically I haven't surrendered,' he stated, as evenly as he could manage.

Le Jeune pulled out his authority letter from Davis and showed it to the sailor, who read it with a heightened sense of dread. He knew the order was coming even before it passed Le Jeune's lips.

'Commander Waddell, I'm directing you to take us to Britain.'

Waddell frowned. 'Now just hang on a minute, Colonel. General Lee has surrendered. The President has been arrested and charged with treason. The war is clearly over.' Steele noted the emotion in the Commander's voice was accentuating his South Carolina drawl. Waddell continued. 'Even before the war finished, it wasn't clear to me the amnesty offered to our soldiers would extend to the navy. Many Federals consider us as nothing more than commercial raiders. If we leave this harbour under these circumstances, there's a good chance we'll be hung for piracy,'

'I understand the difficulty,' said Le Jeune soothingly. 'I admit that legally this is tricky, but the situation is unclear. If it's of any use, the last we heard was that General Kirby Smith was still in the field in Texas.'

Le Jeune could see Waddell derived some comfort from this but he remained unconvinced and reluctant. He needed further persuasion and cajoling. 'In the safe of my hotel there are ten boxes of gold bullion. One of those boxes can be divided between you and your men. Should be at least fifty thousand dollars worth, maybe more.'

Le Jeune paused to let the offer sink in. Waddell was considering the inducement.

'How many men have you got?' asked Steele.

'We're down to about seventy, barely enough to crew her.'

'Only seventy,' repeated Steele, surprised. 'Still, dividing by seventy comes to a tidy sum for each man.'

Le Jeune could see Waddell was still undecided. He required more prodding. 'Look, I appreciate you're not comfortable with this and I'm not going to order you to help us. Would any of your junior officers be prepared to take us across the Atlantic?'

Waddell bridled at this. 'I'm the Captain of the Shenandoah. This is my ship; I'll bloody well take you to England.'

Le Jeune smiled. 'Thank you, Commander.'

Waddell's mind now switched to strategy. 'Though how you expect us to get out of the harbour, under the guns of Fort Charlotte, and passed two Union warships here, and another standing off Hogg Island, is unclear.'

Le Jeune clapped him on the shoulder. 'Don't worry about that Waddell. That's why we have Mr Steele here. That's his department.'

CHAPTER TWENTY

Nassau
Bahamas
28 May 1865

G overnment House was a short walk from the harbour, but despite the afternoon sun losing its midday heat, Steele still sweated profusely. Gangs of thin, idle men, lounging around street corners made him uneasy, but he relaxed a little when he approached the building and saw red coated sentries standing like statues.

The official residence of the Governor was untypical of the New England colonial style, which was so prevalent in Nassau. Its pink colours, and wide verandas, were certainly Bahamian, but its white columns and Palladian frontage evoked both the British Regency period and plantation house elegance.

Steele doubted whether the sentries would have waved him through dressed as he'd been earlier in the day, but now, clothed in a new suit, he sauntered past them. No official would know who he was, so he thought the best tactic was to frighten the junior clerks who dealt with his angry demands to see the Governor.

When this worked, Steele met the Colonial Secretary, a timid official, whom he bullied into believing he was Palmerston's right hand man – which proved enough to get an audience with the Governor. As a last resort, Steele held a letter of authority from the Prime Minister - similar to the one Davis gave Le Jeune - but it had been given to Steele for a very different purpose, and he was reluctant to use it.

As he waited outside the Governor's office, Steele reflected on why he was sticking his neck out to help Le Jeune. He liked Le Jeune, and since Richmond they'd bonded, but that in itself wasn't enough. The gold was certainly an inducement. Steele wasn't a wealthy man and just one of the boxes would free him from his dependence on Palmerston's loathsome patronage. He knew he had an understanding with Le Jeune about the gold, although it was a worry that the exact nature of that understanding hadn't been settled between them.

Another reason why Le Jeune deserved his help was the American's keen sense of honour. Le Jeune had given Davis his word, as a Southern gentleman, that he'd get that sealed envelope to London. Steele admired this. In his world of subterfuge and duplicity, principles were easily dispensable. Having come as far as this and bested so many hazards, Steele was determined that the Shenandoah should reach English shores. To achieve this, the next obstacle to overcome was His Excellency the Governor of the Bahamas, Sir Rawson Rawson, KCMG.

The door opened and the Colonial Secretary waved Steele into a spacious wood panelled office. The gently fizzing lamps had just been lit and Steele inhaled the oily traces in the air. The greying Governor, dressed in an elaborate confusion of lace collars, cuffs and buttons, sat behind an enormous desk which was far too big for him.

'Mr James Steele, your Excellency,' announced the Colonial Secretary.

'Come in, come in, Mr Steele, take a seat.'

Rawson's greeting was warm but Steele sensed nervousness. If Steele was as close to Palmerston as he'd led them to believe, they'd be fearful of him. In some ways it was reassuring that senior officials were as frightened of Palmerston as Steele was himself. 'Thank you for seeing me at such short notice, your Excellency.'

Steele was now polite rather than belligerent. It was important he persuaded them to help him without using the Prime Minister's authority letter. Steele's firm approach had got him this far, so he resolved to continue in the same vein.

The Governor nodded at a black footman who was perspiring heavily under his powdered wig. The footman picked up a silver tray from a sideboard and put it on the desk between Steele and the Governor. On the tray there were three large punch cups flanking an immense punch bowl. Adjacent to the bowl was a huge ornate ladle which bore the Governor's cipher.

'We like to take a glass or two of punch in the late afternoon,' said Rawson mischievously. 'It's my own recipe based on Planter's Punch -

lemon juice, lime juice, pineapple juice, not too much orange juice and plenty of rum, of course.'

With that Rawson sprung out of his chair and grabbed the ladle. Steele watched transfixed, as the Governor's practiced hand hypnotically swung and dipped the ladle repeatedly, splashing the liquid into the glasses with perfect precision, never spilling a drop.

'They say this ladle belonged to the last Spanish Governor,' said Rawson. 'It was stolen from him along with the island itself by Governor Woodes Rogers.' Steele glanced at the ruddy, smiling face of one of Rogers's successors.

The potency of the punch could be ascertained long before the cup got anywhere near Steele's lips. The heady scent filled his nostrils but the taste was pleasant, so Steele downed the measure in one. Rawson was delighted and took the opportunity to refill his own cup at the same time as Steele's.

'Well done, Steele,' said Rawson, 'not too strong is it?'

'Not strong enough,' chipped in the Colonial Secretary.

Steele was having difficulty maintaining the severe countenance he'd intended. 'It certainly packs a punch, your Excellency.'

The joke was old and weak but Rawson and the Colonial Secretary roared with laughter. 'Another glass, Steele?' asked the Governor, topping up Steele's cup before he could reply.

Steele took another mouthful then determined to focus on the purpose of his visit. 'About the Shenandoah, sir?'

Rawson straightened up a little and directed his glassy eyes at Steele. 'Yes, I've been appraised of the situation. Nothing to be done I'm afraid.' He picked up a document from his desk and showed it to Steele. 'From the Foreign Office, just came in, I'm to hand this Confederate ship over to the Federal officers here in Nassau.'

Steele looked at the Governor severely. 'But that is now irrelevant, Sir Rawson, my request supersedes it.'

Despite the punch, Rawson's expression hardened. 'I've no doubt you are, who you say you are Steele, but I can't ignore these orders. I won't risk a diplomatic incident with the Americans based on the say-so of a man who turned up here this morning in a twenty foot boat looking like a vagabond.'

'I'm sorry, your Excellency, but I must insist that the Shenandoah is released to Colonel Le Jeune and myself and given safe passage out of Nassau. I'm on state business for Lord Palmerston who won't be pleased if you ignore my wishes.'

Steele observed Rawson as he pondered the threat. He knew Rawson was a reform-minded, well meaning Governor with an interest in statistics and botany, but as a career colonial administrator he was institutionally averse to risk.

'The Shenandoah will be handed over to the Americans,' he said, firmly.

Steele reached into his coat pocket and handed Rawson the letter which carried the Downing Street cipher:

All of Her Majesty's civilian and military personnel are to give the bearer of this letter, James Steele, their total and unconditional cooperation. Mr Steele, in order to perform the duties with which I have tasked him, has my full authority to direct any and all civilian and military personnel, of whatever rank, as he sees fit. Given under my hand this thirty first day of August, one thousand eight hundred and sixty three and by Her Majesty's command.
Palmerston

Rawson handed the letter to the Colonial Secretary who read it, then noted its contents in an official looking log. Steele knew now there'd be no escaping a reckoning with Palmerston.

Rawson sat back in his chair and sighed, placing his hands behind his head. 'Well, this is awkward,' he said, 'can't see that whatever you're doing is important enough to risk a spat with the Yanks, but no one ever quite knows what's in his Lordship's mind.'

'Long experience of dealing with the Prime Minister has taught me as much,' agreed Steele, relieved he had Rawson's support.

The rum was inhibiting a plan forming in the Governor's mind but eventually he focused and sat forward. Rawson spoke slowly. 'Releasing the Shenandoah is the easy bit. Get one of the sentries to run up to Fort Charles and tell the garrison commander not to fire his guns at anything until further notice. Spike them if he has to. If we accidentally fire on a Union warship there'll be merry hell to pay.' The Colonial Secretary nodded to the footman who disappeared on the errand. 'More difficult knowing what to do about the Union ships in the harbour.' There was silence. Rawson gulped down the remainder of the punch. 'Any ideas?'

'We'll just have to risk it in the darkness, Sir Rawson,' said Steele, 'there isn't much moonlight, I should know, I've just spent weeks in an open boat.'

The Governor nodded, a half smile forming on his face. 'Let's improve the odds though. It's still early. Send word to the officers of the two Federal ships in the harbour. Ask them here for dinner. Most are likely to accept an invitation to Government House.'

'We already have some local businessmen and their wives invited this evening, sir,' pointed out the Colonial Secretary.

'Replace them with Federal sailors; the local dignitaries can miss out on a meal for once if Queen and country demands it.'

The Colonial Secretary bustled out the room. Rawson stood up and guided Steele to the door. 'Best I can do, Steele. You'll just have to take your chances with the Federal ship off Hogg Island.'

'I'm grateful, your Excellency.'

Rawson focused his watery eyes on Steele. 'I trust you'll mention to Old Pam how helpful I've been? The hot climate here doesn't really suit my wife. We preferred Cape colony when I was there as Colonial Secretary.'

Rawson's meaning was clear. Steele suddenly felt fraudulent. Palmerston would be furious when he discovered Steele's brazen misuse of his authority. The Premier had given him the letter to ease his passage to Richmond two years ago, not for helping a Confederate warship evade its pursuers. Whilst Steele would be at the centre of the Prime Minister's wrath, Rawson would get caught on the periphery.

'I'll see what I can do, your Excellency.'

'Good man, now if you'll excuse me. I've a seating plan to rearrange.'

CHAPTER TWENTY ONE

Clinton Street
Washington Square West
Philadelphia
Present Day

'Read it again,' said Purcell, the exasperation clear in his voice, 'out loud!'

Mackay cleared his throat, 'a well regulated Militia, being necessary to the security of a free state, the right of the people to help and bear arms shall not be infringed.'

'Well?' asked Purcell.

'Well what?' repeated Mackay sharply, 'I haven't changed my mind.'

Mackay looked at him and was glad the Supreme Court's recess was over and Purcell was returning to Washington. Mackay rarely agreed with Sally's father on anything, and the interpretation of the Second Amendment to the United States Constitution was no exception.

Whilst Sally was able to tolerate her father and on occasions seemed to enjoy his company, Mackay found him a difficult man. Other than loneliness, Mackay couldn't understand why he chose to stay with them, when the Judge had a grand house in Washington and a summer house in Cape Cod. Mackay acknowledged Purcell was polite and could be charming, but he rarely demonstrated any affection towards Sally.

Mackay glared at him. Their mutual distrust bordered on dislike; hostility simmered during their every conversation.

Earlier, Sally had left for campaign headquarters and foolishly left them at breakfast together. To make conversation, Mackay had asked what case the Supreme Court would be considering when it reconvened. To humour Mackay, Purcell had explained that the court would be enforcing an individual's right to bear arms.

Mackay had unintentionally yawned when Purcell had begun to explain the legal technicalities of the case. This had irritated Purcell, but the argument had really begun when Mackay had accused him, and his colleagues on the bench who supported the Second Amendment, of being obtuse.

'Look Donald,' continued Mackay, 'if it only said 'the right of the people to keep and bear arms shall not be infringed,' I might have agreed with you, but it doesn't, does it, you can't ignore the militia and free state bit at the beginning. Any idiot can see it refers to an army.' Purcell was struggling to suppress his anger, but Mackay didn't notice and ploughed on regardless. 'Even if you're right, the text should be interpreted through a 21st century prism, not an 18th century one. The Second Amendment has no valid function in a modern society and its consequences, which we see on our TV screens every week, are murderous.'

Mackay sensed he'd overdone it. Purcell looked set to explode; his voice shook with emotion. 'If the American people find parts of their Constitution, murderous, to use your word, then there's a mechanism, through their elected representatives, to change it.'

Mackay tried not to frown, but failed, 'fat chance of that happening. Sal's told me how it works. It has to be supported by two thirds of both houses of Congress, then ratified by thirty eight of the fifty states. Really no likelihood of reform happening is there?'

'I'll concede, it's rare.'

'When was the last change?'

'1992. But that's the whole point. It's designed to be difficult to change.'

Mackay shook his head and continued, 'a young, democratic republic finding its way in a world of monarchs and empires. I can see the logic back in the 1780s, but now it's not fit for purpose, especially with judges like you giving a literal interpretation to eighteenth century words, words which result in dozens being killed.'

'Enough,' snapped the judge. Mackay waited for Purcell to launch into the usual personal attack on him, but the passion faded from his face. 'Let's agree to differ then,' said Purcell. He picked up his suitcase and headed for the door. 'I see you've had some legal training, Tom.'

Mackay was surprised at Purcell's sudden change of mood. 'A little, plus I've learnt a lot about your legal system, largely from Sal.'

The judge tried to smile. It was forced and wooden, but it was a genuine attempt. 'I look forward to discussing the imperfections of the British Constitution during my next visit. It's certainly being tested by Brexit.'

Mackay was astonished by Purcell's unexpected civility. 'Er, yes Donald.' Mackay blurted out the only thing that popped into his head, 'the benefits of an unwritten constitution.'

'Quite.'

And with that, the Supreme Court judge was gone.

It was an hour later when Sally rang.

Mackay spoke first. 'I think I've upset your father.'

Sally sounded frustrated, 'Dear God, not again. What about this time?'

'Your Constitution, especially the Second Amendment and gun control.'

'I leave you two together for a couple of hours and it's pistols at dawn. I knew I shouldn't have left you alone.'

'Is that a joke, Sal? Pistols at dawn, the right to bear arms?'

She laughed, 'no.'

'We agreed to disagree. I wouldn't say we parted on friendly terms, but there was a detectable thaw in relations.'

'Yes, he prefers it if you argue with him,' she paused, 'when did he go?'

'About an hour ago.'

'Good. I want you to come over to do some phone canvassing. The latest poll has the President five points ahead.'

Mackay wasn't keen, 'I'm gonna swing the election with a few phone calls am I?' She didn't reply, she often used silence to bend him to her will. 'Besides, I haven't finished the Shenandoah research.' The silence continued for several seconds. 'Ok, Sal, I'll come right away.'

'Glad you saw it my way.'

She hung up. He replaced the receiver, but it rang again immediately, 'what now, Sal?'

'Thomas?'

Mackay recognized Mary Coggins's soft Edinburgh lilt.

'Hello Mary.'

'Thomas,' she said meekly, in her default 'sorry to bother you' voice. 'I'm calling to warn you, some American men paid me a visit recently. I was at your great grandfather's house collating some papers, when they knocked at the door.'

'Go on,' said Mackay, his earlier suspicions about his great grandfather's death now at the forefront of his mind.

'The astonishing thing was, they knew all about our ancestry project,' she said. 'They knew about James Steele, Colonel Le Jeune and the Confederate Treasury. They said they were researching their own ancestors, but I have my doubts. Whilst one man was polite and clearly educated, said he was a history professor, the other was rough looking, a skinhead type I would call him. They seemed more like treasure hunters to me.'

Mackay was concerned. 'That's very astute of you, Mary.'

Her voice became confessional. 'They asked for your contact details. I was alone in the house and, in truth, a bit frightened. They were very polite but somehow menacing. I'm sorry, but I gave them your address and phone number.'

'Don't worry about it, Mary,' he said, reassuringly.

Mackay updated her with what they'd learned in Nassau and the link with the Shenandoah. He fielded her excited questions and absorbed her infectious enthusiasm.

After she'd hung up, he reflected uneasily on what she'd said about the two mysterious American 'treasure hunters.' Could his suspicions about his great grandfather's death be solidifying?

He picked up his coat and looked for his keys. The phone rang again. He looked at it for a moment and was tempted to ignore it. If he was much later, Sally would be cross. He picked it up.

'Tom?' asked a vaguely familiar voice.

'Yes.'

'This is FBI Director, Wade Andrews.'

'I'm just on my way out, Director,' said Mackay quickly.

Andrews allowed the silence to drift, 'I know.'

Mackay was shocked and angry, 'what, are you spying on us?'

Andrews chuckled softly, 'calm down, I'm joking. This isn't the Bourne Supremacy.'

'Very funny. What do you want?'

Andrews's voice was measured. 'I see you've been to Nassau. Did you discover anything which might be of interest to me?'

So, you *have* been spying on us.'

Andrews ignored the question. 'Any sign of those Richmond Papers I mentioned when we met in Florida? Anything from Jeff Davis been found?'

'No, nothing. Even if we do find anything, I doubt Sal will want to tell you.'

There was a short silence. It was time for Andrews to deploy a threat. 'You really should be more helpful to the Federal authorities, Tom. I see your visa has expired.'

Mackay answered quickly, 'I have a K1.'

Andrews laughed. 'You've only got a few weeks left on that, when are you getting married?'

'Soon.'

'Prove it.'

Mackay imagined the lavish wedding he wanted for her. Hundreds of guests, a big church, perhaps even a bishop thrown in; it would take months to plan. 'We thought we'd fly down to Nevada, just the two of us, keep it simple.'

Andrews didn't sound convinced, 'I see.' Mackay waited for the Director's next assault. 'A K1 is dependent on being able to support yourself whilst you're in the United States, Tom.'

'That's ridiculous' said Mackay, firmly. 'I've millions of dollars strewn across several of your banks.'

Mackay could hear Andrews tapping a keyboard. 'So I see, Tom, millions of dollars. If I was to suspect money laundering, of course, all these accounts would be frozen. How would you support yourself then?

I'm not sure how you'd buy a loaf of bread if all you've got is your fancy house in Washington Square. All this would have an impact on your visa as well. It'd be much easier on you, and Ms Purcell, if you just found the Richmond Papers.'

Now it was Mackay's turn to laugh. 'I'm no rule breaker, Andrews. I've always tried to help the police if I can. I even counselled Sal to be more cooperative with you over these damned Papers. I really don't care what they say or what this big secret is. So why don't you take your threats and piss off.'

Mackay hung up.

CHAPTER TWENTY TWO

J Edgar Hoover Building
Washington DC
Present Day

Trying to intimidate Mackay might have been a mistake, thought Andrews. He'd observed in Orlando how the Brit deferred to Sally and rarely spoke. He'd assumed Mackay was a rich, spineless, dimwit, who could be easily threatened. Andrews could see now that wasn't the case.

The threat to deport him had been a bluff. The Director knew any attempt to put him on a plane would easily be thwarted by Sally Purcell. Andrews didn't want her, her team of lawyers, or any of her activist friends weighing down his Department with a flurry of lawsuits.

Andrews returned to the briefing note he was finalising for the President. With re-election seeming more and more likely, the demands from the White House had become more reasonable.

Andrews reflected on his relationship with the President. As he'd risen through the FBI's ranks, Andrews had increased exposure to elected officials, who, at best, he had found irritating. He glanced across the room, his eyes resting on the picture of J Edgar Hoover on the far wall. There was a man who knew that the machinery of government, was best operated by those who'd spent their careers learning how each lever worked. Hoover knew meddling politicians were a hindrance, and that the best way to keep away prying eyes from Capitol Hill, was to ensure every legislator's peccadillo was carefully recorded and filed.

Andrews's cell rang. He could see the call was from the low-key surveillance unit he'd left outside the Le Jeune's home in New Orleans.

Agent Morris headed the unit; his tone was measured and professional. 'Two men, Director, they've tried to enter the Le Jeune house. We've run them through the database and one of them, a Lyle Travis, has a sheet as long as your arm. There's no record of the other man. This Travis has just returned from the UK, a bit of a long trip for a Mississippi redneck like him. Most of them don't have passports.'

That is strange, thought Andrews. 'And where is Ms Le Jeune?'

'At her Country Club. She goes every morning, has lunch, and returns mid afternoon. She's just gone. Looks like these men cased the joint and were waiting for her to go.'

'And they've not got in?'

'No, sir. Pretty good security she's got. They're sitting in their car eating Big Macs. It looks like they're waiting for her to return.'

'You're sure they're not burglars?'

'Yes. One man's dressed in an expensive suit. The sun's blazing down here and being mid morning, it's not a good time for a robbery. It just doesn't feel like an ordinary breaking and entering.'

'Stand by, Morris.'

Andrews deliberated, his mind calculating scenarios and outcomes like a second rate chess player. Should he intervene, another search of the house to find the second part of Le Jeune's journal would certainly be helpful? Tracking down the copy of the Richmond Papers was proving more difficult than he'd imagined. Could these men be linked to the Papers? A trip to Europe by a thug like Travis did seem anomalous.

Andrews couldn't take the risk. He looked at his watch, it was 10.30. At a push he could be in New Orleans by early afternoon. But what about the President's briefing? He'd no choice but to delegate it to someone else - the Richmond Papers were too important. Andrews thought for a moment, he knew Deputy Director Roberts was ambitious, he'd drop everything for face time in the Oval Office - he could do the briefing.

'I'm coming down myself, Morris. Stay in touch. Don't do anything until I get there.'

'As you wish, Director.' Andrews hung up.

At the other end of the line, Morris wasn't surprised. Until last month, he'd never spoken to the Director, never mind met him; now Andrews was heading to New Orleans again. Morris had noticed the

Director hadn't opened an FBI file on this case. That wasn't compliant with procedure. What was going on?

Rebecca Le Jeune had drunk three large glasses of rosé at lunch. Why not enjoy herself? After all, her days were numbered. Lately she'd been feeling weaker and every morning her energy levels dropped a little further, her visits to the Country Club would soon become less frequent.

On Perrier Street, she struggled to get the key in the lock and pushed the door to free it. The key turned as she was shoved gently from behind. She was unprepared and - unsteady from the wine - fell forwards onto the polished wooden floor.

She heard the door close and turned to see two men. The first man was a huge barrel-chested gorilla, with a string of tattoos running up both arms. One of the tattoos was the Battle Flag of the Confederacy. The second man was smooth and well dressed. He spoke in a slow Southern drawl.

'Dear God, I'm so sorry, Ms Le Jeune. My friend here can be a little heavy handed at times. He didn't mean to push you over. Here, let me help you up.'

Her glassy eyes blazed at him fiercely as she pushed him away, and got up unaided. 'Get out of my house,' she roared, with the vigour of a twenty year old.

The well dressed man was unperturbed and got straight to the point. 'I'm a Professor of history, I believe my ancestor and your ancestor knew each other, I was wondering....'

'Out' she repeated.

The man nodded to the thug, who scooped up the tiny ninety year-old and deposited her in a chair in the panelled salon.

The educated man scanned the room and focused on a faded picture of a Confederate officer on the sideboard. He picked it up and showed it to the elderly spinster. 'And this must be Colonel Pierre Le Jeune.' He half turned to his accomplice. 'We know all about him don't we, Lyle?' The question was rhetorical and the smooth man returned his gaze to the old woman. 'Now, if you could tell us all you know about your... great... or is it just grandfather... no matter... about Colonel Le

100

Jeune, we'd be most grateful. Any diaries or his papers from that time would also be helpful.'

She remained silent, glowering at him furiously. Lyle Travis had a short temper. 'Now listen, lady. We've been tracking Colonel Le Jeune for months now. We've come all the way from Scotland to find you, that's Scotland in England, you know.'

She gave the sort of sympathetic smile she'd give to a dumb animal, 'I know where Scotland is you oaf.'

He went to strike her but the Professor took a couple of steps forward and blocked his path. The Professor's smile was so oily it dripped. 'Now Rebecca, Lyle is right. We've come a long way to find you and I'm afraid we're not leaving without some answers.'

She remained silent. The Professor continued to smile but now there was an edge to his voice. 'You've already upset Lyle. I would advise you not to do that again.'

'Go to hell,' she snapped.

The man sighed and nodded to Travis who stepped towards her.

There was a loud knock at the door. 'Open up, it's the FBI,' shouted Agent Morris.

'Help!' yelled Ms Le Jeune.

'Open it, Lyle, quick,' said the Professor, a note of alarm in his voice.

There were two blows on the door before Travis got there. As it swung open, FBI agents streamed in and pinned the two intruders to a wall.

Andrews followed them in. His immediate concern was for the old lady's welfare. 'Are you okay, Miss Le Jeune?' he said gently.

She suddenly felt very tired. The fall, her illness, the large lunch, the wine and the excitement, all had drained her energy. 'I'm fine Director, but I need to rest. I'm gonna have my afternoon nap now.' She headed for the stairs, 'you can tell me all about these men when I get up.'

'Of course, Ms Le Jeune,' said Andrews. He signalled to Agent Morris, 'bring that one here.' Two agents manhandled the suited man into the warm leather chair left empty by Rebecca Le Jeune. Andrews circled around the chair, peering down at the man. 'And who might you be?'

CHAPTER TWENTY THREE

United Kingdom
Present Day

Mackay swung his legs out of bed and looked across the cabin at Sally. She was still asleep, so he sat beside her and gently caressed her face. She stirred.

'Where are we?' she asked, sleepily.

'Somewhere over Scotland, I think. They're doing breakfast soon.'

'What is it?'

'Salmon and scrambled eggs.'

She yawned. 'Good, I'm hungry.'

One of the benefits of wealth, reflected Mackay, was that it brought comfort to travel. The British Airways Sleeper service, from Philadelphia to Heathrow, had delivered a good night's sleep and a tasty breakfast.

Then more coffee, pastries, and a shower in the airport lounge, prepared them for their journey north to Liverpool. Mackay knew the five hour drive was by motorway, so at the car rental he chose a BMW 7 cruiser.

Mackay's research had revealed the CSS Shenandoah evaded her Federal pursuers for weeks, before surrendering to the British in Liverpool, months after the war had ended. There was no mention of Le Jeune or Steele in any online records, so he had decided a long weekend in North West Britain, scouring original documents, was the best way to look for clues.

Although the in-flight beds had enhanced their sleep, the beds couldn't cure jet lag, so they shared the driving. In Liverpool, they drove to the UNESCO Heritage dock area and checked into the Titanic Hotel, a huge redeveloped warehouse on Stanley Dock. The elegant mass of brick, glass and steel impressed them, as did their Hartley Suite, which they soon found was the size of a small house.

'A fair amount of Confederate cotton was shipped through this very building,' said Sally, flicking through a local tourist guide.

Mackay held the hotel information booklet. 'And tobacco and Nassau rum. Look, they even have a rum bar downstairs. I'm not flagging yet.' He reached out and pulled her towards him. 'Only one way to test whether it's up to Nassau standards.'

She smiled. 'Indeed, let's go.'

There were no Goombay Smashes on offer in the dark wood - all leather bar - but there were Floridian Rum Runners. Two drinks each, and the adrenalin dam, which had kept their jet lag at bay, was breached; they were in bed by 8pm.

Having woken early and despite the onset of autumn - well wrapped up - they braved an alfresco breakfast on the hotel's colonnade, overlooking the River Mersey.

'Where's that ship going?' asked Sally, through a mouthful of cheese omelette.

Mackay looked up from his English breakfast, and saw a large white ferry gliding westwards through the dull, grey water.

'Belfast or the Isle of Man.'

'Is the Isle of Man part of Ireland as well?'

Mackay thought for a moment. 'No. It's an odd one. I don't think it's actually part of the UK.'

She looked perplexed, 'but it lies between England and Ireland?'

'Yes. It is strange. I've never thought about it before. I know the Queen is the head of state on the island but I couldn't tell you why it's self-governing. It must be a historical accident.'

He could see his responses didn't satisfy her inquisitive mind but she changed the subject. 'So we're in Liverpool, with the 'Liver' pronounced the same way as the organ which processes my Rum Runners, but you say the city is named after these mythical Liver birds, with the 'i' in Liver, pronounced the same way as the organ I see through... why?'

He felt like a city tour guide with insufficient training. 'Again, I don't know, Sal, but I'll be sure to find out for you today.'

She pushed her knife and fork together on the plate. 'Alright then, let's go and find out about the CSS Shenandoah and these Liver Birds.'

They walked up river, passing dock after dock, each one bigger than the last, all now bereft of the shipping which was once the city's life blood. The scale of the place was difficult to absorb, it was vast, immense, the sense of emptiness acute.

'Bet this was busy back in the day,' observed Sally, clearly impressed.

Mackay nodded. 'Liverpool was dubbed the second city of the Empire. It's little wonder the Shenandoah surrendered here.'

She pointed to a large grey building crowned by a pair of clock towers. 'There are those mythical birds, on top of the towers.'

'Yes, the Liver Birds, guardians of the city.'

'Can we go up?' she asked.

Mackay feigned an annoyed expression. 'Yes, we can, but we've got work to do first, Miss. We need to find the Shenandoah's log book.'

As he said this, they turned the corner of another huge warehouse and found themselves at the entrance of the Merseyside Maritime Museum.

'This looks like a good place to start,' she said, accelerating away from him and bypassing a group of Chinese tourists who were massing near an anchor by the door. Mackay caught her up, and nosed in, before the sizeable queue could solidify.

'This way to the Archives Centre,' floated in the air, as she disappeared up the stairs. He took two steps at a time in pursuit. Was there no end to her energy?

The morning came and went. Lunch was a sandwich from the café. They drank a gallon of coffee.

With few records digitalized, they had a good workout fetching log books and worn paper files from the shelves. Passenger lists, emigration records, crew lists, merchant seaman papers and Royal Navy archives, all were examined, but none mentioned Colonel Pierre Le Jeune or Mr James Steele.

Sally was exasperated. 'Perhaps they didn't board in Nassau after all.'

Mackay was frustrated. 'They must have. I'm sure of it. I'm convinced they're not mentioned because they weren't officially on the ship. There's lots about Shenandoah's crew. Some stayed on here. Some even went to Argentina; we saw that in the emigration records.'

Sally looked at her notes. 'Quite a few went back Stateside when their pardons came through.'

A bell rang, the Centre was closing. 'What a waste of time that was,' he said, snapping a log book closed.

Sally gathered up her notes and pulled on her sweater. 'I think that's all the research we can do on this. What's next?'

He thought for a moment, then sighed deeply. 'What's next is an early supper. Let's try that seafood restaurant we passed near the waterfront. Jolly ourselves up with a beautiful sunset and some great fish.'

Sally had grilled sea bass and Mackay devoured monkfish and king prawns. The sun, setting across the Mersey, was stunning. Mackay signalled to the waiter to bring another bottle of crisp, chilled Chardonnay.

He glanced out of the window as the sun was obscured by a passing ferry. When it reappeared it caught Sally's golden hair with a halo effect. She looked angelic.

The angel spoke, 'I don't want to be a killjoy but we may be at the end of our search. I can't think where else we can try.'

Mackay picked up the bottle and splashed the wine freely into their glasses. 'No, he conceded, it's a dead end for now.' He thought for a moment. 'I suggest we do a bit more sightseeing in Liverpool tomorrow, then pop up to see my parents. They'd love to see you.'

She wasn't convinced, 'how much further up the road is it?'

'A couple of hours.'

'It'll mean a long drive back to London for our flight.'

'No problem, I'll...' Mackay was cut off mid sentence by his cell ringing. He usually ignored calls when eating, but he could see it was an American number, so he connected.

'Tom Mackay?' asked the caller, the accent was southern, Mississippi or Alabama.

'Yes, who is this?'

'My name is Doug Calhoun,' said the caller, in a friendly tone.

The name was vaguely familiar. Mackay had read it that day somewhere. 'What can I do for you, Mr Calhoun?'

'I understand we're looking for the same thing,' drawled the American. 'Nine boxes of Confederate gold. I can help you find it.' The American allowed the words to impregnate the conversation before continuing. 'I'm guessing from the ring tone that you're across the Pond. Bet you're in Liverpool right now.'

Mackay was surprised at the accuracy of Calhoun's guesswork. 'What if we are?' he said, neutrally.

'You won't find any mention of Colonel Le Jeune or James Steele in that city,' said Calhoun, with the air of a conjurer preparing for his best trick.

Sally was looking at him intently across the table. Another ferry blocked out the sun. 'But surely they got on the Shenandoah in Nassau,' said Mackay.

'Yes, sir, they did,' confirmed Calhoun, 'but they didn't disembark in Liverpool.'

'Then, where did they get off the ship?' he asked quickly, his curiosity unchecked.

'That would be telling, Tom, that would be telling,' teased Calhoun. 'We need a business arrangement before I disclose that information.'

Mackay hesitated. This man's claims needed verification. 'How do you know all this? About me, my great grandfather, about Le Jeune? Where they got off the Shenandoah - how?'

'From a letter,' answered Calhoun, 'from my great grandfather's letter. He wrote it all down. You can read it yourself if we get a deal.'

'And who was your great grandfather,' queried Mackay, feeling more convinced the caller was genuine.

Calhoun paused for dramatic effect, 'he was Lieutenant Henry Calhoun, sixth officer of the CSS Shenandoah.'

CHAPTER TWENTY FOUR

FBI New Orleans HQ
2901 Leon C Simon Boulevard
Present Day

Calhoun ended his call with Mackay, and looked across the table at Andrews with a syrupy smile.

'Were they in Liverpool? Have they agreed to meet you?' asked the Director, impatiently.

Calhoun glanced down at his notes. 'Yes, in Liverpool, at the Titanic Hotel. They're gonna wait there for me.'

The news relaxed Andrews and he reclined in his chair, he was back in control of events. 'You'd better get going then.'

Calhoun pushed out his greasy smile. 'Sounds more like an order than a request.'

Andrews's laugh was wooden. 'Naturally it's a request. You don't work for me or the Bureau.'

Calhoun hesitated. 'Maybe not, but flying to England at short notice, business class, that won't be cheap.'

Andrews shook his head. 'Your expenses aren't part of the deal. You're an independent treasure hunter, whose interests temporarily align with the Bureau's.'

Calhoun decided to test his new relationship with Andrews. 'In that case I'd better look for an economy ticket. It might be next week before I can get to the UK.'

Andrews grimaced. 'Don't push your luck, Calhoun. God knows how you escaped prosecution over your conduct at De Forrest University, but intimidating old ladies in their homes is still an offence. Those charges haven't gone away, they can easily be resurrected.'

'We didn't break in and there was no harm done to Ms Le Jeune. I'll take my chances in court,' responded Calhoun.

He's a gambler thought Andrews. It was tempting to make the De Forrest business a Federal matter, but that could be kept in reserve. For now, it wasn't worth the fight. 'Very well, I'll give you five thousand dollars in cash for you and your sidekick to get to England; you'll have to manage on that.'

Calhoun's face lit up with delight. He sensed something wasn't quite right here. There were no other agents in the room, no notes were being taken, and Bureau disbursements in cash were unusual. What was the Director up to? Andrews had declared no interest in the gold, so these Richmond Papers were clearly important to him. It gave Calhoun leverage.

'From what you say about Mackay, this hotel is gonna be five star. Five thou won't cover it.'

Andrews was compliant. The benefits of Calhoun working for him as a quasi independent contractor were real. 'Ten then, that's it.'

Calhoun had struggled with authority figures his whole life so he couldn't resist needling the Director. 'You're a hard man to do business with,' he said sarcastically, 'ten it is then.'

The Director found dealing with Calhoun distasteful, so he delegated the disbursement of the cash to Agent Morris. Andrews knew Morris wasn't happy with another departure from Bureau procedure, but the Agent executed his Director's wishes. Calhoun was soon on his way to Louis Armstrong New Orleans Airport.

Andrews considered the latest developments. Calhoun's letter provided the next piece of the jigsaw, but not all the answers. It suggested the officers of the Shenandoah had realised Pierre Le Jeune was carrying something more valuable than nine boxes of gold, but it seemed Le Jeune had successfully kept his secret from the crew. It would have been better for Le Jeune, better for everyone, better for America, if those damned Papers had gone up in flames with the rest of Richmond in 1865.

Andrews had long wondered why Davis didn't try to recover the Richmond Papers after the war. He knew from his research, the disgraced President had visited Britain in the late 1860s. Even if he didn't try to get them back, why didn't he reveal their contents as an act of vengeance? Andrews sighed and closed the file, reflecting that some truths were forever lost to history.

CHAPTER TWENTY FIVE

Fort Monroe
Virginia
20 April 1867

The wind howled across the narrow isthmus, seemingly bent on flipping the carriage directly into the Hampton River - spray soaked both driver and horses.

The carriage's sole occupant pulled his cloak tighter around him, trying to get the collar to obscure his face as best he could. He was mad to have come, he knew that, but there was something in the note that rang true.

Suddenly, the grey murk cleared and he glimpsed the huge fort looming above him. The carriage stopped at the massive gate and the sergeant of the guard approached.

'State your business,' said the sergeant.

The passenger was keen to keep his visit as low key as possible, especially if he *was* on a fool's errand. His journey through Virginia - aided by appalling weather - had gone largely unnoticed, but now anonymity was impossible. He opened the window and leant out. 'I'm here to see General Miles.'

The sergeant's eyes widened in recognition, he hastily saluted and waved the carriage through.

Once inside, the passenger was guided through the dank and foreboding complex by a duty officer, who knocked at the General's door. The passenger went in unannounced and found Miles working on papers at his desk.

'What's this?' bawled the General, without looking up, 'you'll wait to be invited into my office.'

'Your Commander-in-Chief needs no invitation, General,' said President Johnson, firmly. Miles stood and saluted.

Johnson returned the salute. 'He's not dying is he?' continued the President, with some urgency, 'I don't want a martyr.'

Miles's moustache twitched nervously. 'He's weak. He sits in his chair all day and barely eats. I accompany him when he can be coaxed into taking a walk.'

Johnson hung his cloak on a chair opposite Miles's desk. 'And what of his mind? I hear he's very despondent.'

Miles wondered who the President's source was. It was disconcerting. 'I give him books and newspapers to read.'

President Johnson looked Miles up and down disapprovingly. 'I can understand it's not easy for a soldier to become a jailer. Please take me to him.'

Miles led Johnson through a series of passages to Casement Number 2. The room contained a bed, a table and a single chair. On the table was a jug of water and a wash basin.

Jefferson Davis sat on the bed and barely stirred when Johnson entered. Johnson hadn't seen him since they'd both been senators - many years ago - and barely recognized him. He'd lost a lot of weight, his skin was paper thin, and there were marks on his ankles where the leg irons had been.

Johnson half turned to General Miles. 'I'd like to speak to him alone.'

Miles left the room and Johnson pulled up the chair by the bed.

Davis eyed him fiercely. 'Did you order the leg irons?'

Johnson shook his head. 'That was Miles's own idea.'

'He's a bastard,' declared Davis.

Johnson resisted the temptation to mention Andersonville. He studied Davis's face, then asked the question which had been on his mind for over two years. 'Did you order Lincoln's assassination and the attempts on me and Seward?'

Davis looked startled. 'You know I didn't.'

The wind howled against the casement window, sending a damp draught surging through the room. Davis winced at the colder air. It was clear to Johnson, that the conditions in the cell were the cause of the traitor's poor health.

Despite the risk of martyrdom, thought Johnson, Davis's death would solve a lot of problems. A treason trial would damage the

111

Reconstruction and hamper the country's healing process. As part of his defence, Davis would lay out the contents of the Papers he'd dispatched to London on his last day in Richmond. Of course, without the documents themselves as evidence, their sentiments could be denied, but their effect would still be devastating on America's fragile process of reconciliation.

Although Davis didn't have possession of the Papers, Johnson had to assume he knew of their whereabouts, and could produce them with the aid of his supporters. He presumed Davis had suffered in this cell for two years, because he wanted to use his trial to make the Papers public with the utmost fanfare, thereby destroying what little unity was building between the States.

Davis had read Johnson's thoughts, 'you got my note then, Mr President?' he asked, spitting out the last two words as if he'd chewed something rancid.

'Yes, Jeff,' replied Johnson, flatly, 'that's the only reason I'm here. I don't give a damn about your welfare. Swinging from a rope or dying in this cell, it makes no odds to me.'

Davis gave a hollow laugh. 'I don't believe you, Andy. What happens to me *has* political ramifications for you. That's if you survive your impeachment that is.'

Johnson was taken aback. 'You know about that?'

'Miles gives me the newspapers.'

Johnson looked at Davis, hoping to convince him he was being sincere, hoping to convince him his life was in peril. 'Then have you worked out that I'm your best chance of avoiding the rope? With no Vice-President, Senate President Wade will be in the White House if I'm impeached. He's determined to hang you.'

Davis remained calm and composed. 'I'll take my chances at the trial. I've not committed treason anyway. When Mississippi seceded I was no longer a US citizen.' Davis paused for maximum impact, 'and as you know, as I said in my note, I will produce an affidavit which strengthens that argument.'

Johnson sighed and slumped back in his chair. He could call Davis's bluff. What was so important about this document anyway? Davis had called it an affidavit.

Johnson had never read the affidavit himself. He'd only learnt of its existence during the brief and only meeting he'd had with Lincoln - after the inauguration - just hours before Lincoln was shot. Lincoln hadn't read the affidavit either, and referred to it simply as Madison's Folly.

During their conversation in the White House that fateful day, Johnson had pressed Lincoln to be tougher on Southerners, but Lincoln had seemed more interested in making Johnson aware of this affidavit – which President Buchanan had told Lincoln about, the day he'd taken office himself in 1861. Buchanan had also told Lincoln, no President had read it since Madison, but all had known its contents.

If the document was as bad as Lincoln had suggested, then Johnson acknowledged the damage done by publication would be immense. On the whole, perhaps it was best to avoid scandal in these troubled times - it was better to offer Davis a deal.

Johnson sat upright in his chair and opened the palms of his hands expansively. 'Look Jeff, here's what I think we should do. I'll see you get released from this cell immediately. In terms of your trial, Vanderbilt says he and a few others will put up $100,000 in bail, which should be enough for the Circuit Court in Richmond. Then, assuming I survive the impeachment, and after a suitable period, say a year or so, you can apply for a presidential pardon which I'll grant. After that, you'll agree to keep your mouth shut, whilst I get on with cleaning up the mess you've made. I don't ask you to support my Reconstruction policy, but you'll keep silent about it.'

Davis hauled himself up from the bed and peered into the wet greyness out of the window. 'I would certainly welcome getting out of here,' he mumbled. He turned sharply to face Johnson, but I won't apply for your pardon. I've done nothing wrong. You can give me one if you wish, but I repeat, I won't ask for it.'

Johnson nodded, relieved. 'And you'll instruct your lieutenants in Britain to surrender this document or documents, whatever they are, to my Federal agents.'

Davis had no intention of complying with the President's last request, but he stepped forward and took Johnson's hand, declaring, 'it's a deal.'

CHAPTER TWENTY SIX

'That must be them over there,' said Sally.

Mackay looked up and saw two men entering the bar. The taller man wore a sports jacket, lilac shirt and jeans. His dark, slicked hair, shone like his polished brogues. He had a scar on his jaw which was still healing. The other man had missed out on 40,000 years of evolution, and resembled a clothed Neanderthal.

Mackay stood up to shake their hands, but Calhoun had already taken Sally's and kissed it like some eighteenth century French aristocrat. 'Enchanted,' he said, perfectly fitting the stereotype.

Calhoun had a ready smile which he fixed on Mackay, 'and you must be Tom. This is my associate, Lyle Travis.' Travis also matched his stereotype and grunted a primeval greeting.

They were all staying in the hotel but Mackay elected to be host. 'Can I get you some coffee? Tea?'

Calhoun flashed his smile. 'Two lattes would be great, thank you.'

Mackay signalled to the waiter.

'So, are you professional treasure hunters?' asked Sally.

'Part-time,' replied Calhoun, 'I'm a....I was a history professor at a university in Mississippi. I'm looking for a new post. I specialise in the US Civil War which has been good for this project.'

Calhoun didn't drop his stare from Sally and she began to feel uncomfortable. In response she passed the conversation to Mackay. 'It's extraordinary that Doug's ancestor knew your great grandfather, Tom,' she said.

Mackay nodded. 'Yes, what can you tell us about James Steele, Doug? How come you waited until now to hunt for this gold?'

The Professor subconsciously fingered the scar on his jaw before answering. 'I researched Lieutenant Henry Calhoun some time ago - it's my field after all. I knew he was on the Shenandoah and I found out that he'd stayed in England for a few years after the war. When President Johnson's general amnesty came through, he returned to Mississippi and spent the rest of his days on east coast commercial steamers.'

Calhoun had been speaking to Mackay but his gaze still lingered on Sally. From across the table he was entering her personal space. The intrusion was becoming difficult to ignore.

Four lattes arrived and at last Calhoun shifted his stare, first to his cup, then to Mackay, who continued his questions. 'But why have you only recently started looking for the gold?'

Calhoun waited to clear his mouth of coffee. 'I didn't know anything about it until my cousin died a few months ago. Henry Calhoun's letters had gone down that side of the family. My cousin had no kids and I found the letters going through his things. The letter you're interested in was written by Henry to his fiancée, Emma Forbes.'

Calhoun had locked his eyes onto Sally's body again like a military grade searchlight. Mackay saw her shift uneasily in her chair. The Professor's interest in her had moved beyond friendly to sexual.

Calhoun placed a folder on the table in front of them. 'You can both read the letter tonight, in bed, if you wish.'

Mackay leaned forward to pick it up but Calhoun jerked it back. 'We need a deal first, Tom,' he said, with a creamy smile. 'You also need to know all the answers ain't in there. There's a clue, sure, but we'll need to work together to find the next piece of the jigsaw.'

To his left, Mackay heard Sally exhale loudly through her nostrils, the thought of working more closely with Calhoun clearly didn't appeal to her. 'What sort of split have you got in mind, Doug?' asked Mackay.

Calhoun flicked his eyes away from Sally and looked at Mackay. 'I'm not greedy - 50/50 will do.'

Mackay considered the proposal, then continued. 'How many boxes are there?'

'Six were put off the Shenandoah,' said Calhoun, then he hesitated, anticipating Mackay's next question. 'That's about ten million dollars a box at today's gold price.' Calhoun felt a caveat was needed, 'if the boxes were full of gold that is.'

Talk of sixty million dollars drew a response from Travis who growled in appreciation.

'I hadn't appreciated there'd be that much,' murmured Mackay, almost to himself. 'You're sure Lieutenant Calhoun saw gold inside the boxes?'

'Nope.' Calhoun gestured to the folder. 'All he says in there is that it took two strong men to lift a box. Say that's one hundred and forty kilos of gold per box. It gets you to nine or ten million depending on the spot price.'

'And there are six boxes,' added the Neanderthal.

'An equal split seems fair to me,' said Mackay, 'Sal?'

She paused to think. '50/50 of what we get is fine. But what do you propose to do with the gold. Pitch up to a bank and ask them to swap it for sixty million in cash. The ownership of it might also be an issue.' She was thinking as she spoke. 'The bullion belonged to a state which ceased to exist 150 years ago. And even when that state did exist, no other country recognised it. No, Uncle Sam will want it back. The FBI will come and claim it.' She paused again, 'the best we can hope for is a finder's fee. At say...twenty percent, that would still make twelve million.'

'You raise a valid legal point,' said Calhoun, who feigned interest, whilst reflecting on the promise made by Director Andrews that the FBI didn't want any gold.

Mackay chipped in. 'Might be even more complex than that. If they buried it on the British coast somewhere, and if ownership can't be proved, under our law the Crown will take half.' Mackay continued to think through his reasoning. 'Or if a court did decide it was still owned by the Confederate Government, it might sit in the Bank of England until a bona fide representative of the Confederate Government comes to claim it. I know it sounds far-fetched, but the Tsar's gold is still rumoured to be in the vaults under Threadneedle Street to this day, unclaimed, because the Bank of England didn't recognise Lenin's Government as the Tsar's legitimate successor.'

Calhoun would make a poor poker player thought Mackay. The Professor had given a clear tell when Mackay had suggested the gold was buried somewhere on the British coast. The Briton glanced down at the folder on the table in front of him. Was the exact location revealed in there?

'The lawyers will have a field day,' declared Sally.

'I thought you were a lawyer?' asked Calhoun.

'Not this sort,' she replied, looking away from the Professor, who tried to hold her stare.

'I think we're getting ahead of ourselves,' said Calhoun, who had no intention of sharing the gold with anybody. He'd already researched a boat charter to take the bullion to Lebanon, where it could be exchanged for dollars, no questions asked. He looked at Sally and fantasised about throwing her into the hold along with the gold - she certainly would make his cruise through the Mediterranean much more pleasurable.

Mackay decided there was no point worrying about what to do with the gold until they'd found it, so he concluded the negotiation. 'OK, we'll go 50/50 on what we get. It may be a finder's fee, or face value, whatever.' He paused, 'one more thing though Doug, was it you who spoke to my great grandfather's friend, Mary Coggins, up in Scotland?'

The Professor switched on his auto-smile but his hand instinctively went to the scar on his jaw, 'yes, it was Tom. Very helpful she was too. Nice place you have up there in Scotland,' Calhoun paused, 'I don't want to seem presumptuous, but we could all stay there tomorrow night.'

'What?' said Mackay, 'Le Jeune and Steele got off the Shenandoah in Scotland?'

Calhoun tossed him the folder, 'read that, you'll see.'

In their hotel room later, Sally voiced the dislike for Calhoun they were both feeling. 'He's creepy,' she said, 'he couldn't take his eyes off my breasts. He can get a hotel tomorrow; no way is he staying at Norlands.'

Mackay nodded as he turned the yellowy pages of Henry Calhoun's letter.

Sally continued to tap her phone. After a couple of minutes she suddenly sat upright in bed. 'I knew it, look at this.'

She showed him the screen which displayed an extract from a local Mississippi newspaper.

'History Professor Resigns after Sex Probe.

Professor Doug Calhoun, head of history at De Forrest University, resigned yesterday after the De Forrest County Sheriff's Department dropped all charges against him. The serious sexual allegations made by three of Professor Calhoun's female students could not be proved, said the Department, and the State would no longer be pursuing the matter. In a statement, Professor Calhoun said the State's decision proved he was innocent of all the charges and he would be instructing his lawyers to consider libel actions against the students concerned.'

'Bet those libel actions never got off the ground,' said Mackay.

'No. There's no mention of them anywhere else,' confirmed Sally. 'The lower burden of proof in a civil court was no doubt too risky for him. Looks like the University paid him to go, hoping to salvage their reputation. God he's a creep.'

Mackay continued to read Henry Calhoun's letter. She sensed she didn't have his full attention and poked him in the ribs. 'I want you to understand, Thomas, that if we find this gold, we're handing it over to the FBI, or, if appropriate, the British authorities.'

'Of course, Sal,' he responded, a little too automatically.

She reached over and snatched the letter. 'I know you; you sometimes bend the rules too much for my liking. I'm serious.'

'I'm serious too,' he declared with a smile, 'I wouldn't have a clue how to fence ninety million in gold anyway, if fence is the right word.'

'I guess fence assumes we stole it,' she pondered aloud, 'and stealing it is not what we're doing.'

'No,' he said. 'And are we handing these Richmond Papers over to the FBI as well?' He knew she'd see that 'treasure' very differently. 'Director Andrews seemed very interested in them.'

She put down her phone. 'Depends what they say. If it's so important to Andrews, it sounds important to the American people. They should know what the Papers are about.'

He smiled. 'I thought as much. Therein lies the difference between us. You're more interested in some ancient history and a dull principle than ninety million dollars.' He paused, 'now, would you mind giving me the letter back?'

She gave it to him; he found where he'd left off and was immediately transported back to nineteenth century Nassau, and the mind of Lieutenant Henry Calhoun.

CHAPTER TWENTY SEVEN

CSS Shenandoah
River Mersey, Liverpool
8 November 1865

*D*earest Em,

I have so much to tell you, where do I begin?

I will start with my present circumstances.

I write to you from my cabin on board the CSS Shenandoah. We are anchored next to a British warship, HMS Donegal, in the River Mersey, Liverpool, England.

Yesterday, Captain Waddell met Captain Paynter of the Donegal and together they went ashore and walked up the steps of Liverpool Town Hall, where the Captain surrendered himself and the ship to the Mayor. I understand the Mayor was at a loss what to do with us, and is still awaiting instructions from the British Government in London. We have been treated well by the British, but we are fearful of being handed over to the United States Consul, who may deem us as pirates.

You're probably wondering how we got here?

Over a year ago we sailed as ordinary passengers from this very port on the steamer Laurel, bound for Funchal. The Shenandoah had been bought in secrecy by Confederate agents in Liverpool, and because of British neutrality, her conversion to a warship occurred off the Portuguese island of Madeira, of which Funchal is the capital.

Equipped with cannon, we set about disrupting Federal shipping. We captured six union ships before we reached the Cape of Good Hope, and then took another prize in the Indian Ocean.

I have been to Australia, Em! From the Indian Ocean we sailed east, and then spent a month refitting in Melbourne, Victoria colony.

After sinking dozens of Yankee whalers in the Bering Sea, Captain Waddell decided to attack San Francisco, but he changed his mind when he learnt of General Lee's surrender - from a newspaper we found on board a captured ship. Unsure whether the report was true - and if we would be treated as pirates by the Federals if we were captured - we sailed around Cape Horn, seeking a friendly British port.

Knowing the authorities in Nassau had permitted blockade running and had been sympathetic to our cause, the Captain decided to lay up there until our fate could be determined. The British told us President Davis had been arrested, so the Captain asked the Governor if he would accept our surrender. By this stage we were keen to hand ourselves over to the British because three Union warships had arrived in Nassau.

Then events took an unexpected turn. At the beginning of my watch one day, a crewman hailed me from the bow and pointed to a small sail boat which was tacking gracefully into port. Through my telescope I saw the occupants were extremely ragged. It seemed likely they were our countrymen who had fled from Florida. Indeed, one of the men wore a tattered, threadbare, grey uniform.

After a few minutes the boat disappeared behind a Packet Steamer and I thought nothing more of it. I spent the rest of my watch ensuring the crew remained vigilant as groups of hungry islanders were continually stealing from the ship.

I was about to hand over to Lieutenant Grimball when the men from the small boat, I'd seen earlier, approached the gang plank. I was astonished at their appearance. Both were shaved and tidy looking, with the officer's uniform repaired and cleaned. I could now see he was a Colonel and I showed him into Captain Waddell's cabin.

I finished my watch and headed for the wardroom. My fellow officers were discussing their plans to get off the island. Small traders carrying fruit, salt and sponges, regularly left Nassau for Havana. From Cuba it was possible to obtain passage to Argentina, where the Executive Officer and a few others were going to try their luck gold prospecting. I intended to take the Royal Mail Packet to Southampton and stay with my relatives in Bristol, until it was clear the amnesty given to our soldiers would be extended to Confederate sailors.

All these thoughts were cast aside when we were summoned to the great cabin and told to prepare for a silent exit from Nassau under cover of darkness. It turned out the Colonel and his British companion carried State papers and seven boxes of gold vital to the future of the Confederacy. None of us relished grappling with the Union warships in the harbour and those officers who'd favoured going to Argentina were displeased, but I was happy the Shenandoah would complete her circumnavigation of the globe, and also for the free passage to Britain.

As soon as it was dark we greased the cables thickly, doused the lights and slipped silently out of Nassau. It was astonishing we weren't challenged by the Federal ships in the harbour. Soon we could see the lights of the Union warship stationed off Hogg Island, but our local pilot was experienced and had us quickly round the headland and out of sight.

Captain Waddell told us later the British Governor had asked the Federal Officers to dinner and intended to ply them with gallons of rum. Whether it was drunkenness or carelessness, we didn't care, because no one had stirred and we escaped the island unnoticed.

Unfortunately our hasty departure had meant we'd taken on little coal and were therefore dependant on the wind to get us across the Atlantic. To evade our steam powered pursuers, we hid in an inlet off Wood Cay which was known only to our helpful pilot (who'd been lent to us by the Nassau authorities). We were well provisioned and the offshore breeze kept the sun's intensity and mosquitoes at bay. It was idyllic.

We caught fish, played cards on deck, and lazily swam to the beach. For what seemed like endless days we felt as if we were on a pleasure cruise, with the war, union warships, and all thoughts of piracy charges, a world away.

However, our tranquillity was disturbed on a couple of occasions by disagreements between our Captain and Colonel Le Jeune. The Colonel was frustrated by the delay and was desperate to deposit the bullion and the State papers in the Confederacy's account in the Bank of England. The Captain prevailed but was soon keen to get underway himself, as discipline began to wilt in the blissful conditions.

Sitting here in cold, dark, murky Liverpool, I now find it remarkable that the crew didn't throw us officers overboard and take the ship and the bullion to the South Americas. The midshipmen picked up rumblings, but it is a testament to the men that there was no serious plot.

We gave the pilot our gig to sail back to Nassau and proceeded into the wide blue Atlantic. With no steam power and no smoke from our funnel, we were difficult to spot, so initially made good progress. But then the wind turned against us and we were finally spied by a Union warship, which meant turning west again to evade her.

And this was the pattern for months, battling against the wind and advancing several hundred miles east, before being pursued for days and reversing our progress. This routine became wearing on both the officers and men and couldn't have contrasted more with our idyllic existence at Wood Cay.

Eventually the coast of Ireland was sighted and the Captain called us to the great cabin. He needed our counsel on what to do with Colonel Le Jeune, his gold, his companion, and the State papers they'd brought with them all the way from Richmond. I was the last to enter the cabin and took my place in one of the seats which fanned out from the Captain's desk in a loose semi-circle.

Colonel Le Jeune was speaking with some emotion in his voice. 'The problem with sailing straight up the Mersey into Liverpool, Waddell, is that everything on board will be impounded and we'll all likely be arrested. It's too much of a risk. I haven't come all this way to fall at the last hurdle.'

Waddell nodded in agreement, 'I concur, Colonel. The question is where to put you off?' He pointed to the maps of Britain strewn out on the adjacent chart table, 'where on the charts will we find a safe deserted anchorage? We lack local knowledge and we can't ask a pilot.' He scanned the room, 'I'm open to suggestions, gentlemen. Any of you know these waters?'

There was silence. In the absence of any other ideas, I related what I'd overheard John Parker talking about on my watch. 'Old Parker, sir. He was gossiping the other day about an elderly hand he'd sailed with on the Constitution. Turns out this old hand first enlisted in the Continental navy on the Ranger, under John Paul Jones, during the Revolutionary War. This old hand told Parker they'd found a deserted anchorage off a small island in the Solway Firth.'

'Get Parker in here, Calhoun,' ordered the Captain, and I left at once to find him. You've probably heard of John Paul Jones, Em. He was the founder of the American Navy and during the Revolutionary War he harassed British shipping in the Irish Sea. He also did some coastal raids, one of which was an attempt to kidnap an Earl near to where Jones was born, at a place called Kirkcudbright. He was hoping to exchange the Earl for Americans who'd been pressed into the Royal Navy, but the Earl wasn't at home, so Jones left with the family silver instead. Anyway, I digress.

I fetched old Parker to the Captain's cabin and presented him to the officers. The old man was uncomfortable in front of his superiors but he confirmed what I'd said, and when pressed by Waddell, remembered the island was called Hestan. Waddell soon found it on the chart. 'Looks just the spot, Colonel. We'll put you off there at high tide.'

'You'll give us a boat to get to the mainland then?' asked Steele, the Briton.

'No need,' replied Waddell. 'There's a causeway at low tide. I'll have the carpenter fashion you some sort of cart for the boxes,' he paused, 'you'll be leaving one box with us, of course, that was the deal.' Le Jeune nodded.

And that's what transpired, Em.

We gave the Ulster coast a wide berth to avoid Royal Navy ships, then sailed up the Solway Firth to Hestan Island. The day we put the Colonel ashore was bright

124

and sunny, and I was thankful I'd been selected to accompany the Captain in the shore party. The charming island was no more than half a mile long, with stunning views across the water to England and the Cumbrian hills.

The cart our carpenter had made did have wheels and did move, but it was an odd design, so rather than bring further attention to himself, the Colonel had changed out of uniform. We put the cart into a low shepherd's hut where Le Jeune and Steele intended to stay out of sight until dark, when the low tide would also mean they could reach the mainland across the causeway.

After that, Em, back on ship, we used the last of our coal to steam for Liverpool. We anchored at the mouth of the Mersey estuary but the pilot refused to take us upriver unless we flew a flag. So we hoisted the Battle Flag of the Confederacy for the last time, much to the delight of the crowds on the river bank, and proceeded towards the docks. Hoisting the flag unnerved three of the crewmen though, who swam ashore in cold autumnal water rather than risk piracy charges.

And here we've been anchored for two days, Emma, awaiting our fate. Lord knows when I will be able to see you again because even if we are paroled by the British, the US Consul has told us there is no immediate prospect of an amnesty, so I may be stuck here for some time.

Take care my darling.

Your loving fiancé

Henry

P.s. I write this quickly. We are preparing to leave the ship. Since I wrote yesterday, the British have confirmed those members of the crew who are not British will be paroled. I laughed earlier today when the crew was mustered in front of Captain Paynter for roll call. About a dozen crewmen are British but they affected Southern accents when questioned by Paynter as to their nationalities. Five crewmen clearly hailed from the banks of the Clyde rather than the Mississippi but, no doubt following secret orders from his superiors, Paynter ignored the discrepancy and declared the whole crew to be American. And so I am free to leave the ship, Em, after twelve months and 55,000 miles around the globe. Part of me is sad but part of me longs for an amnesty so I can travel home and see you again. H x.

CHAPTER TWENTY EIGHT

Hestan Island
Kirkcudbrightshire, Scotland
Present Day

Horizontal rain probed the windscreen of the BMW like rods of steel and the car shook as it absorbed penetrating blasts of wind.

'How do you people live in this country?' asked Sally, 'apart from a single day in Liverpool, I haven't seen the sun.'

Mackay pulled open the plastic sleeve of his service station sandwich. The bread was like balsa wood and the cheese like putty. 'Christ,' he said, 'I didn't expect much, but this has been made by a joiner.'

She offered him the remains of her wilted salad bowl, 'not much better but at least you can chew it.' He took it and forked a soggy tomato into his mouth with the plastic utensil.

'Put the wipers on,' she said.

Mackay obliged and through the murk they saw the shape of the causeway emerging from the grey brown water. Mackay glanced to his left and saw Calhoun reaching for his coat from the back seat of his rented Ford.

Sally did the same. 'Come on then,' she said, 'according to the tide table we've only got an hour.'

It was easy to see why they had such a narrow window. As they approached the shoreline, the water was retreating faster than they could run and the causeway was already clear.

About half way across, a low flying fighter jet roared above them - drowning out the sound of the crunching shingle underfoot. They instinctively ducked and as Calhoun straightened he laughed nervously. 'You should have warned me about that. I nearly had a coronary.'

'I think the RAF use the Solway for training,' said Mackay, 'it happens often but still gives you a jump scare every time.'

'Wish we had a SUV,' grunted Travis, 'would have saved this walk.'

Ten minutes later they stepped onto the green grass of the island and strode up the gentle elevation towards a low white building. Mackay saw the structure was a single storey Galloway cottage with a chimney at each end. 'It looks like a holiday let,' he muttered, 'it might be built on the shepherd's hut, they put the bullion in when they got off the Shenandoah.'

'No, I think that's the hut over there,' said Calhoun, pointing to the roofless remains of a small structure.

'I'm telling you there won't be anything here,' drawled Travis.

Calhoun sighed with irritation, 'we still have to look though, Lyle, maybe there's a clue.'

'Let's split up,' said Sally, 'Tom and I will take the south side by that lighthouse. You two can take the hut and the cottage.' Calhoun nodded and they divided.

The small lighthouse was a modern metal structure. As they approached, they were startled by hidden sheep scattering from behind a rock. 'I didn't fancy searching the cottage,' declared Sally, 'that large padlock was a deterrent.'

'I agree, best to leave any illegal activity like breaking and entering to Travis.'

The rain had eased off to a drizzle, the wind had gone, and the sun was trying to break up the cloud over the Lake District to the south. Suddenly a single shaft of light penetrated the whitening grey and locked onto an opening in the rock.

They bounded towards the outcrop and found the opening led to a dry airless tunnel.

It was exciting. Mackay spoke first, 'so, like a rainbow the ray of sunlight points us to a crock of gold.'

Sally giggled, 'yes. Bit like that scene in Raiders of the Lost Ark where Harrison Ford is in the tomb with his staff.'

Mackay pulled out his phone. 'Let's see if this cave is marked on the Ordinance Survey Map.' The signal was poor and he took a few seconds to find the right page. 'I think it's a mine shaft. There's another one further south towards Daft Ann's Steps, whoever she was. They've both been disused since the 1840s.'

'I'm not holding my breath but it would be a good place to hide a cache of gold,' observed Sally.

'Switch on your phone torch,' instructed Mackay, as he tapped on his own.

The cave was remarkably dry and airless. The tunnel, if you could call it that, was irregular and gently descended towards sea level. There was evidence of Victorian miners' chisel marks and small pyramids of spoil lay haphazardly on the ground.

'This looks like it was tough work,' said Sally.

Mackay kicked a loose stone which clattered downwards into the darkness, then splashed. 'Yes, it wouldn't have been much fun down here. I don't know what sort of rock it is but it must be hard, the miners haven't even bothered to prop it up.'

They followed the tunnel as it sloped downwards; searching every man made gap in the rock and every natural crevice - for a space large enough to hide a box of gold.

After a few minutes they reached the bottom of the mine which was filled with water.

Sally was disappointed. 'Where have they put it?'

'Not under the water there, that's for sure.' Mackay paused for thought. 'There were a couple of big boulders back up the way. They moved a bit. I'll see if I can shift them with Calhoun and Travis. There might be something underneath?'

There was only rock underneath and their search of the other mine was also fruitless. Calhoun had found nothing in the cottage or the dilapidated shepherd's hut.

On leaving the second mine, Sally glanced out to sea and saw the water racing in. 'Look how fast the tide is coming in,' she said.

'We've been here more than an hour,' noted Mackay urgently.

When they reached the causeway the water was already lapping at its edge. At the midpoint Mackay looked back and saw where they'd been was already submerged. With two hundred metres to go the water was ankle deep - so they began to run. At fifty metres they were wading and for the last ten the water was approaching chest height.

'Man, that's a fast tide,' spluttered Calhoun. As they stood by their cars, panting for breath, soaked through and cold.

'Folk drown all the time on the mudflats further up,' said Mackay, breathing heavily, 'they get caught in the open and can't outrun it.' Mackay lifted the boot of the BMW and opened his suitcase. 'Let's warm up a bit in the cars then change into some dry clothes, we'll meet you at the Steamboat Inn in Carsethorne for a drink. We can decide there what to do next. It's a twenty minute drive.'

Calhoun nodded.

'I'm not getting changed with him leering at me,' declared Sally, as soon as they were alone in the BMW.

'OK' said Mackay, starting the engine, 'I'll find a secluded lay-by.'

As they pulled away, a minibus - plastered with Duke of Edinburgh stickers - parked opposite the causeway. A group of young women got out and began assembling camping equipment. 'What, in this weather?' exclaimed MacKay with astonished respect, 'strewth they're hardy.'

Soon the three Americans and Mackay were warming themselves in front of a roaring log fire in the Steamboat Inn, the chill from the Solway's cold water already a memory. One of the bar stools was a horse's saddle which Travis gleefully jumped onto rodeo style.

'You look right at home' said Calhoun, with his auto-smile.

'I know you Americans aren't keen on real ale but Sal here has acquired a taste for it. Can I tempt you?'

'I'll try one,' said Calhoun.

'A Bud,' growled Travis.

Calhoun ignored the redneck and scanned the room. 'Interesting maritime memorabilia.'

Mackay knew the pub would appeal to the former history professor. 'Carsethorn was a major emigrant port. Tens of thousands of American settlers would have drank in this very pub. The same for Australians and New Zealanders.'

'I'll get the drinks,' said Sally, who promptly disappeared to the bar.

Mackay continued, 'your man John Paul Jones is from here, about a mile to the west. A place called Arbigland.' Calhoun's eyes lit up. 'The museum's good. It's in the cottage where he was born and is usually stuffed full of retired US navy types on holiday. On Independence Day your navy still sends your nearest Admiral to unfurl a flag or something.'

'I'll be sure to go,' said Calhoun enthusiastically.

Sally returned with the drinks and Mackay took a gulp of bitter. 'This beer's called Galloway Gold,' he said, 'maybe a sign that we're on the right track?'

Mackay's wishful thinking elicited a grimace from Travis.

'I agree with Lyle,' declared Calhoun, observing Travis's expression. 'It doesn't look like there's anything on Hestan Island but Lyle and I will return with metal detectors, just to make sure. It'll take a few days to sweep it properly.'

Mackay nodded his head slowly. 'If you think it's worth it but I don't believe they buried the bullion there. The whole crew of the Shenandoah knew where they'd been put off. There was a risk that some of the sailors would come back later to steal it. Plus I think Le Jeune still wanted to follow his orders and deposit it in London.'

Sally had already drunk half her pint. What a girl, thought Mackay. He was astonished when she drained the rest, then spoke. 'Tom and I will go to Norlands. We'll see if Mary Coggins has missed anything. Given what we know now there may be clues she's seen but wouldn't have attached any importance to.'

'Okay,' agreed Calhoun. 'Let's stay in touch.'

An hour later, Mackay and Sally were on the coast road back to Dumfries. The storm had passed and left a clear blue sky. Bright autumn light shone across the Firth.

They rounded a corner and entered a village of single storey houses. Sally was enchanted. 'This is a charming place. What's it called?'

'New Abbey,' replied Mackay. 'They call it New Abbey but it's probably seven or eight hundred years old.' Mackay knew the road well and what was round the sharp bend they were approaching. They turned almost ninety degrees, 'and this,' he said, like a compere introducing his star act, '... is Sweetheart Abbey.'

The low sun picked up the deep red sandstone of the magnificent ancient building like an orange filtered stage light. The building felt artificially illuminated and contrasted starkly with the greens of the trees and grass around it.

'Wow,' exclaimed Sally, 'let's get out for a closer look.'

The place was deserted, so unhindered, they explored the crumbling nave, transepts and cloisters. 'Why Sweetheart Abbey?' she asked.

Mackay knew the story well. 'It was built by a noblewoman in memory of her husband. She was so devoted to him that when he died she embalmed his heart in an ivory casket inlaid with silver, and always carried it with her. When she died herself she was buried with this 'sweetheart' of her husband lying on her bosom.'

Sally momentarily seemed choked with emotion. 'How romantic,' she gasped, pulling him towards her. She kissed him passionately then drew back to look at him. He had very dark brown hair, almost black, which was curly in places and falling haphazardly over his brown eyes. The focal point of his face was his cheeky grin which hinted - when combined with his dark skin and swarthy looks - at a touch of Irish ancestry.

'Come on then, let's see if we can find these medieval lovers,' she said.

They found the resting place of several Scottish nobles and the grave of the founder of the Bank of England, a William Paterson, but of the sweethearts' tomb, there was no trace.

'Oh we must find them, Tom.' Mackay was surprised at her sentimentality. She could be tough, even severe sometimes, like her father, but there was a side to her that was utterly endearing. They searched again but still drew a blank. Finally he accosted a friendly looking caretaker who was mending a fence.

'They're buried round here somewhere' said the man, 'though I'm afraid the exact location is lost. Building work over the centuries, then the Reformation, when half the place was pulled down - most of the village is built of stone from here you know. No, the best you'll get is the effigy in the south transept, but even that's sixteenth century so doesn't fit.'

'OK, thanks,' said Mackay. He looked at Sally and saw the disappointment in her face.

They drifted slowly to the south transept and examined what remained of the carving of the noblewoman. Mackay turned to Sally and smiled broadly. 'I do hope you'll put my heart in an ivory casket inlaid with silver, then carry it across your bosom until you die?'

She laughed. 'Of course I will. One big difference though.'

'Oh, what's that?'

'The casket won't be forged from silver; it'll be forged from Dixie gold.'

CHAPTER TWENTY NINE

Sally turned the page of the leather scrap book. 'This has been meticulously laid out,' she said, 'Mary's done well - James Steele's life is all here.'

Mackay was a few feet away, but still caught the musty smell of the leather. 'It's a pity she isn't here.'

'Where's she gone?'

Mackay closed the Victorian biscuit tin which held Steele's military records and reached for an old shoe box. He opened it gently. 'Train tickets,' he exclaimed, 'hundreds of train tickets. I can't believe James Steele kept all these.' He tipped the box upside down and they cascaded onto the desk like a rainbow coloured waterfall.

'Why so many colours?' asked Sally.

'Different colours for different train companies, different travel classes and different destinations. I remember this type of ticket as a boy. You don't have a colour coding system in the States?' She shook her head. 'How backward,' he teased, 'sounds a bit like your dollars, all green. I can't tell a ten dollar bill from a twenty, far better to have different colours for different denominations.'

She laughed. 'You must be stupid if you can't tell a number 10 from a number 20, and besides, our economy is doing just fine with the system we've got.'

There was silence as she turned the next page of the scrap book.

Mackay dealt a handful of tickets like playing cards. 'Oh, to answer your question,' he said, 'Mary is in Greece somewhere on a tour, following in the footsteps of Alexander the Great. I didn't like to bother her with this; she's already been very helpful.'

Mackay picked up another handful and resumed dealing. He was disappointed there were no tickets stamped 1865.

'I wonder how Calhoun is getting on?' said Sally. 'I don't trust him. If he finds anything he'll disappear and we'll never see him again.'

'More than likely,' replied Mackay, 'but I agree with Travis on this one. I'm sure there's nothing on the island.'

Half an hour later, Mackay took a call from Calhoun which confirmed this.

Sally was puzzled. 'I thought they were going to spend a couple of days sweeping the island.'

'Calhoun's had a rethink. He crossed the causeway with Travis in the dark this morning - then spent the day on Hestan until the next low tide - and swept the whole island.'

Sally looked alarmed. 'I hope those Duke of Edinburgh girls we saw yesterday had their tents zipped up. The thought of Calhoun creeping about in the dark makes me shudder.'

Mackay was only half listening - his last scoop of tickets had yielded 1865. 'Look Sal,' he said, 'here's one stamped 15th October 1865, from Dumfries to London Euston.'

He handed it to her. She took it between her thumb and index finger and looked at it closely. 'The date fits.' She flipped it over and saw a name on the back written in Steele's flowing handwriting. 'Who is this James Heffer?'

Mackay was already searching on his phone, 'he was the Confederacy's main spy in Britain.'

'It's a clue!' declared Sally excitedly.

Mackay continued to flick his phone screen. 'Nothing more here, but they must have met.' He echoed The Clash, 'sounds like 'London Calling,' Sal.' Gathering up the tickets he flung them into the shoe box. 'We'll drive down after breakfast. It'll take about six hours, so we'll have to push the flight back till Thursday if we want a day in London. Can you get the extra time off the campaign?'

'It shouldn't be a problem.'

'Good, it'll give us time to go to the Bank of England and look through the archives. See if we can find whether the gold was deposited in the Confederacy's account.'

'Will they let us do that?' she said.

Mackay shrugged his shoulders and walked over to the side table. He picked up the decanter. She nodded and he splashed two large measures of Highland Park into the crystal glasses. 'I'll call Calhoun and tell him the plan,' he said.

She felt the heat of the scotch in her mouth and nostrils. 'That gives us the evening free. What shall we do?'

Mackay looked directly into her eyes. 'Not that,' she said.

Mackay put down the decanter and picked up his glass. Next to the decanter was an old family board game. 'You haven't had a go at this yet, Sal. All Mackay family members or prospective family members must be initiated.'

She wanted to watch a movie but feigned interest, 'what is it?'

Mackay was enthusiastic. 'We call it the Great Game of Wealth. It's a family tradition that we play it at Christmas. It's a bit like monopoly - the aim is to amass wealth. But rather than making money through property, players go on a kind of treasure hunt around the board and perform tasks to get the next clue.'

Sally looked at the homemade square board, consisting of forty small boxes quote like Monopoly. There were two decks of crudely cut cards in the middle, one set were called Challenge Cards and the other was called Prodigy Cards. The Challenge Cards were nearest to her and she picked one from the top. It said, *'Do a handstand for two minutes.'*

'Sorry, too energetic for me,' she said quickly, 'I want to watch a movie.' Her heart sank when she saw the disappointment in his face.

'The Prodigy Cards are general knowledge questions or riddles,' he said hopefully. 'You don't need any energy for them.'

But she was resolute. 'Movie!'

CHAPTER THIRTY

Royal Automobile Club
89 Pall Mall
London
Present Day

'This building feels French,' she said, as they left the cab, 'a bit like the Place Vendome or Place de la Concorde in Paris.'

Mackay was impressed. 'How observant you are. It's French inspired and was designed by the folk who did the Ritz Hotel. After the Entente Cordiale, the Edwardians were big fans of the French and wanted to reflect this in their architecture.'

They checked into a junior suite and after a quick pint in the Long Bar, went to the Great Gallery.

'Now I really am at Versailles,' declared Sally.

Mackay scanned the room, taking in the opulent details and fittings, the neo classical frescoes and the high ceilings. 'Is that Louis XIV sitting over there?'

'Very funny,' she said, picking up the menu.

After a few minutes she put the menu down on the table. 'Having a millionaire fiancé does have its uses I suppose,' she said with a smile.

Mackay understood. 'The Tasting Menu with matching wines then,' he said. She nodded and the waiter was duly commissioned.

Their conversation was subdued as they feasted on Orkney scallops (Cotes du Rhone), pan seared fois gras (Royal Tokaji), pan fried sea bass (New Zealand Sauvignon) and soy marinated venison (Bordeaux).

'It's a taste sensation,' she said, through her final mouthful of venison.

Mackay was happy he'd pleased her. 'I think to finish it's pistachio parfait with a Spanish sherry.'

She giggled, 'I don't think Travis and Calhoun will be eating as well as this.'

Mackay agreed. 'No. The Travelodge on the Euston Road isn't widely known for its fine dining.'

The next day after breakfast, Sally and Mackay walked across St James's Park towards the District Line. As they crossed the Mall the morning sun caught the gilded bronze of the Victoria Memorial.

'Look, the Queen's at home,' said Mackay, pointing to the Royal Standard which hung limply from the roof of the palace.

'Are you much of a royalist?' she asked, hooking her arm through his as they entered the park. A duck suddenly appeared at her feet; she stumbled to avoid it and used his arm as a prop.

It was comic. What's going on Sal, are you still unsteady from last night's booze?'

'Not funny, Thomas.'

'No, Sal. I'm not really a monarchist, but I believe it's better than the alternative. I can't see us ever going for an elected head of state like you guys. The head of state and head government in a single office, it doesn't work well, a point I've made to your dear father on a number of occasions.'

She laughed. 'Another heated debate whilst I was absent?' The question was rhetorical so she gestured towards Buckingham Palace then continued. 'The beauty of a Republic is that you don't need any of this ridiculous anachronistic frippery, crowns, coaches, and palaces - great in a Disney movie, but really, in the twenty first century?'

Mackay really didn't care but decided to be defensive. 'The tourists love all that stuff. Bet if you did a cost benefit analysis you'd find the Royals pay their way.'

'Don't get me wrong,' she said, 'I love all the history.'

Mackay wanted to have the last word, 'besides, you have a hereditary monarchy of sorts yourself.'

'How d'you work that out?'

They crossed the Park Bridge and headed towards Birdcage Walk. 'President Bush senior, President Bush junior, President Clinton, Secretary of State Clinton, and that's without mentioning the Roosevelt Presidents who I understand were related. What you have across the pond is a semi monarchical republic.'

She couldn't take his assertion seriously and tried not to laugh. 'We'll have to agree to differ on that, Tom.'

Having missed the morning rush, it was easy to get a seat on the Tube all the way to Monument. At the station, a glance at Mackay's watch confirmed they were in good time. They walked to Threadneedle Street and saw the Americans waiting by the entrance to the Bank of England. As they approached, Travis finished his cigarette and stubbed it out on the pavement.

Calhoun fixed his easy smile on Sally. 'I've found the gold already, just like that - it's in the vault under our feet.'

Sally humoured him. 'How much is there?'

'There's about 400,000 bars. It's the second largest deposit after the Federal Reserve. Twenty billion pounds at today's prices.'

'Wow,' said Sally, 'all owned by the British Government?'

'Hardly any of it,' grumbled Mackay, 'most of it was sold by the last Government at ludicrously low prices, something like two hundred dollars an ounce.'

Calhoun exhaled loudly. 'Jesus. The price has been over $2,000 recently.'

'Who owns it now then?' asked Sally.

Mackay sighed, 'other Central Banks mostly. I told folk not to vote for the last government but I was ignored by millions.'

They skirted past the pink liveried footman and up the steps to the grand foyer of the Bank - Sally asked a hostile looking receptionist where the Archives were.

'Do you have an appointment?' asked the receptionist sharply. Sally shook her head. 'Do you have two forms of ID, one showing a photograph and the other showing your address?'

'I only have my American passport,' said Sally, 'and my address is on my driver's licence.'

The receptionist held the licence in her hand as if it was plagued. 'I can't accept this. I'll need to check if it's legitimate. Can you come back tomorrow?'

Sally was exasperated. 'It's issued by the State of Pennsylvania.'

The receptionist looked pleased at her own awkwardness. 'I'm sorry. I'll need to ask my supervisor if it's valid.'

Calhoun had also been searching his pockets for some form of ID, but without success. 'Looks like I'm going in by myself,' declared Mackay, 'handing over his passport and UK Driving licence.'

Travis turned and left, leaving, 'I'm gonna get a Bud,' hanging in the air. Calhoun saw an opportunity. 'I'll buy you a coffee, Sally.'

'I've just had one thanks,' she replied evenly, 'think I'll go shopping on Oxford Street.'

Calhoun tried again, 'I'll come with you if you like - I need some souvenirs for the family.'

'Sorry, I prefer shopping alone,' she said firmly. She turned to Mackay, 'let us know when you're finished Tom.'

They left and Mackay proceeded into the bowels of the building. The silence, the décor, the staff perched on row upon row of wooden desks reminded Mackay of some nightmarish Kafka novel. The cavernous Bank felt very empty, Mackay reflected that only the public sector could afford to utilize space so poorly.

Mackay began with the Bank's daily accounts book for 1865, a slab like ledger which he needed both hands to lift. The first few pages detailed the huge sums borrowed by dozens of companies during the Victorian railway building frenzy. Mackay noted that one such firm, London and North Western Rail, was due to repay £825,000 in early 1866, a vast amount then, and millions now. With two thirds of Britain's railways ripped up in the 1960s, the waste, thought Mackay with sadness, was colossal.

Next, came pages of other redeemable security holders, from the Borough of Manchester, to more exotic sounding borrowers like the Panama New River Company. Mackay doubted whether - during the age of unfettered capitalism and speculative adventures - any of the Panamanian bonds were ever repaid.

140

Then he found a page of bullion imports and saw the American column was by far the most active. He read that in November 1865, £487,000 of gold was deposited in the Bank of England from America. Were Le Jeune's boxes part of that, he thought? If they were, which account were the funds credited to?

Now it became more difficult. There was no Microsoft search function in 1865 so Mackay hauled out ledger after ledger and read page after page of customer accounts. Whilst the Confederacy hadn't been recognized by Palmerston's government as a sovereign state, it had been granted belligerent status, and so trade, via blockade runners, had continued with Britain. Consequently huge amounts of wealth had continued to flow through the Bank from Confederate states.

Towards the end of the war - when it became clear the Federal Government would pursue President Davis and his cohorts and try to find the wealth they'd squirreled away - Mackay saw large deposits had been made in the Bank by a firm called Fraser, Trenholm and Co. Calhoun had told Mackay that this firm, which was headed by the Confederate Treasury Secretary, George Trenholm, was effectively the Confederacy's overseas bank.

Mackay noted the firm was based in Liverpool. Why then hadn't Le Jeune deposited the gold there? Had Trenholm's associates told Le Jeune it was safer to put the bullion in the Bank of England to avoid Federal lawyers? Mackay's research suggested Trenholm's firm was certainly transferring its own assets into the Bank of England at that time.

Mackay continued to trawl through the records for the rest of the day but found no evidence of Le Jeune's gold. He looked for accounts under several names; Le Jeune, Davis, Steele, Heffer and the State of Virginia, but he couldn't find a bullion deposit that fitted. Mackay became frustrated. He called Sally and then Calhoun, and arranged to meet them in the Long Bar of the RAC.

'Could you have missed something?' asked Calhoun, in a way that suggested a history professor was more thorough than an accountant.

Mackay was unfazed. 'It's possible of course. What's more likely is they deposited the gold under another name. Without that name we'll never find out what happened to it. The Bank had thousands of accounts in 1865.'

Calhoun didn't look convinced and was confident of his superior research skills. 'I'll have another go in the archives tomorrow.' He paused for thought, 'we also need to consider that the gold and the Richmond Papers have been separated.'

There was an awkward silence. They hadn't discussed the Richmond Papers before. Sally was surprised, 'you are interested in these Papers?' she said. 'They weren't mentioned much in Lieutenant Calhoun's letter.'

Calhoun sipped his pint whilst he thought of a response. He'd let slip he'd been aware of the documents. He hoped they wouldn't deduce he'd learnt about their importance from the FBI. Of course, as a historian, he *was* interested from a historical perspective, but he didn't really care what happened to them as long as he got the gold.

Calhoun spoke in a professorial tone. 'No, they weren't mentioned specifically by Lieutenant Calhoun but it's well known amongst Civil War historians that key Confederate State papers were never recovered - documents of undoubted historical importance. Of these, we think a letter or some form of affidavit written by President Davis, somehow purports to cast doubt on the validity of the United States. Any ordinary historian would make his name discovering the whereabouts of such a trove.'

'You, no doubt, exclude yourself from the category of ordinary historians,' jabbed Sally. Calhoun smiled but didn't respond. His inadvertent disclosure about the Papers had heightened Sally's suspicions and loathing of him.

'Look,' said Calhoun, aware that he'd irritated her, 'we've done well as a team to get this far. But don't forget if my cousin hadn't died and left me Lieutenant Calhoun's letter, you'd still be wasting your time in Liverpool.'

'That's a good point,' interjected Mackay with excitement. Sally scowled at him. 'No, I don't mean it's a good point we'd still be flapping about in Liverpool. I mean it's a good point the death of Doug's cousin took us a step forward.' Sally was still smouldering and didn't speak.

'What do you mean?' asked Calhoun.

'My own cousins,' said Mackay, 'the Steeles. They emigrated to New Zealand. Like your cousin they might have family papers. I've always been a bit surprised that Mary found so little correspondence from James Steele. Perhaps my Kiwi cousins have got some in an attic buried under a foot of dust?'

'It's worth a try,' said Calhoun, 'but I'm still going to have another go at the Bank tomorrow.'

'I need to get back to the States for the last phase of the campaign,' said Sally.

'Then we'll have to stay in touch by phone, Doug,' said Mackay, with little expectation that he'd hear from the professor again if Calhoun found anything of use at the Bank.

Calhoun flashed his oily smile. 'For sure, I'll reach out if I find anything.'

CHAPTER THIRTY ONE

Clinton Street
Philadelphia
Election Night

Mackay refilled the crystal tumbler and sank back into his wingback armchair. The brown leather was faded and worn but perfectly moulded itself to his body, the comfort was unparalleled. It had been decadent to ship the chair from the UK and when it arrived, Sally had hidden it in a rarely used recess, but gradually, over time, he'd inched the chair into prime position in front of the living room TV.

Draping his legs on the soft leather footstool he took a sip of Highland Park. To gain a British perspective he pressed the remote control and switched from CNN to the BBC. There was no doubt the President was ahead and there was no doubt the BBC reporters, despite the Director General's frequent attempts at impartiality, couldn't hide their disappointment. Director Generals, Chairmen, charter renewals, they'd all come and gone over the years, but the Corporation's left leaning bias was still firmly embedded in its DNA. Mackay changed over to Fox News. The channel had been a success, he thought, perhaps rivals like talkTV did stand a chance in the UK, but against a taxpayer subsidized rival like the BBC, it would be an uphill struggle.

The projection for Virginia flashed blue, bagging Ruth Callaghan 13 Electoral College votes, but a few seconds later Florida and its 29 votes flashed red for the President. Mackay sighed. Sally and the team in Market Street would be disappointed. The polls had always put the President ahead in the national vote but she'd left Clinton Street that evening believing that key swing states were too close to call. His cell rang, it was Sally.

'Looking grim,' he said.

'I'm not so sure,' she replied, the optimism clear in her voice. 'Our internals show the President is way ahead in the popular vote but the swing states, Michigan, Pennsylvania, Georgia, even Arizona, are all close, very close.'

Mackay was surprised, 'I might have another Scotch then.'

'I want you to come over here,' she said, 'we have champagne on ice.'

The streets of Philadelphia were deserted as Mackay traversed Walnut Street, then Chestnut Street, before turning right into Market Street. Campaign headquarters were located in a drab concrete tower in front of City Hall. Sally was waiting for him in the foyer and swiftly whisked him past security up to the fourth floor.

Dozens of campaign staffers were ringed loosely around a huge TV screen on the far wall. Mackay could see Ruth Callaghan, her husband, and former President Alex Freeman, at the front. The atmosphere wasn't quite despondent but certainly it was tense.

Over the next couple of hours, as each key state was coloured blue, it felt like some hidden hand had dialled up the voltage in the room. Then Pennsylvania projected for Callaghan, releasing a further frisson of electricity amongst the staffers.

'That's us on 261,' declared Mackay, stating the obvious.

'There'll be a recount in Penn with that margin but yes, it leaves North Carolina,' said Sally, pulling him towards her with a smile, 'Ruth's own state.'

Mackay kissed her, 'you've won then.'

She nodded.

'When can we decently open the champagne? The scotch is wearing off and I'm feeling sleepy.'

She laughed, 'be patient!'

Half an hour later North Carolina declared for President-elect Callaghan.

'Astonishing turn around in three hours,' said Mackay, 'that makes 276.'

Sally's face turned to disappointment as the final popular vote flashed up. 'My God! The President's got seven million more votes.'

'I told you, the Electoral College is a failed system,' he said cheerily.

She shot him a fierce glance. He realised the timing of his observation was poor. 'That's not helpful, Tom.'

She sat down on a desk and took the glass of champagne he had procured. 'No popular mandate, the Senate controlled by the Republicans and the House on a knife's edge. It's going to be difficult to get much done.'

Callaghan had been working the room, now it was their turn and the President-elect joined Sally on the desk.

'Congratulations Ruth,' said Sally, with a wide smile.

Mackay looked at Callaghan more closely. She wore her clothes well. Her shimmery blue top and black skirt were relaxed, her long brown hair was tied back but still half fell to her shoulders. It may have been her role as the Iron Lady which framed the image in Mackay's mind, there was certainly a likeness - Callaghan reminded him of Meryl Streep.

The President-elect was sharp and highly sensitive. She immediately detected the uncharacteristic flatness which Sally tried to hide, 'what's up, Sal?'

Sally half smiled, 'it's a win, sure, but only because of a quirk in the system.'

Callaghan's expression briefly hardened before softening again. 'Well, let's see if we can't improve it. Why don't you have a look at the Constitution for me, as Deputy White House Counsel? I know it'll be difficult getting anything meaningful through Congress given my thin mandate, but I intend to run a collegiate administration.'

Sally's eyes lit up, 'thank you Ruth, I'd relish the chance.'

There was a buzz from the front of the room. The President had appeared on screen for his concession speech. 'Excuse me, but I want to listen to this.' Callaghan nodded an acknowledgement at Mackay and headed off.

Alex Freeman took her place on the desk. 'A worthwhile job,' he said, 'White House Counsel got me through a number of scrapes.'

'I'm honoured to be offered it,' said Sally.

Freeman smiled at her and then paused to allow a natural change of subject. 'And how did you get on in the Bahamas? When we last met you were hunting for a secret document written by Jefferson Davis, the Richmond Papers, I think you called it.'

Mackay chipped in, 'our hunt has taken us across the Atlantic. Seems the document and some gold were taken by a Confederate warship to Britain in the final days of the war. We know it was put off the ship in Scotland and a Confederate officer then went to London. That's as far as we've got. We're hoping my relatives in New Zealand might have family documents from that time that will give us a clue, but they've not replied to my emails or letters yet.

'I see,' said Freeman. 'And has Director Andrews been troubling you?'

'No,' replied Sally 'we not seen or heard from him since Orlando.'

Freeman spoke to Mackay. 'Sally is aware but you may not know that Andrews was interim Director for a short time on my watch. Looking back now I can see why the Republicans were pushing him at me for the job permanently. My instincts told me there was something dark about him which he hid well. I found his ideas on government diverged significantly from my own and I got rid of him. I wasn't surprised when the current President appointed him.'

Sally nodded, 'yes, I sensed his outlook was akin to a Soviet era policeman, the KGB or the Stasi. His view and more worryingly his belief, is that illegitimate, even criminal actions by the state, are all justified by the greater good.'

'You sum him up well, Sally,' agreed Freeman with a smile. He got up from the desk. 'Keep me in the loop on these Richmond Papers. I'll be seeing you in the White House. Ruth is intending to have me hanging around as some sort of adviser.'

Sally beamed. 'Of course, Mr President.' Freeman left to rejoin Callaghan.

Mackay turned to Sally and looked into her eyes. 'Well then, shall I start looking for a house to buy in Washington tomorrow?'

CHAPTER THIRTY TWO

The Residence
Te Koi Lodge
Nelson
New Zealand

Sally yawned. 'What time is it in Philly?'
'About three o'clock yesterday afternoon,' he replied drowsily. 'Did you manage any sleep?'
'A bit.'
'I'm zonked,' he said, 'I've never known jet lag like it. He got out of bed and idled through to the lounge. He opened the glass doors and flopped into a chair on the outside deck. To signal his arrival, the warm morning sun skirted out from behind a white fluffy cloud, bathing the Waimea Estuary in golden light. They'd arrived in the dark and had no sense of their orientation. 'Come and look at this, Sal, some view.'

She padded out to join him in her bare feet. 'Stunning,' she confirmed. 'Where's this you've booked us then.' She looked around the secluded two bedroom bungalow and saw their private spa pool had panoramic sea views. Before he could reply she'd disrobed and plunged into the water naked. 'Now, I feel awake!' she yelled. He threw off his dressing gown and joined her.

'It's called the Residence,' he said, softy splashing water at her, 'it's got a luxury price tag, but I couldn't resist it, I thought we could pretend we're in our own 'White House' Residence.'

Her face darkened. 'That's if Ruth ever gets there. The President withdrawing his concession was a shock.'

'I can't see this recount in North Carolina making much difference,' he said, 'Ruth's 8,000 ahead. Even if the odd postal vote ended up in the wrong pile it won't be material.'

She frowned. 'I won't tell you again - we call them mail-in-ballots, not postal votes.'

He kissed her. 'Alright Sal, no need to snap. I'll put your mood down to jet lag and frustration with the President. But really, this recount and court case are going nowhere.'

Her expression softened. 'You're right. But it's not this business in North Carolina that troubles me. There's widespread discontentment, even amongst some Democrats, given the President won the popular vote by such a wide margin. The President's supporters are voicing their anger and the clamour is growing. I sense it's leading somewhere, I'm sure the Republicans are up to something, this court case and the recount in North Carolina are just smokescreens.'

A black and white image of Kirk Douglas appeared in Mackay's mind. 'A coup attempt?'

She read his mind and laughed, 'you mean Seven Days in May. No, not a military coup, a Republican led constitutional coup.'

'Not sure what that means and frankly, after months of it,' he feigned a yawn, 'I'm bored of American politics.'

She opened the palms of her hands and splashed him back. 'What a shame. You've only got another four years of it coming up.'

He sighed as the sun dipped behind a cloud. 'Come on, let's get dried and head into the Lodge for what's billed as a gourmet breakfast. We haven't spent a day getting to New Zealand to simply lounge around in a spa pool.'

After breakfast they took a cab into Nelson, passing through a suburb called Richmond on the way. Mackay consulted his phone. 'That has to be good karma,' he said, 'this suburb and Richmond, Virginia, are both named after Richmond in London.'

She laughed, 'must be the link we've been looking for. We're clearly onto something.'

They arrived at Collingwood Street which Mackay suspected was unchanged since Victorian times. The grand weather-board houses with their red tin roofs formed a charming palate of traditional colonial colours.

The finest house on the street, which boasted large verandas on both the ground and the first floors, had been white, but was now more of a dirty grey. Through the overgrown foliage Mackay could see there was significant dilapidation. They had travelled several thousand miles to reach this house.

The Briton forced open the rotten gate and guided Sally along a stone path partially hidden by weeds and overhanging branches. One of the four panes in the front door was cracked and another had been replaced by cardboard. The bell didn't work so Mackay knocked on the door. There was no response. Mackay put his mouth to the cardboard pane and shouted, 'hello, Mr Steele.' There was silence. 'You try, Sal.'

'Mr Steele, Mr Steele,' she said loudly. 'My name is Sally Purcell. I'm here with my fiancé, Tom Mackay. He's your cousin. We're researching the Steele family history and we've come all the way from America to see you.'

The inside of the house was still and noiseless. She began to think it was empty, but the creak of a floorboard halted her turn back towards the road. 'Tom's written a few times,' she said to the cardboard pane, 'but he hasn't had a reply. We really have come a long way.'

Another floorboard creaked and an elderly Kiwi voice emanated from the cardboard. 'What do you want to know about the Steeles?'

'My great grandfather was James Steele. I believe he was your grandfather. We've been researching him for months now.'

'You're not American,' said the voice, in an accusational manner.

'No. I'm British. My name's Tom Mackay.'

'That's what your girlfriend just said,' snapped Steele, 'I got your letters. Just because you send me a letter it doesn't mean you're related to me.'

Mackay sensed Steele was more receptive to Sally and he tilted his head towards the cardboard, suggesting she speak. 'Can we come in Mr Steele; it would be helpful if we could talk.'

One, two, three bolts were drawn back, a key was turned, then the door slowly swung open. The old man stood propped on a walking stick. He was frail and his face was chequered with blotches where cancerous moles had been removed. His fair complexion and gingery white hair suggested his battle with the fierce New Zealand sun had been a long one.

There was evidence Steele had made an attempt to keep up his appearance, but he'd missed some buttons on his shirt and his belt was not properly buckled. He tried to prevent his de facto scowl from softening but it was plain he'd taken an instant shine to Sally, as most men did. 'You'd better come in then,' he said, with artificial gruffness.

Steele hobbled into the musty living room and sat in a leather wingback chair similar to Mackay's own favourite. The room, the house, Steele himself, seemed lost in some Victorian time warp more suited to a museum.

The old man looked at Mackay. The lad was dark and pale but there was something about the set of his eyes which suggested family. Steele pointed to an old grandfather clock in the corner. 'Would you please wind that up for me, the key's hanging underneath.'

Mackay did as he was told and reset the time. He then joined Sally on the sofa, propelling a cloud of dust into the room as he sat.

'Do you live alone?' asked Sally gently.

He chuckled. 'The house is a mess you mean. Yes, I'm the last of the Steeles. My wife, my brothers, my sister, all dead. Not a single child between us would you believe. No cousins either. Only that damned social worker trying to get me into a home.' He cackled again. 'I don't let her in. Hours she's spent on that doorstep. Sometimes she ambushes me when I go out though. I can't do much about that.'

Mackay sensed Steele had turned evading his social worker into a sport. The old man waited for Mackay to speak but it was Sally who took up the conversation. 'If you've read Tom's letters, Mr Steele, you'll know why we've come.'

Steele switched his rheumy eyes from Sally to MacKay. 'Your letter prompted me to search for some stuff in the attic. I nearly broke my neck getting up there. I found my grandfather's journal though. There's quite a lot in there. Man, his adventures in 1865 read like a novel.'

Mackay exhaled loudly and Sally gasped before speaking. 'I can't tell you how helpful it would be if we could read it, Mr Steele.'

The old man knew he now had their undivided attention. 'Please call me Bob.'

Mackay pushed too quickly. 'No need for you to get up Bob. I can get the journal for you.'

151

The old man shook his head. The silence was broken only by the peaceful ticking of the grandfather clock. Steele first examined Sally, running his eye over her in an appreciative way, then he studied Mackay, and saw in his handsome face a degree of straightforward sincerity.

Steele sat back in his chair and emitted a thin mist of dust. He cleared the air with a wave of his wrinkled hand and spoke to Sally. 'You want this journal. Fine, you can have it, but we need to make a deal first.'

'A deal?' said Sally.

'Yes, a deal,' repeated Steele with sudden energy. 'I'm going to make a couple of calls as soon as you've gone and you're going to come back here this evening to take me out for dinner at the Urban Oyster Bar.'

Sally beamed at him and reached forward to place her hand on his arm. 'No problem Bob, about seven?'

The old man put his hand over hers. 'See you then.'

Mackay was concerned, what sort of deal?

CHAPTER THIRTY THREE

The jet lag and the warm tropical breeze floating through The Residence meant drifting to sleep that afternoon was easy. Around 3pm they woke, and Sally's polka dot bikini emerged for its first South Pacific outing.

Refreshed from their swim in the Lodge's pool, they dressed and called for a cab. This time their driver took the coast road into the city and they marvelled at the stunning greens, blues and golds of Tasman Bay. Compared to dirty, reeking London, Mackay knew the Bay must have seemed like paradise to his Victorian ancestor. At Tahunanui Beach the road and coast became one as they motored passed the tree lined Haulashore Island and Nelson Yacht club. At the commercial port they turned inland towards the heritage city, and within five minutes were at Collingwood Street.

Steele had managed to wrestle himself into a military looking blue blazer which complemented his Panama hat. 'I can't go out without a hat, Sally. My skin's wrecked from years on the farm without sun block. No one wore hats in the 1950s. I don't want skin cancer back. After all,' he paused for dramatic effect, 'I don't fancy an early death.'

She smiled at his joke and took his arm for the short stroll to Hardy Street. The intensity of the early evening sun surprised her. 'I see what you mean, Bob, the sun is still strong.'

Steele pulled his hat further down in response. 'It's because the ozone layer is depleted over this part of the Southern Hemisphere.'

They took a shaded table outside and consulted the menu.

'Don't bother with that, Tom,' said Steele, 'it has to be oysters in here, with the fish sharing platter to start.'

Mackay nodded and read the wine list. 'It also has to be a Nelson Sauvignon Blanc I guess, although I'm surprised it's so expensive given its local. I'll go for a Neudorf.'

'Yes. Sadly most of it goes for export,' added Steele.

During their mutual dispatching of the fish platter, Mackay began to warm to the old man, for sure he was crusty and direct, but there was a likeable honesty to him. It was no surprise that Steele had immediately taken to Sally, but Mackay also felt the old man was growing attached to himself - his only known relative. Their friendship was clearly developing but it didn't prepare Mackay for what Steele said next.

'When you left this morning, I called my solicitor.' Steele chuckled. 'The young fellow was very surprised to hear from me, he thought I'd been dead for ten years.' Steele laughed again. 'Anyway, I told him the deal I'm proposing and he'll prepare the documents.' Sally looked at Mackay who returned her puzzled stare. Steele continued. 'You want my grandfather's journal; you can have it, along with everything else, my house, my savings, my whole estate.'

Mackay was astounded. Sally was shocked.

'Before you thank me, there's a catch, in fact several conditions. Whilst I know you are who you say you are, Tom, you know what lawyers are like. He wants you to take a DNA test, just to make sure we're related.'

'Really, Bob, I can't accept...'

Steele interrupted, 'wait 'til you hear the rest first, it's not a freebie, you've got to earn it.'

Mackay fell silent and Steele continued. 'First, you need to help me fix up the house. Repair it. Make it suitable for a geriatric like me. A stair lift, that sort of thing. I can't cope by myself; you can see that from the state of the place. I need help. If you don't help, my social worker will cart me off to a home.' He took a mouthful of oyster and a sip of wine. 'Then I want you to sort out some day care for me. I read about old folk being abused in their homes by their carers all the time. I'm not asking you to live in Nelson, but you need to visit, monitor my care. I know it's a long way from the States, but say every couple of months. Check I'm

154

okay. Look after my financial affairs while you're here. I'll give you power of attorney.'

Mackay exhaled slowly and loudly. Sally spoke, 'that's a lot to take in, Bob.'

Steele decided to push further. He wouldn't insist on his final condition but along with the oysters and the Sauvignon he put it on the table, just to see their reaction.

He looked at Sally. 'You don't get off scot free either. He doesn't get a penny unless he marries you.'

She laughed, 'you're quite the matchmaker, Bob.'

Mackay was dumbstruck. Steele looked at him, his eyes twinkling as he spoke. 'It's a lot to take on, Tom. Monitoring my care is one thing, but my financial affairs are also complex. My grandfather arrived here in Victorian times with a box of gold. You could buy a lot of land cheaply then. And he did. At one stage, me, my brothers and my sister, we had nine farms between us. I've got assets all over the place.'

Mackay was already wealthy but he'd noticed Washington house prices were double Philadelphia's. Nelson was a great place and would appeal at the time of year when Washington was under several feet of snow. He looked at Sally, it seemed both US immigration and his distant cousin wanted him to marry her. He knew Bob was joking but it *had* brought the question up again.

But what about the rest of the deal? Given his bonhomie it seemed likely the old man would throw in James Steele's journal, but even retired farmers could drive a hard bargain. Logistically, Mackay did have time for a few trips to Nelson every year, but Sally would struggle after she joined the White House. He wanted to help his cousin and was inclined to accept his offer. 'I can't speak for Sally about your last condition, Bob, but helping you stay in your home is quite an inducement. For my part I accept your terms.'

Steele was pleased but thought it best to backtrack on the marriage condition in case they'd taken him seriously. 'Please don't feel you have to plan a wedding yet, Sally, think about it.' She smiled and nodded. Steele raised his glass. 'A toast to my new family.'

They clinked glasses and Mackay called over the waiter. 'I think we'd better have a bottle of your best champagne.'

CHAPTER THIRTY FOUR

Executive Lounge
Auckland International Airport
New Zealand
Present Day

The early part of the week had been hard work, lawyers, DNA tests, builders, banks; even Steele's social worker had received a visit. Then the conversion of the house on Collingwood Street into a deluxe retirement home had been arranged with a contractor, and a project plan agreed.

To allow Mackay to supervise the work remotely, the contractor had offered to send daily video updates of his progress; all Steele had to do was open the door every morning to let him in. The bespoke upgrade was going to cost a lot of money, but there was a lot of money to go around. Mackay discovered Bob's New Zealand farms had sold for £1-2 million each, and there'd been nine of them.

Mackay and Sally had a chance to relax the second half of the week and they meandered back to Auckland. On their way north, they did wine tasting tours at several Marlborough vineyards before collapsing onto the ferry at Picton, inebriated. The residual jet lag and the wine resulted in the Cook Strait being largely missed, but on reaching the North Island, they felt refreshed enough for a lightening tour of New Zealand's delightful capital.

After Wellington, the train took them to Otoroharga. From there they transferred to Peter Jackson's Hobbiton, where Mackay - a big Lord of the Rings fan - overindulged in the Green Dragon. The next day they rejoined the train at Hamilton for the last leg to Auckland, where, despite the disruption caused by the construction of the new underground, they found the city vibrant and conducive to cocktails overlooking the busy harbour.

In Auckland's international terminal the airport lounge was half empty - so accessing the bar has been made too easy. Mackay returned again with two large gin and tonics. Sally grabbed one. 'After this I'll doze all the way to LA,' she said.

He took a mouthful himself and sat back on the sofa. 'Thirteen hours, then another six to Philly. Our body clocks will be in meltdown.'

'We can plan in more touring next time we visit, Bob,' she said, 'our sightseeing was a bit hurried this week.'

Mackay took her hand, 'remember you agreed we'd do the UK for Christmas with my folks, perhaps we can come to New Zealand from there, go completely around the world.'

'We'll see,' she replied, which probably meant no. 'And what was your highlight of our short tour, Thomas?'

'Had to be Hobbiton,' he said quickly, 'you know I'd love to retire to Rivendell.'

She laughed. 'I really liked Wellington - it had a great energy - even if it was a bit windy.' She glanced at the departures board. 'That's us, go to gate.'

She gestured to the leather journal which lay on the table in front of them - a departing gift from Bob. It was embossed and had a Tree of Life on the front. 'Are you going to delve into James Steele's journal on the flight?'

They'd wrestled over it all week and devoured its contents like starving hyenas. Mackay nodded and referenced the International Date Line east of Fiji that they'd soon be flying over. 'Yes. I'll read the next bit when we cross into yesterday.'

CHAPTER THIRTY FIVE

Savile Row
London
October 1865

This part of Savile Row was poorly lit and Le Jeune was thankful that the lights of the Brougham illuminated the door of the building. Behind him he heard Steele pay the driver and as the vehicle pulled off he was plunged into darkness. His eyes soon adjusted to the feeble streetlight and he knocked at the door. The three storey building was narrow, the ground floor window was a single bay. The upper floors each had three small windows, none of which displayed any light.

'Are you sure this is the right address?' asked Steele, pulling his coat closer to him to combat the unseasonably chilly wind.

Le Jeune shielded his hands to light a match. He pulled a piece of paper from his coat pocket and read it. 'Yes. This is the house they told me about in Richmond.'

Steele put his face to the glass and peered in the bay window. 'There's a faint light coming from a room at the back. Maybe they think we're Federal agents and they're hiding.'

'Maybe,' said Le Jeune, knocking at the door again.

Someone must have been listening to Le Jeune's southern drawl from the other side of the door, because bolts were rapidly slid back and it smoothly swung open.

A balding man in his early fifties, with dark darting eyes and whiskers almost a foot long, blocked their entry. 'If you're not Federal agents, then who are you?' he said.

Le Jeune was easy going but for some reason he took an instant dislike to the man. He ignored the agent's question and asked his own. 'Is this the Confederate Commercial Agency?'

'It was the Agency,' said the man, 'who wants to know?'

'I am Colonel Pierre Le Jeune. I left Richmond in April. I am tasked by President Davis with bringing certain items to London.'

Now the man looked interested and beckoned them in. 'James Heffer,' he said, offering his hand, 'I am ... .I was the agent here.'

He showed them to a parlour at the rear of the house where a low fire struggled for life. Heffer jabbed at it with a poker and threw on some coals - which immediately spat and crackled - and soon thick yellow smoke was woven with flame. He pulled up some chairs - half circling the fire - and gestured that they should sit.

Heffer spoke in a conspiratorial tone. 'We've had quite a few escapees through here since the summer. Secretary of State Benjamin is still in London I believe.' Heffer picked up some tongs and grasped a glowing shard of coal which had landed on the stone floor by Steele's feet. 'There are Federal agents everywhere. They believe the money to finance Lincoln's assassination came from here. They're hunting anyone with a connection to James Wilkes Booth. Friends of mine simply disappear overnight and the British turn a blind eye.' He glanced at them furtively. 'Does anyone know you're in London?' Le Jeune shook his head. 'Keep it that way,' said Heffer.

Le Jeune's temper was beginning to fray. He'd travelled several hundred miles from Scotland on a series of draughty trains and this unpleasant man had neglected to offer him any kind of refreshment. Le Jeune was usually calm and composed but on this occasion was struggling to hide his irritation. 'Difficult times, Heffer, difficult times. But what shall we do with the bullion we've brought from Richmond?'

Heffer pursed his lips and involuntarily put his hand on his head. 'Tell me where the gold is and I'll make sure it's deposited into the right account.'

Le Jeune's dislike of the man grew, but Heffer *had* been appointed by the Confederate government, so Le Jeune reasoned they had to trust him. Steele sensed otherwise and interrupted. 'If you make the arrangements, we'll deliver the gold to the bank you suggest ourselves, and see it's safely deposited.'

Steele saw Heffer bridle at this but Le Jeune missed the agent's grimace.

'Very well,' said Heffer, 'how shall I contact you?'

Steele stood to leave. 'We'll come here at noon on Thursday.'

Outside the house, as they stood trying to hail a cab on Savile Row, Steele voiced his concerns. 'I don't trust him. The war's over, he's going to take the gold for himself.'

Le Jeune didn't want to believe their efforts had been a waste. Six months, five thousand miles and countless near misses with death couldn't all be for nothing. He stalled, refusing to face the inevitable. 'We can't produce the gold by tomorrow anyway.'

Steele raised his arm but the Hansom clattered by. 'No. But we'll get an idea of the best bank to put it in. I'll make sure I'm armed when we meet Heffer again.'

Steele turned and faced Le Jeune full on. He looked him straight in the eye and spoke earnestly. 'Listen, Pierre. I've held my counsel until now but no longer. I must tell you what I think.' Le Jeune looked at him quizzically. Steele continued, 'C'mon, you must be hungry, I am. I'll buy you dinner at Simpsons.'

Le Jeune nodded in agreement.

They walked down Regent Street, through Piccadilly, down Haymarket and via Trafalgar Square onto the Strand. Just before entering the restaurant, Steele suddenly spun round and saw a shadow ducking into a doorway.

'Is there a problem?' asked Le Jeune.

'I'm not sure, but I sense we've been followed since we left Savile Row.'

Le Jeune looked back up the street. 'They must be the Federal agents who were watching Heffer's house,'

Steele nodded, 'must be.'

The Grand Divan dining room was brightly lit and the highly polished wood panelling reflected the lamps like glass. 'There aren't many chess players in tonight,' said Steele, almost to himself. Le Jeune looked puzzled, the remark needed explanation. 'All the big chess tournaments are played in here,' said Steele, 'sometimes against other clubs, those runners in the top hats over there carry news of each move.'

'I see they do a good roast,' said Le Jeune, observing a waiter wheeling in a silver trolley laden with beef.'

It only took an hour before their own joint, with all the trimmings, potatoes and greens, was wholly washed down with a quart of claret.

Le Jeune turned a glassy eye on Steele. 'Now, tell me James, what's on your mind?'

Steele sat back in his chair and drained his glass. He'd travelled with Le Jeune for six months and learned of the American's acute sense of honour. Steele respected him, liked him, trusted him, and was afraid his proposal would damage, or even break their bond.

He began cautiously. 'I admire how resolutely you've carried out your orders. It's not been easy getting the document and the gold to this island all the way from Richmond, but we've done it, you've done it.'

Le Jeune began to feel more sober. He noticed the claret had stained Steele's teeth. He knew what was coming before Steele said it. 'The war's long over, Pierre. Heffer, Davis, Benjamin, people like them, they don't care about the cause anymore, you can surely see that, they're just out for themselves.'

Steele recharged their glasses from a fresh bottle. He could see that Le Jeune, who was normally so open and frank, was on this occasion difficult to read. Steele was uncertain how he'd react. 'I think we should keep the gold, Pierre, and give the Federals the documents you received from President Davis, which Davis himself got from Lord Palmerston, via me.'

Le Jeune was expressionless. The American reached forward and drained his glass in one. His face remained blank when he spoke. 'James, the Federal government will destroy the documents. Since the US government last had possession of them fifty years ago, we've had a civil war which has threatened the very existence of America. No. Your Lord Palmerston is right. The documents are now a huge problem for them. They will burn them, so why don't I keep one copy and you keep the other.'

Steele nodded. 'And what shall we do with the gold?'

Le Jeune was stony faced. 'The gold belongs to the South and will be needed to rebuild. I will not give it to Heffer. I will keep it myself and take it to Louisiana to put to good use.'

Steele was disappointed but understood. Le Jeune broke into a smile. 'Of course there'd be no gold at all without you, James. It's only fair I allow you a commission.'

Steele quickly mixed the arithmetic with fairness and covetousness. 'Nine boxes left, so a box would be a commission of about 11 percent. That seems fair to me. What do you think?'

Le Jeune beamed and knocked over Steele's glass as he reached across the table to take his friend's hand. 'That, Mr Steele, is a deal.'

Steele shook Le Jeune's hand and flung out his arm to signal to the waiter. He was rich. 'Waiter, bring a bottle of your very finest Champagne please.'

CHAPTER THIRTY SIX

10 Downing Street
London
October 1865

Steele knocked on the Downing Street door. A footman showed him into an anteroom. A few minutes later an under-secretary arrived.

'I'd like to see the Prime Minister,' said Steele.

'I'm afraid he's not here, sir.'

'Is he at Cambridge House or Broadlands?'

'I'm not at liberty to say, sir. If you'd like to make an appointment, I'll...'

'Get Barrington please,' snapped Steele, 'it's important.'

Steele had no identification, but Palmerston's Principal Private Secretary, Charles Barrington, had been present when the Premier had given Steele his commission two years earlier.

The under secretary was in a dilemma. 'I'm afraid Mr Barrington isn't here either, sir.'

'It's important,' repeated Steele.

The under-secretary looked at Steele closely. The man seemed credible and given Palmertson's temper, no official dared to risk delaying intelligence from reaching the Premier. 'His Lordship is at Brocket Hall, sir.'

Steele nodded his thanks and left the building. He didn't want to delay his meeting with Palmerston any longer. The use of the Prime Minister's authority to get out of Nassau, and the assistance he'd given first to Le Jeune, and then to the Shenandoah, would now be known by the Premier. Steele didn't want to contemplate the retribution he knew Palmerston would exact.

It was too late to call on Palmerston that evening, so he resolved to catch a train from Kings Cross the following day. He toyed with the idea of sending a boy home to fetch Le Jeune for dinner at Rules, but instead hailed a Hanson cab and went back to Cheyne Walk himself.

The lock and hinges of his front door were recently oiled, so Steele entered his hallway silently. Instantly, he saw the bloody carnage before him. Heffer was standing, snarling over Le Jeune's crumpled body, as his three accomplices reigned blows on Steele's friend with fists and boots.

'Where's the gold?' growled Heffer, before turning his head to see Steele silhouetted against the door. One man pulled a knife and sprang towards the Briton, but Steele had already levelled his pistol. He fired at the man's head. The man fell to the stone floor, dead.

Le Jeune saw his chance and wrestled with Heffer for the knife. A second thug went for Steele, but as the man vaulted over the body of his fallen comrade, Steele killed him instantly with a shot to the temple.

Steele turned to see Heffer plunge the knife into Le Jeune's belly and withdraw it for a second stab, but the Briton's third bullet thudded into the American's arm and the knife clattered to the floor - Heffer howled with pain. With the battle over, the third attacker turned and fled towards the parlour at the rear, but Steele dispatched him with two quick shots to the back.

Steele pointed his pistol at Heffer and walked up the hallway. He glanced down at Le Jeune's face and saw a swollen pulp of red cuts and bruises. Steele knew the belly wound was serious.

'He should have told me where the gold was,' said Heffer, with a grimace. Heffer cradled his shattered arm, then looked at Le Jeune's stomach wound and sneered. 'He'll have no use for gold where he's going.'

Steele snapped. 'You greedy bastard,' he yelled with savage fury. He pulled the trigger and Heffer recoiled onto the stairs with a thud.

Then there was nothing but the acrid smell of gunpowder, clouds of smoke, and Le Jeune's groans. Steele examined the injury more closely and could see there was little hope. He pulled a handkerchief from his coat and partially staunched the flow.

'Hold this, Pierre, I'll send a boy for a doctor.' Le Jeune pressed the handkerchief to his wound and shrieked with pain.

On Cheyne Walk there were no runners but a cab was passing - Steele gave the driver a sovereign to fetch a doctor. He returned to find Le

Jeune as white as snow. As Steele's bent over him, Le Jeune gripped his friend's hand and gasped. 'Promise me you'll write to my wife, James, tell her I love her.' Steele nodded. 'Send her some gold and the document. Tell her to keep the document safe. Tell her she's not to read it.'

'Don't worry about such things now, Pierre,' said Steele gently.

Le Jeune tightened his grip, 'please promise me, James. If America is to heal, this document must be kept secret for many years. Maybe a hundred years from now politicians and historians can study it dispassionately and use it to do what's best for the country. Promise me James. Make all that we've been through worthwhile. Make my life mean something.'

Steele placed his hand on the dying man's shoulder. 'I promise, Pierre.'

A man burst in through the open door, 'I'm a doctor.'

Steele felt Le Jeune's grip weaken, then fade, and the American's arm fell to his side.

Steele turned to the doctor. 'A wasted journey for you I'm afraid. He's dead.'

CHAPTER THIRTY SEVEN

Cheyne Walk
London
October 1865

With five bodies strewn across the hallway like a small battlefield, it was clear Steele needed to see Palmerston immediately; explaining this butcher's yard to a Scotland Yard inspector would be far too difficult. He told the suspicious doctor he was going to fetch a constable but instead took a cab to King's Cross station. From there he caught the last train to Wheathampstead, a small stop on the Dunstable branch line.

Outside the station, a man with a horse and cart waited for the last passengers of the day. Only Steele got off the train, so the carter was asked to take him to the home of Lord Palmerston's wife, Brocket Hall.

The light was fading but Steele could see the Hall was a small, red brick country house, which overlooked its own parkland to the South West.

The carter was unsure of Steele's social status. 'Shall I take you to the North façade door, sir?'

'Is that the main entrance?'

'Yes, sir.'

'The North façade it is then.'

The carter's remark prompted Steele to cast an eye over his appearance. At King's Cross he'd noticed some of Le Jeune's blood on his coat. Now, in the half light, he couldn't tell whether he'd washed it all off with the station water pump. He feared if there was a stain, the punctilious Prime Minister would be sure to notice it.

By calling at this hour, at his wife's home, when Palmerston would be at dinner, Steele was taking a risk. He knew there was a good chance the Premier would refuse to see him.

A stony faced footman opened the door and when he handed him his card, Steele noticed it had blood on the corner. He reached into his pocket and saw his spares were also bloodied. The footman snorted and escorted him into the library. 'Wait a moment, sir.'

Steele waited and waited. After an hour of standing his legs began to ache so he took a seat by the fire. At that very moment Palmerston walked in.

'Why don't you make yourself at home, sir,' he snarled sarcastically, 'really Steele, does your impertinence know no bounds.'

Steele leapt to his feet, 'please forgive the intrusion, my Lord, if I could just ...'

'You, sir, are a disgrace,' continued the Premier vehemently. 'My wife's home, during dinner,' he hesitated, noticing Steele's appearance, 'with a blood stained coat and, what's that, is that blood under your fingernails?'

'If I could just explain, my Lord.'

Steele saw Palmerston was ashen. His red rimmed eyes flashed fiercely but there was no energy in his posture and he gulped for air. His outburst had drained him and the Premier swayed slightly before collapsing into a chair.

Steele had met the Prime Minister many times and had never once seen him seated. 'Are you alright, sir?'

'Yes, yes, I'm fine,' he said, but clearly he wasn't.

Steele remained standing and prepared for the second onslaught, but it never came. He knew that was out of character for Palmerston, he must be very ill. 'Can I get you some water, my Lord?'

'No,' snapped the Premier. For a moment there was quiet, and only the muffled voices of Lady Palmerston and her guests could be heard from the distant dining room.

Palmerston had recovered sufficient strength to continue. 'Before you explain why you're covered in blood, tell me why you deemed it necessary to use my authority to help a Confederate warship escape from Nassau.'

Steele proceeded as cautiously as possible. Advocating the arguments he'd rehearsed for months in preparation for this encounter. 'With the war lost, sir, I thought you'd want the document you gave me brought back to London for your future use. I remembered what you'd told me about the growing power of the United States and the threat that country poses to our dominance.'

Palmerston growled his agreement, 'go on.'

'I also had with me boxes of gold bullion which would have been seized, along with the document, by the Federal warships which were in Nassau harbour.'

The aggression was gradually subsiding from the Premier's unhealthy looking eyes, 'a small fortune in gold, eh?'

'Yes, my Lord,' confirmed Steele, who sensed he was making some headway.

'Ah, that explains why the American ambassador has been so belligerent over this. I sensed there was something more behind it. They don't know for certain we assisted the Shenandoah escape, but I know they suspect it.'

Steele saw Palmerston's anger was ebbing away. The thrill of the game of global politics he'd been playing for fifty years had gripped him. The Premier looked at Steele, 'and what's this business with the blood?'

'The Confederate agent, James Heffer, tried to beat the whereabouts of the gold out of the officer I'd travelled from Richmond with, a Colonel Le Jeune.'

'Heffer's a reptile,' interrupted Palmerston, 'please continue.'

Steele was relieved the Prime Minister disliked Heffer. 'A reptile no longer, sir. He, his three accomplices, and Colonel Le Jeune, are all lying dead in my hallway.'

'They're in your house in Chelsea?'

'Yes, my Lord.'

Palmerston looked astonished. 'For God's sake, what a shambles. Yet more leverage for the US ambassador.' He coughed violently, 'and the police?'

'They weren't there when I left, sir, but I think they will be at my house by now.'

Palmerston sat back and assessed the situation. He moved the diplomatic, criminal, and monetary factors about in his mind like pieces on a chess board. On the global chessboard, he was still the King.

169

'Where is the gold and the copies of the document now?' Steele told him. 'Very well, Steele, this is what we're going to do. I need you out of London. You need to get away from here. I have in mind a senior posting to the New Zealand police force. There's a gold rush on the South Island. Lots of lawlessness, just the job for a man like you.'

Steele was disappointed. 'But it's the other side of the world, my Lord. I need to be here for....'

Palmerston raised his hand to silence him. 'You will also turn over all copies of the document and hand them, and the gold, to me.'

'The gold to you, my Lord?' said Steele, surprised.

Palmerston saw Steele thought he wanted the gold personally and his aristocratic anger flashed in his eyes. 'You think I'd enrich myself in this grubby manner? I'll use it for my secret service fund; it'll keep Parliament from prying into my affairs. When I ask them for money to undertake necessary state business, they ask too many awkward questions.'

'Of course, my Lord. But if you don't mind me saying, this is a one sided deal.'

Palmerston laughed weakly. 'You're in no position to negotiate, Steele. I imagine the police are filing murder charges against you right now. There'll be a manhunt across London as we speak. If I throw my weight behind the prosecution you could be facing the gallows. A bunch of criminals killing each other over a cache of gold, that's how the Yard will see it, you mark my words.' Palmerston let the threat sink in before continuing. 'Alternatively, I can compel the police to make the whole thing go away. A robbery that's gone wrong, that sort of thing.'

Steele was furious but had no option. 'Very well, my Lord.'

Palmerston pulled the bell cord and a footman appeared. 'Show Mr Steele out at once. Then ask Barrington to prepare a dispatch for Commissioner Mayne at Scotland Yard.'

Steele was no aristocrat and expected to be treated with disdain by the aloof Prime Minister, but where did Palmerston expect him to spend the night. 'The last train to London has already left, my Lord.'

Palmerston's whole body shuddered as he coughed again. 'Not my problem Steele. You can't expect to stay here. Try the Plough or the Royal Oak in the village. Now go.'

Steele left Palmerston spluttering in his chair.

CHAPTER THIRTY EIGHT

Presidential Suite
Watergate Hotel
Washington DC
Present Day

Mackay took in the view of the Potomac before shutting the balcony door against the December chill. 'Where did Nixon's men do their spying?'

'The adjacent office block. You probably can't see it from here.'

'I suppose your Constitution did work on that occasion,' reflected Mackay. 'You managed to get rid of him.'

Sally didn't respond to his jibe. She was on her phone, focusing on houses they were going to view.

Mackay tried again, 'so in the 1970s Ford wasn't even elected. In 2000 and 2016 the candidate with the least votes became President, and now the President has lost against Ruth, despite getting millions more votes than her.'

'C'mon,' she said, grabbing her coat and ignoring him again, 'let's walk over to our first viewing. I'll show you the sights on the way.'

They left the hotel and took the river path to the Lincoln memorial. Mackay was impressed by the twenty foot statue of the sixteenth president. 'I wonder if James Heffer, the Confederate agent Steele encountered, *was* actually involved in his death. I wonder if he did get the finance together in London for the assassination.'

Sally took his hand. 'If he was involved, it's nice to know justice was meted out by your great grandfather.'

They turned and walked along the Reflecting Pool towards the Washington Monument, taking a diversion to the John Paul Jones memorial en route.

'John Paul Jones came a long way from a small village in Scotland to here,' said Mackay.

She nodded. The bronze statue prompted Sally to think of their unfruitful trip to Scotland, although the trip had in the end, led them to New Zealand, Bob Steele, and James Steele's journal. 'It still doesn't fit together for me,' she said. 'If James Steele gave Lord Palmerston both copies of the Richmond Papers, as well as the gold, how come Director Andrews and Calhoun seemed to know about them?'

Sally's analysis induced Mackay to halt at the foot of the Washington Monument. 'Yes, that's a good point, Sal, I've been thinking the same myself.'

She looked up at the six hundred foot obelisk, and continued, 'also why was there nothing in James Steele's papers from 1866. There was every other year except that one.'

'And Bob Steele said James arrived in New Zealand with a box of gold,' said Mackay, warming to her theme. 'How did he have a box if he'd given all the gold to Palmerston?'

'Yes. Something's missing. I've no idea how we find out more though.'

Mackay noticed a queue of tourists waiting for an elevator. 'You can go up it?' he asked.

'If you have tickets,' she said, 'producing a couple from her jeans pocket with a smile. They took the elevator to the five hundred foot observation deck, and enjoyed the views of the National Mall and the DC skyline.

'This was the tallest building in the world until the French built the Eiffel Tower,' she said, with a sense of national pride.

'It's certainly worthy of the Father of the Nation,' replied Mackay, 'but the Egyptian feel seems a bit incongruous to me. Doesn't quite fit with these other neoclassical buildings.'

She feigned a look of horror. 'I wouldn't advise burning it down just because you don't like it. Your countrymen have already had a go at that.' He laughed. 'C'mon, we'd better go,' she said, 'our first appointment is in twenty minutes.'

They viewed apartments and houses in Downtown DC and Foggy Bottom. Property values in the capital soon dispelled Mackay's lingering hopes of a house with an indoor pool - he feared for his waistline, he'd have to join a gym instead. To his dismay, Sally favoured a four storey town house by Lafayette Square, adjacent to the White House south lawn. Dating from the 1880s, the six bedroom house exuded period elegance and Mackay was charmed by it, it was the seven million dollar price tag he took issue with.

'Are you planning on having five kids?' he asked, as they walked back to the Watergate Hotel. 'It's too big for only you and me.'

'We'll have your family over and your British friends. And I can see us doing more entertaining.'

He smiled. 'Oh I can see it all now. We'll be hosting parties attended by senators and Washington's political elite. After four years of networking you're gonna run for the White House yourself. The youngest President, ever.'

She laughed. 'Building up my contacts will certainly help if I ever did decide to run for some sort of office. And I'd only be a few years younger than JFK. You'd make an excellent First Gentleman, Thomas. You could model yourself on....er.... Mrs Thatcher's husband.'

'Dennis.'

'Yes. Dennis Thatcher. You told me once he wielded significant influence over the Prime Minister.'

He looked at her and she stared back, the amusement clear in her eyes. 'So, let me get this straight,' he said. 'On the off chance you decide to run for elected office, I'm to shell out seven million bucks in the hope that one day I get to play some American version of Dennis Thatcher.'

'You've summed that up nicely. By the way, you'll also be on point with the kids.'

They'd reached the hotel and Mackay opened the door to the Presidential Suite. He followed her into the room and gestured to the bar before speaking. 'If I'm going to buy a house, it's only fair that you fix the drinks. I'll have a G&T please.'

She disappeared and he heard ice falling into a glass. Mackay loitered by the balcony window, observing the first pin pricks of artificial light appearing over the city in the enveloping dusk. He switched on the TV and saw the networks were leading on a developing political story.

'You'd better come and look at this, Sal,' he shouted, through to the kitchen. She arrived with a drink in each hand and gave him a glass. 'There's something going on in Harrisburg, wherever that is,' he said.

'It's the state capital of Pennsylvania.'

'What's happening?' he asked.

She was transfixed by the screen and didn't answer. There was panic in her voice when she eventually spoke. 'Dear God, they can't do that.'

'Do what, Sal?' pressed Mackay, trying to understand the crawl. 'I don't get it. What does faithless elector mean?'

She wasn't listening to him. 'I knew they were up to something. I told you the Republicans were plotting.'

'What is this, Sal?'

She turned to him from the screen and steadied herself with a gulp of gin. 'It's the constitutional coup I warned you about. I was only joking at the time, but it's come to pass.'

Mackay was still confused. 'So Ruth won Pennsylvania by a few hundred votes. I thought that meant she got all twenty of Pennsylvania's Electoral College votes. That's what the networks projected on election night, and that's what the actual count has confirmed. How can ten of these Pennsylvania electors then vote for the President?'

Sally hadn't fully recovered from the shock. She stared blankly at the TV, her hopes and dreams evaporating as fast as Ruth Callaghan's.

Mackay was still absorbing the news coverage. 'One of these ten electors is giving a press conference,' said Mackay, almost to himself. 'This elector says he can't ignore the President's big win in the popular vote, it gives the President a national mandate, that's why this elector's overlooked the Penn vote at state level and is voting for the President in the Electoral College.' Mackay looked over to Sally and could see she was still upset. 'Don't worry, Sal, they can't act illegally like this, their Electoral College votes will be overturned in some court.'

She looked at him despondently. 'Electors in some states are not bound by state law to vote for the winner of their state's popular vote. Pennsylvania is one of those states.'

He was astonished and realised the seriousness of the situation. 'That's crazy. This country never ceases to amaze me. What happens now?'

'Each state sends its Electoral College votes to Congress early in January. Then in a joint meeting of the Senate and the House, the votes are delivered in two mahogany boxes and counted. The presiding officer of the House, who on this occasion is the Vice President, will declare the result of the vote and certify who is elected President.'

'Well at least by then we should be in Washington ourselves to see it,' he said, in an attempt to cheer her up.

She turned to him and spoke sharply, the raw exasperation in her voice was acerbic, 'you don't get it do you, Tom? There's no Washington for us, because if this happens there's no Deputy Counsel job for me.' He still looked confused as she continued, 'Ruth has now only got 268 electoral college votes.'

His brain grasped what the ten electors switching their pledge now meant, 'I understand, that means the President has got...'

'272,' she bellowed.

CHAPTER THIRTY NINE

J Edgar Hoover Building
Washington DC
Present Day

The dynamic had changed, the ten Pennsylvania electors - now known as the 'Harrisburg Ten' - had seen to that. The staffer on Callaghan's transition team, who'd liaised with Andrews, had been shocked when he'd stopped taking her calls. 'Your boss is no longer the President-elect,' he'd told her with relish. With the President's grip on the White House tightening, Andrews's own tenure at the FBI seemed more assured.

The Democrats' legal challenge quickly reached the Supreme Court, so the President had asked Andrews to prepare a briefing to assess which way the justices would vote. Andrews's conclusion, was that the five Republican judges, would, in accordance with Pennsylvania state law, uphold the right of the 'Harrisburg Ten,' to vote for whom they pleased.

But the President had been unhappy with this slim 5/4 split in his favour, and had asked Andrews if more justices could be pressured into backing him. Even Andrews had been uncomfortable with this request, but he'd nonetheless prepared a strategy to 'persuade' one of the Democratic judges to vote for the President.

The actions of the 'Harrisburg Ten,' had again tested the resilience of the Constitution, and prompted Andrews to accelerate tying off the Richmond Papers. With the Constitution under constant strain, and its legitimacy as the framework for the nation repeatedly questioned, Andrews feared the publication of the Richmond Papers would deliver a fatal blow, and chaos would ensue.

There was a knock at the door and Doug Calhoun was shown in. Andrews gestured lazily to the chair in front of him, like some nabob. The meaning was clear to a scholar of the nineteenth century, like Calhoun. 'Don't expect me to kowtow, Andrews!' said the disgraced Professor.

The Director half laughed. 'I haven't summoned you before me like an Eastern Potentate.'

'It feels that way, with the veiled threats you made on the phone.'

Andrews's expression hardened. 'I merely mentioned my Federal colleagues in Mississippi are keen to speak to you about your activities at your former university. It would seem a fourth student has come forward. I gather she corroborates what the other three said.' He let the implied threat hang in the air before continuing, 'you'd think, being the Director, I'd have a degree of control, but really I have little influence on what goes on at state level.'

'What do you want?' said Calhoun sharply.

'Update me on your activities in Liverpool, with Ms Purcell and her British boyfriend?'

Calhoun was apprehensive. He'd been unaware of a fourth student making a statement, and coming back from the UK empty handed, meant he'd nothing to trade with. Sally and Tom seemed honest, and when they'd told Calhoun the gold and both copies of the Richmond Papers had been confiscated by Palmerston, he'd believed them. If the missing copy of the Richmond Papers *was* in the British State archives, there was no chance of secretly obtaining it, but to keep Andrews and the prosecutors in Mississippi at bay, Calhoun needed to pretend it could still be obtained.

Calhoun told Andrews about the Shenandoah, anchoring near John Paul Jones's birthplace. He related their search of the copper mines on Hestan Island, and their investigation into the Bank of England's archives. He told Andrews about Sally and Tom's trip to New Zealand.

Andrews had been tracking Sally's passport and already knew her movements. That Calhoun had volunteered and corroborated this information, added credibility to the Professor's assertion that the missing copy of the Richmond Papers could still be acquired.

'Why do you think Sally's holding out on you, Professor?'

Calhoun was relieved that Andrews still had faith in him. 'I sense she's not holding out on me. It's more likely she's missed a clue. After all, they're only amateurs at this.'

'Mmm. Will they let you examine this journal they got from Mackay's Kiwi relative? Maybe you'll see something they've missed.'

'I'm sure they will. They trust me,' said Calhoun.

An image of Sally's attractive face appeared in Andrews's mind, and he laughed. 'Trust you! I bet she wouldn't want to be alone in a dark room with you.' The Professor grimaced, but didn't respond. 'Anyway,' continued Andrews, 'you'll soon find out whether they trust you or not, when you see them.'

Calhoun began to speak, 'rather than go to Philadelphia, I'm sure Tom could digitally....'

Andrews interrupted him. 'No need. They're here in DC, in the Watergate Hotel. They checked in yesterday.'

Calhoun was no libertarian, but even he baulked at the kind of surveillance that was available at Andrews's fingertips. It dawned on Calhoun that the actions of the 'Harrisburg Ten,' had handed Andrews a further four years of spying on fellow Americans. 'I guess you must be pleased with developments in Harrisburg, Director. It looks like it'll get you and your boss another four year term.'

Andrews ignored him, and reached across his desk and picked up a folder. He began reading it. 'I don't want to see you again without the Richmond Papers. You know your way out, Professor.'

'It's certainly unique,' said Mackay, scanning the bar from end to end. The hotel's Next Whisky Bar, was softly illuminated by thousands of whisky bottles, sunk into its curved walls. 'I'd better have a Scotch in here. What do you two, want?'

Calhoun shook his head. 'You're in the States now, Tom. It has to be Bourbon. Get three Blanton's.'

With the drinks ordered, Sally quizzed Calhoun. 'No Travis today?'

'He's in Freedom Plaza, over by the White House, a rally in support of the President.'

Sally sighed. 'Why doesn't that surprise me?'

Calhoun looked at her. 'You worked on the Callaghan campaign didn't you, Sally? You must be disappointed with what's happened.'

179

'It's not over yet,' she said defiantly.

Calhoun formed a greasy smile, 'your father's a Supreme Court Justice, isn't he? It's a bit ironic you worked on the Callaghan campaign, and he'll vote to keep the President in the White House.'

She avoided the question and turned to Mackay. 'Is there a purpose to this meeting, Tom?'

'Yes, let's change the subject. You wanted to see my great grandfather's journal, Doug.' Mackay reached into a bag by the side of his chair. 'Here it is. You're welcome to look through it. I'm pretty certain we've not missed anything, though.' Calhoun started flicking through the pages. Mackay continued, 'like I said to you on the phone, Le Jeune and Steele got tangled up with Confederate agents turned robbers in London, and Le Jeune was murdered. To clean up the mess, and to avoid a diplomatic scandal, we believe Lord Palmerston confiscated the Richmond Papers and the gold.'

Mackay had voiced this last assertion in a faltering voice, which suggested to Calhoun that Mackay wasn't convinced it was true. Calhoun knew, through Andrews, that both copies of the Richmond Papers hadn't been confiscated. The Professor sensed the pair still didn't know where the gold or the Papers were, but he also felt they knew all the documents weren't in the British State archives either. But if not in London, then where?

Calhoun took a slug of Bourbon, then closed the journal. 'Ok. It won't do any harm to have another pair of eyes look over this. I know you two are thorough, but I'm a professional, and may pick something up.'

Sally yawned at his default arrogance, but Calhoun ignored her and finished his drink.

Sensing conflict between Sally and Calhoun, Mackay ended the meeting with some inane pleasantries, and they went up to the Presidential Suite. In the privacy of their room, she gave him a hostile look.

'He might pick something up, Sal?' ventured Mackay.

'He's creepy. It feels like he's following us. How come he just happens to be in DC when we're here?

'Travis's rally?' suggested Mackay.

'I doubt it. I think Calhoun's a Democrat. But I sense he knew we were here.'

Mackay thought of their encounter with Director Andrews in Orlando. 'You're thinking Calhoun has a powerful friend.'

'It would explain the coincidence,' she said. 'If the FBI's been spying on us again, I'll be furious.'

CHAPTER FORTY

The Supreme Court of the United States
Washington DC
Present Day

If the courtroom's architects had intended to evoke Imperial Rome, they'd succeeded; Mackay felt like an extra in Gladiator. Only the winged bench where the justices sat looked incongruous, had a dais with the Emperor's throne replaced it, then the classical look would have been complete. It was a fitting forum to determine who would - like Caesar - become the most powerful person in the world, the President, or the President-elect, Ruth Callaghan.

The atmosphere inside the chamber was electric. To the left of the bench sat the court clerks, to the right the marshals, and occupying the tables in the centre, were the attorneys. A bronze railing divided the court clerks from the red benches where the Press were seated, and in the middle of the chamber, assorted dignitaries were flanked by the judges' guests.

As family of Justice Purcell, this was where Sally and Mackay were perched; without this connection, they would've been jostling outside the building with the crowd. Mackay scanned the chamber and estimated three hundred people were crammed in. Amongst the VIPs, he could see several prominent Democrats and Republicans, including the Vice President and the Vice President-elect.

There was uproar as the nine justices filed in and occupied the black leather chairs behind the bench. Mackay saw Sally's father was next to the Chief Justice in the centre. Sally looked at Mackay in surprise, when the senior clerk announced Justice Purcell would deliver the opinion of the court.

Mackay thought back over the last frantic fortnight. The chaos caused by the actions of the 'Harrisburg Ten,' had necessitated an emergency sitting of the Supreme Court. Sally didn't want to miss anything, so instead of returning to Philadelphia, they'd invited themselves to Justice Purcell's grand Washington mansion. They'd gone there directly after one night at the Watergate Hotel, but on arrival their reception had been cool.

'Don't you want us here, Dad?' Sally had asked.

'Why did you choose to stay at the Watergate Hotel when I own this huge house?' the Judge had replied.

'We didn't want to bother you. We were only intending to stay in DC for a night, whilst we looked for a house to buy. What happened in Pennsylvania changed our plans.'

'I can understand that,' he'd replied.

After a few days it had become clear to all three of them that lodging with Sally's father had been a mistake. Whilst Purcell wanted them to stay, he'd underestimated the stress he'd be under, deciding if Ruth Callaghan was going to be the next President. The furore was unrelenting, and even the American press, which Mackay deemed to be tame by UK standards, intruded into their lives on a daily basis.

That Sally had worked on Ruth Callaghan's campaign, suggested to many a conflict of interest, and the clamour for Justice Purcell to recuse himself was deafening, but after Purcell had spoken to the Chief Justice - who was terrified of a 4/4 deadlock - he'd remained on the case. As the Chief Justice had pointed out, there *was* no higher court which could determine whether Anthony Purcell was conflicted or not.

Relations between Mackay and Purcell had been cordial for most of the time, but the mood was edgy over breakfast, after they'd sparred over their favourite topic - the Constitution.

'But Tom, your judges are just as political as we are here. Your Supreme Court's ruling to reverse Prime Minister Johnson's prorogation of Parliament, is a case in point.'

'Yes, for some people that was very political and was viewed by Brexiteers as the Establishment trying to thwart the will of the people,' said Mackay. 'But Anthony, that's not my point, with a flexible unwritten constitution like the UK's, obstacles like the Supreme Court's ruling, an obstructive Speaker of the House of Commons, and half a dozen MPs playing God, were all swept away by a General Election which voiced the

People's frustration. That would never happen here, your legislature, through which the American People express their will, is never strong enough to overturn what you, and your eight colleagues, decide. You nine unelected judges really make the law in America, not Congress.'

Mackay took a mouthful of bagel, chewed, then continued. 'Today you'll decide who'll be the most powerful person in the world. Not the one hundred and fifty million Americans who voted, you nine.'

Purcell drank some orange juice. 'You know it's not quite as simple as that, Tom.'

Mackay was in full flow. 'No, I'm sure you and your colleagues will dress it up in legal jargon, but at the end of the day, it is just as simple as that. Federal Law, State Law, previous Supreme Court rulings, the whole thing is an unholy mishmash. You need to start the Constitution again from scratch; a blank bit of paper is what's needed.'

Purcell looked reflective. 'So, what you're saying is that I should find some legal contrivance to give effect to the will of the people, and keep the winner of the popular vote, the President, in office.'

Mackay checked Sally was out of earshot. 'You're going to do that anyway. You and your four colleagues, who were appointed by Republican Presidents, will of course rule to keep a Republican President in the White House.' Mackay took another bite of his bagel. 'As to your wider point, and I'd never say this in front of Sal, with nearly seven million more votes than Ruth Callaghan, the President did win the election, irrespective of what the Electoral College says.'

Purcell smiled. 'I suspect Sally believes the same in her heart of hearts.'

Mackay was jolted back to the present by the voice of the senior clerk, trying to make himself heard above the din. Eventually the noise subsided to a low murmur.

The clerk declared,

'Pennsylvania Department of State, Petitioner, v James Millard, David Burlison, Michael Boam, Julian Skingley, Michael McCabe and others.'

Justice Purcell delivered the Opinion of the Court.

'Every four years, millions of Americans cast a ballot for a presidential candidate. Their votes, though, actually go towards selecting members of the Electoral College, whom each state appoints based on the popular returns. These 538 electors then choose the President. The States have devised mechanisms to ensure that the electors they appoint vote for the Presidential candidate their citizens have preferred. Article II of the Constitution gives the States the authority to appoint electors 'in such a manner as legislature thereof may direct'. Nothing in the Constitution expressly prohibits States from taking away presidential electors' voting discretion. Federal law does not therefore prevent the ten Pennsylvania electors, in this case, from exercising their discretion and voting for the Presidential candidate who won the national popular vote.

Indeed this court observes that several states have enacted legislation to give precedence to the winner of the national popular vote rather than the winner of the popular vote in their own state, but the majority of this court holds that Pennsylvania is not one of those states. This court observes that although a bill aimed at electoral reform has been laid before legislators in Pennsylvania, it has not been enacted.

Therefore the majority in this court holds that the Pennsylvania Department of State can compel the ten electors in question to vote for the winner of the popular vote in the state of Pennsylvania, namely the Democratic candidate. Furthermore, we find that the Pennsylvania Department of State may replace the ten electors with alternative electors who will pledge to vote for the winner of the popular vote in the state, namely the Democratic Candidate.

The ruling of the Supreme Court of Pennsylvania is affirmed.'

Half of the chamber erupted into cheers. Sally was choked with emotion. 'I can't believe Dad's done that.'

185

The room quietened again as another Justice began reading the dissenting opinion of the four judges in the minority.

'The nine haven't split on party lines,' said Mackay, 'two of the four dissenters were appointed by Alex Freeman.' He took her hand. 'I'm glad for you, Sal. We'd better get a house bought in Washington asap.' He gripped her hand tightly, 'but I don't think it was necessarily the right result. The President won the election fair and square. I'm sorry, but there it is.'

She smiled at him. 'In truth I'm conflicted myself. I know the country will be better off with Ruth, but the President's win in the popular vote can't easily be ignored.'

'I said it to your Dad this morning, and I'll say it again to you now, the way you folk elect your leader is a mess. It needs sorting.'

She sighed. 'And that's part of my new role at the White House. Let's see if we can improve things.'

Mackay thought she'd no chance, but didn't want to rain on her parade. 'At least we can have a stress free Christmas now,' he said.

'Remind me, when are we leaving for Scotland?'

'Wednesday.'

CHAPTER FORTY ONE

Hadrian's Wall
England/Scotland Border
Christmas Eve

The single tree stood framed by Hadrian's Wall in a dramatic dip in the landscape.

'No one leaves without a picture, Sal,' said Mackay. He pushed her in front of the tree and stood back. It was a grey day and the auto flash on his phone responded by accentuating her golden hair. 'It's called Sycamore Gap. Remember the Bryan Adams video, 'I Do It For You', it was shot here. So was the Robin Hood movie, Morgan Freeman sat here, and Kevin Costner was over there.'

'I remember the song,' she said.

He laughed, 'who could avoid it. It seemed to be number one for a lifetime.'

'It was the same in the States.'

They followed the path up the hill by the side of the Gap. For seventy miles east and west they could see the remains of the Wall. Sally was reflective. 'Not much has changed in 2,000 years, Tom. Emperor Hadrian built a wall to keep out the Picts, and the President has built a wall to keep out the Mexicans. Is that progress?'

He smiled. 'And don't forget that only sixty years ago the Soviets built a wall to keep in the East Berliners.'

She sighed, took his hand, and headed back to the car.

Overnight, the cloud had cleared and Christmas morning was heralded with a heavy frost. From the library window, Mackay saw the fields which fell away to the sea seemed to be covered in a white metallic film. The distant waters of the Solway glinted like silver in the sun. The frost defined, sharpened, edged.

In the hall, a huge Christmas tree was encircled at its base with a low wall of multicoloured gifts. Through the door, Mackay saw his mother place a metre-wide silver tray, laden with smoked salmon blinis and bucks fizz, on a low table by a branch. She yelled an invitation, and the family began to gather en masse to guzzle salmon and exchange gifts.

Sally and Mackay had travelled to Norlands via London. In the capital, Mackay had secretly sourced wrapping paper emblazoned with images of the White House. Sally was delighted with the gesture. She ripped off the paper and underneath found an old shoe box which contained a key. The key was attached to a letter from Mackay's attorney. The letter confirmed the purchase of the house near Lafayette Square.

Mackay smiled at her. 'I don't think we'll have completed in time for the inauguration though.' She was pleased and kissed him so vigorously that his parents felt compelled to look away.

After breakfast they called Justice Purcell, who was just getting up, and then Bob Steele, who was just going to bed. It was the first time Mackay's mother had spoken to her Kiwi cousin.

The call to Sally's father was remarkably light hearted. Sally had brought the Judge's gift to Mackay with her, which Mackay opened whilst Purcell senior was on the phone. Mackay's gift was wrapped in Stars and Stripes paper and felt like a couple of picture frames. 'Very funny, Anthony,' laughed Mackay, as he tore off the paper - underneath were framed prints of the US Constitution and the Declaration of Independence.'

Later that day, with turkey and all the trimmings devoured, and several bottles of a fine Margeaux despatched, the family slumped down before a roaring log fire, to listen to the Queen's Christmas message. Mackay always found her Majesty's voice relaxing, and he immediately began to doze.

Suddenly, he awoke with a jolt, as a model helicopter landed on his head. On a good day, Mackay found his sister's son irritating, but now, armed with his incessantly buzzing new toy, he was infuriating.

Sally recoiled as the chopper whizzed about her ears. Mackay's sister was seemingly oblivious to the havoc. Mackay prepared for sharp words, but the boy's father sensed the awkwardness and guided his son into the garden.

With his nephew gone, a tranquil calm pervaded the room once again.

'It's time to play the Great Game of Wealth,' said Mackay's sister. She went to the library and returned with the game, placing it on the footstool before the fire. Mackay's parents, his sister, teenage niece, and his American fiancé, pulled up their chairs.

Mackay selected a wooden plane as his piece, and soon accelerated around the board, amassing wealth faster than Cornelius Vanderbilt. But it was Mackay's mother, who - after fifty years knew all the answers - raced ahead. Sally again drew the *'Do a handstand for two minutes,'* Challenge card, and regretted wearing a skirt.

Towards the end of the game, with only a few cards remaining, Mackay clumsily snapped his piece. He reached into the box for a replacement, and brought out an old coin. Mackay had played the game dozens of times and had used the coin before, but he'd never looked closely at it. Now he recognised it was a silver half dollar. On one side was Miss Liberty with the date 1861, and on the other, was a shield with seven stars supported by stalks of sugar cane and cotton - it was a Confederate coin.

As the significance of the coin began to dawn on him, Sally read aloud her next Prodigy card; *'The First Bill of the Bank of England was minted from gold.'*

This card had never struck Mackay as unusual before, but now, after the events of the last few months, it took on a whole new meaning. Sally looked at him - she was thinking the same thing. She smiled. He smiled.

This game, the game his family had played every Christmas for decades, he now knew has been designed by James Steele. Mackay reached for the card and she passed it to him. He recognised for the first time the lettering was written in gold, whereas all the other Prodigy cards were inked in black. And was that James Steele's handwriting on the card - it certainly looked like it.

'Bills aren't minted from gold,' said Mackay.

Sally was astonished. 'No. They're made from paper.'

Mackay's family were bemused. 'What is this Tom?' asked his father.

'Treasure,' replied Mackay excitedly, 'buried Confederate Gold.'

Sally continued. 'The Prodigy card doesn't mean the first monetary bill issued by the Bank of England in the seventeenth century; it means the first Bill, or William, who founded the bank.'

Mackay's father was puzzled, 'you mean William Paterson? He was born around here somewhere wasn't he?'

'Yes he was,' continued Mackay, 'and he's buried in Sweetheart Abbey.'

Mackay's father laughed and his tone suggested disbelief, 'you don't seriously mean to tell me that William Paterson, founder of the Bank of England, is buried in Sweetheart Abbey with a cache of Confederate gold?' Mackay was too wrapped up in his own thoughts to answer. His father continued, 'here, in sleepy Dumfriesshire - that's incredible.'

CHAPTER FORTY TWO

Sweetheart Abbey
South West Scotland
Boxing Day

A couple of hours after dark, they arrived at the Abbey. The place was deserted and poorly lit. Sally climbed over the low fence without difficulty, Mackay followed. Gingerly, they crept through the eerie ruins in the murk, fearing to show any torchlight.

Suddenly the wind picked up and howled through the precinct walls like a banshee.

'Christ, I half expect to see Boris Karloff,' said Mackay.

'It is a bit eerie,' agreed Sally nervously.

Mackay reflected on the situation. Jefferson Davis had tasked Le Jeune with taking the gold, and the Richmond Papers, to the Bank of England. Had Le Jeune and Steele intended irony by burying the cache with the actual founder of the Bank? To chance upon William Paterson's grave after they'd put ashore from the Shenandoah, must surely have amused them. During their last visit to Sweetheart Abbey, Mackay and Sally had walked on top of Paterson's grave. Since then, they'd travelled half way around the world in search of the cache; little knowing they'd already stood six feet above it.

Mackay wasn't sure what the law said about digging up graves, but he knew they'd need permission from somebody. That could take weeks, consent might be withheld, and there might be nothing under the ground anyway - the wait would be excruciating, they had to know now.

Their eyes had become accustomed to the dark, but Mackay still failed to see a low grave, and he fell forwards, sending his spade clattering noisily against a headstone.

'For God's sake, be careful, Tom,' she whispered.

He picked up the spade and guided her to Paterson's grave.

'Are you sure about this?' she asked anxiously.

'I don't like it either, but we have to know.' He placed the spade at a forty five degree angle to the turf, and pushed with his foot.

She laughed and grabbed his arm before he shoved again. 'Wait!'

'What?'

'Look, I don't think Paterson's is the right grave, 'she said.

She shone her torch on an adjacent head stone. Like William Paterson's, the graves in this part of the Abbey were seventeenth century, but Mackay saw instantly, that this stone was less weathered. Then he noticed the inscription, and laughed out loud.

The inscription read, 'Here lies David Jefferson, died 9th May 1865, aged four, wishing he was in the land of cotton.'

Sally smiled, 'they must have returned at a later date and put the head stone on?'

He nodded. 'Maybe they did hide the bullion on Hestan Island when they got off the ship, then reburied it here.'

There was silence as the wind suddenly dropped. 'Go on then,' she said.

Mackay had feared another sharp frost would make digging impossible, but light rain, and the Abbey's coastal location, rendered the ground firm, rather than hard. Mackay's first shove hit something solid. 'There's no coffin buried here,' he said excitedly.

The top of the stone chamber was only a shovel deep, so Mackay quickly cleared the surface. Then he dug around the sides to try and free the lid.

'It's like a Roman sarcophagus,' she said.

Mackay was breathing heavily and sweat poured from his brow. 'I didn't think to bring a jemmy, it might snap the spade when I try and lift it. It looks to be perfectly sealed.'

'Make sure all the earth is cleared from the join,' she said, unhelpfully.

The physical exertion had made him snappy, and he sarcastically replied, 'thanks for the useful tip, Sal.'

She lit the area where he worked and her beam followed him around the stone rectangle.

'This corner looks the loosest,' he gasped, 'see if you can get your fingers in the gap.'

She did as he asked. Next, he inserted as much of the spade as he dared into the corner. 'Ready' he said. 'On, three. One. Two. Three.'

He pushed down the handle and the end of the spade juddered against the stone. 'Again,' he spluttered, 'at the same time.' This time the stone moved an inch. 'Again.' He pushed down forcefully on the handle and she pulled as hard as she could. The corner vibrated for a moment before the lid suddenly jolted away. Mackay fell backwards onto the headstone and shrieked with pain. Sally withdrew her fingers and the lid fell.

'I've caught my shoulder.' She went over to him and bent down to pump his arm. 'Bloody Hell, Sal,' he cried.

'A bruise rather than a break,' was her instant, unsympathetic diagnosis.

The lid was now off centre and a small gap had appeared at the far corner. It was heavy, but they were able to revolve it ninety degrees to form a cross with the sandstone base. A whiff of stale air confirmed the chamber had been perfectly sealed. Sally shone her torch into the compartment. There were four wooden boxes, each stamped with a faded, 'CSA'.

'Oh Tom,' she whispered, 'CSA ....Confederate States Army.'

'Yes,' he murmured, the adrenalin masking the pain from his throbbing shoulder.

In the centre of the chamber, flanked by boxes on each side, was a Huntley and Palmers biscuit tin. Sally reached for the tin whilst Mackay prized open a box with his spade. The wood wasn't decayed but it was soft, and split easily. As the wood fractured, the light from Sally's torch caught the gold of the bars, which lit up like a radiant flare.

'It's here,' he mumbled. But she didn't hear him - she was mesmerized by the document in her hand.

'What is it, Sal?'

CHAPTER FORTY THREE

City Tavern
Philadelphia
17 September 1787

Kelly raced up the Tavern steps two at a time, and burst into the main hallway. He saw the coffee rooms were packed with rowdy delegates, and that upstairs, the Long Room was also crammed. Edward Kelly entered a private dining room and sat at the empty table. Pulling out the note from his coat pocket, he reread it in the fading daylight. He wasn't mistaken. It requested a meeting at this hour, and at this place. It was unsigned, but he knew the handwriting.

The door opened and a hooded man entered. Out of habit, Kelly stood up, but the man gestured that he resume his seat. The man sat down and spoke in a quiet tone. 'Good to see you again, Edward.'

'Good to see you, sir,' replied Kelly.

A servant brought in two bottles of claret and some relishes. There was a roar from the Long Room, as the delegates drank another toast to the new Constitution.

'What is your view of our proposed Constitution, Edward?'

'You know me, sir; I leave the politics to others.'

The man nodded slowly. 'We need the Constitution. Our problems are mounting - the British fomenting trouble with the Indians, insurgents in Massachusetts who want the Crown back, several States near bankruptcy - and there's no national government to deal with it. What we have here is our revolution, so hard won, on the brink of failure.'

The man picked up his tumbler and drained it of claret. Kelly instinctively did the same. Kelly's former Commander refilled the tumblers and continued in a low voice. 'It's vital this Constitution is ratified, so a strong Federal government, with a single President, can be established. Only then will our revolution be truly secure.'

'What is required for ratification, sir?'

The man waited for a fresh roar from the Long Room to subside. 'Nine of the thirteen States. Nine,' he repeated, almost to himself.

Kelly could see the anxiety in the Commander's face - it was clear ratification wasn't going to be easy.

'Pennsylvania, Massachusetts, Virginia and New York - they are critical states, Edward. Especially here, in Pennsylvania, it's here that ratification will be attempted first. Push Pennsylvania over the line and the others will be easier to cajole.'

Kelly was surprised, 'but, sir, with the Convention just ended here in Philadelphia, surely the Constitution will be warmly accepted by the people of Pennsylvania.'

Kelly saw the man looked exhausted. The strain on his face and the hollowness of his eyes, reflecting the four month battle to get the draft Constitution agreed. Now, securing ratification by nine states, across thousands of miles, would be challenging. Kelly began to see how he might fit into the Commander's plans.

The Commander's voice was tired. 'A number of states know a Federal government will curtail their power. By definition, a Federal system wouldn't work otherwise. Anti-federalist forces are already assembling, Edward. We must do the same.'

The Commander took a sip of claret, then slammed down his tumbler on the table. Somehow there was now energy, power, and iron in his words. 'Nothing will prevent this ratification from happening, and I mean nothing. You, Edward, are going to see to that.' The man's passion and fervour, which had so inspired Kelly during the war, gripped him again. 'Are you still in touch with officers from your regiment?' asked the Commander.

'Yes, sir, most of them.'

'Then Colonel Kelly, this is what I want you to do.'

CHAPTER FORTY FOUR

Market Street
Philadelphia
September 1787

The Commander had tasked Kelly with, 'getting Pennsylvania over the line first.' Kelly reflected on the reasons for this. Firstly, outside Philadelphia itself, Federalism was unpopular across the State, so to avoid ratification falling at the first hurdle, a win in Pennsylvania had to be 'guaranteed.' Secondly, other wavering states would follow the lead of a big state like Pennsylvania. And thirdly, the Pennsylvania State Assembly was currently sitting, so there was an opportunity to call a Pennsylvania ratification convention quickly - the Commander had made this Kelly's priority.

To achieve this, Kelly had been instructed to call at the home of Pennsylvania's effective leader - a graceful townhouse through an alleyway on Market Street. Kelly knocked at the door and was shown into an elegant salon, where an obese, elderly man, was writing at his desk.

The man looked up and smiled, 'I remember you, Edward, forgive me for not getting up. Is all well?'

'Yes, sir, all is well.'

Kelly saw at once that all was not well with Benjamin Franklin. His weight had ballooned since Kelly had last seen him, and his breath was laboured. 'Eighteen years I've been writing these memoirs, Edward. I fear I shall not finish them before I meet my maker.' Kelly fished in his mind for a pleasantry to contradict the great man, but none was forthcoming. 'Please take a seat. Your wife and children are prospering, Edward?'

Kelly nodded. Like most military men, Kelly wasn't known for his small talk and he came straight to the point. 'I've come about the proposed Constitution, sir.'

Franklin sat back and pushed his straggly white hair behind his ears. He knew Kelly was a resourceful soldier, but he wasn't known for his political acumen. 'You're in favour of it?'

'I am, sir.'

Franklin looked at him closely. 'And you've come here of your own volition?'

Kelly was a poor liar and shifted his weight nervously from one foot to the other. The Commander had made it clear to Kelly, that his involvement in the plot was to remain secret, and that Kelly must appear to act alone. 'I have.'

Franklin looked unconvinced, but as a keen advocate of the Constitution, continued anyway. 'How can I help?'

'We....that is to say I,' stammered Kelly, 'would like to get ratification in Pennsylvania done quickly, but I'm a soldier, sir; I don't know the ways of assemblies, conventions and such like.'

A gust of wind rattled the lead frame of the window. It wasn't cold, but Franklin gestured to the wood pile beside the fire. Kelly threw on a couple of pieces which immediately spat noisily. 'Don't ever get old, Edward.'

Franklin spoke quickly. 'This is what you need to do. First, you must send an express rider to New York to get an official copy of the Constitution. Then you must bombard the Pennsylvania Assembly with petitions, asking that the Constitution be adopted quickly. Get some copies of the Constitution printed, not too many though, we don't want to circulate it too widely, especially in the back country. Two thousand English copies and one thousand German copies should be enough.'

Franklin was breathless and paused to refill his aged lungs. 'Then you must ensure the Assembly doesn't adjourn on the 29th of this month, before a ratification convention has been scheduled for, say December. The anti-federalists will try and force an adjournment, hoping the elections in October will return an Assembly more sympathetic to their cause. This must not happen. I will give you a list of the names of people who will be helpful to you.'

Kelly, now he had his orders, stood up to begin executing them.

'Come back and see me when a date for the ratification convention has been set,' said Franklin. 'Then we'll plan how to ensure that goes our way.'

Kelly looked at Franklin. The excitement, the exertion, the effort, all had exhausted the old man. Kelly thanked him and turned to leave.

'One more thing, make sure there's a big noisy crowd to hear the Constitution being read out in the Assembly.' Franklin hesitated. 'Are you sure you're here of your own accord, Edward?'

Kelly smiled, and headed for Market Street.

The next morning, the Constitution was read aloud to a large group of citizens, who stood in the public gallery of the Pennsylvania State House. A keen observer may have noticed the cheering of every word somehow seemed artificial, commercial almost. Astute commentators may also have noted, that the clothing worn by much of the crowd was ragged, even threadbare, and that the chop houses and taverns of the city were full later that day.

As Kelly himself sat in the dining room of the City Tavern, enjoying a chop, he reflected on how cheap it was to hire a crowd. The cost had barely dented the £1,000 the Commander had given him for 'ratification expenses,' so he'd decided to share several bottles of fine claret with the two former officers from his regiment - captains Merrick and Clive - who'd helped him 'gather' the crowd.

'A good day's work, Colonel,' said Merrick, 'what's next?'

Kelly finished his tumbler. 'Next, we ensure the Assembly doesn't adjourn before a convention has been scheduled. To do this we need a blizzard of petitions to land on the Assemblymen.' Kelly pulled out a piece of paper from his coat pocket. 'I have a list of Philadelphia merchants here. Those who don't submit petitions freely will be induced to do so.'

Merrick had been out of the army too long, and had signed up to Kelly's project hoping for some combat. 'What sort of inducements do you have in mind, sir?'

Kelly's expression was blank, but his meaning was clear. 'We'll try financial pressure first, then if that doesn't work...'

Kelly divided the list between them. 'Gentlemen, we're going to get through some shoe leather in the next few days.'

Within a week, the Assembly was weighed down with petitions, strangely all from the Philadelphia area, and George Clymer - who'd represented Pennsylvania at the Constitutional Convention - had moved a resolution calling for a ratification convention.

Kelly reported to the Commander that things were going well, but on the morning of the 29th September, he received unwelcome intelligence from Franklin.

Kelly met Merrick and Clive in the City Tavern to pass on the news, and form a plan. 'Nineteen assemblymen intend to absent themselves from the State House today, 'said Kelly, 'to deprive the session of a quorum.'

'What does that mean?' asked Merrick.

Kelly continued. 'Today is the last day the Assembly sits before its elections. If Clymer's resolution isn't passed today, it may never be passed. No ratification convention will be held in Pennsylvania, which means there'll be no ratification of the Constitution. If the Constitution is rejected here, it'll be rejected in Massachusetts, Virginia and New York. No new Constitution means no Federal government, and no United States.' Kelly paused for breath. 'I don't want to sound too dramatic, but the Confederation will wither and die, and the British and the Spanish will pick over the carcass. The Revolution will be lost without a shot being fired.'

Merrick reflected on the horrors of the eight year tussle with the British, families divided, farms torched, and the cost in blood. 'We don't want that again, sir. What can we do?'

Kelly sighed, 'there are sixty eight members of the Assembly, with forty four pledged to attend. We need to force two of the nineteen dissenters into Independence Hall, to gain the two thirds needed for a quorum.'

'Where can we find them?' asked Merrick.

'Follow me,' ordered Kelly.

The three soldiers went to Boyd's Boarding House on Wentworth Street. To his dismay, Kelly saw at once that gaining entrance to the building was impossible. The red brick house was part of a block, with a solid front door accessed by four stone steps.

'I know this house,' said Merrick, 'Alexander Boyd owns it. He was a major in the Pennsylvania militia.'

Kelly knocked at the door and waited. He knocked again but there was no response. Laughter came from a raised window to his left. From his position by the door, Kelly's view was obscured. Merrick and Clive were on the street. 'What can you see?' asked Kelly.

'There looks to be about a dozen of them brazenly having breakfast,' replied Clive.

Kelly was getting angry, and tried in vain to appeal to the innkeeper's military background. 'Major Boyd. My name is Kelly, Colonel Kelly. I order you to open this door.' The door remained shut.

'There's too many of them anyway, sir,' said Merrick. 'I suggest we ambush a couple when they come out in smaller numbers.'

Kelly withdrew to the street, and was nearly hit by a coach and four which sped close by. Kelly turned to yell abuse at the coachman, but noticed instead, another member of the Assembly running between a line of trees on the far side of the street. In pursuit of the man, Kelly spotted the Assembly's Sergeant-at-arms and a clerk.

Kelly was middle aged and Merrick was portly, but Clive was lithe and quick. Clive also pursued, running parallel to the fugitive - hidden by a farmer on a trotting horse - until they reached Christ Church, where Clive intercepted him. He caught the Assemblyman by the waist, but the man elbowed him and half wiggled free. Clive caught him again and held him like a vice, until the Sergeant-at-arms arrived to hold his arms. Kelly arrived a few seconds later, panting heavily. Clive laughed, 'you're out of shape, sir.' Then Merrick rolled in. 'What's your excuse, Merrick? I've see a faster baggage train!'

The prisoner was red faced and incandescent with rage. 'What is the meaning of this outrage?'

'You're needed at the State House, sir,' said the Sergeant-at-arms evenly, 'be a good gentlemen and please accompany me there.'

'I will not, you can't...' But they could, and he was pinned between Clive and Merrick and escorted to Independence Hall.

The Sergeant-at-arms turned to Kelly. 'I owe you my thanks, sir. Could I presume on you yet further. I require one more Assemblyman for a quorum.'

'Lead on,' said Kelly.

At Assemblyman McCulmont's house, the maid confirmed he was at home and went upstairs to fetch him. She returned twenty minutes later, and addressed her remarks to Kelly.

'I'm sorry, sir. I'm mistaken; he's not in the house.'

Kelly pushed past her and bounded up the stairs. He found the astonished Assemblyman in his bedroom, half dressed.

'How dare you, sir,' yelled McCulmont, reaching for the fire poker. Kelly was too quick, and sent the weapon clattering to the hearth with a punch to the man's hand. He pinned McCulmont's arms back and handed him over to the Sergeant-at-arms.

'Come along, sir,' said the official, you're needed at the State House.'

At Independence Hall, the two kidnapped Assemblymen protested, but the majority ignored them, and proceeded to debate Clymer's resolution. As the Speaker called a vote, McCulmont bolted for the door, but Clive blocked his exit and pushed him back in.

The resolution was carried by forty four votes to two.

CHAPTER FORTY FIVE

Pennsylvania
November 1789

He could see the road narrowed ahead as it entered a small wood. Robbers were known to frequent this part of the road, and it was a good place for an ambush, but the State messenger was unconcerned, because he carried nothing of value. Bedford County was in west Pennsylvania and would take him days to reach, so the State messenger had planned - at the taxpayers' expense - a leisurely journey via the finest inns.

He entered the wood and was suddenly accosted by masked men from all directions. Pulling his pistol was futile. 'I've nothing worth taking,' said the messenger to a well dressed man, who appeared to be their leader. Looking around he saw all the men were well dressed, and when their chief spoke, it was clear he was educated.

'What have you got in your saddlebags?' asked the chief.

'Just papers,' replied the messenger.

'What sort of papers?'

These men were no ordinary robbers thought the messenger. 'I'm on State business from Philadelphia - carrying copies of the new Constitution for folks in the back country. There's to be a Convention to ratify it later this month.'

'Give the copies to me,' ordered the man.

'But they're of no value, sir.'

'I'll be the judge of that. Now, give them to me and continue on your way. I don't want to see your face in Philadelphia until December.'

The surprised messenger emptied his saddlebags, kicked his horse, and then trotted round a bend.

Clive had a bunch of Constitutions in his hand, 'what shall I do with them, Colonel?'

'Burn them,' replied Kelly, 'we don't want them circulating in the back country.'

Kelly and his two men stopped for cheese and bread at the next inn, where two hundred copies of the Constitution were thrown onto the fire.

'Where next, Colonel?' asked Merrick.

'Dobbs County. There's an election there for five Convention delegates - Franklin tells me it's too close to call. We need to ensure that only supporters of the Constitution are elected. '

They reached Kingston - the county town of Dobbs County - by late afternoon. At the court house, Kelly and his companions found the elderly Sheriff conducting the ballot - they waited in a tavern.

At sunset the vote closed, and the Sheriff began pulling the ballot papers from the box. As the Sheriff read them out, the officials, federalists, and anti-federalists, all kept count.

Kelly and his two companions waited in a corner of the courthouse, which, as the natural light faded, was poorly lit by candles.

'That's 282 so far. How many electors are there?' whispered Clive.

'372,' said Kelly.

Clive did the sums in his head, 'that means there's less than sixty to go, with all five anti-federalist candidates ahead.'

Merrick had come for a fight and pulled a club from under his coat. 'We'd better do something about it, sir.'

Kelly nodded. 'Yes. Usual drill, you two knock out the candles. I'll go for the ballot box.'

Merrick and Clive shuffled slowly from the dark recess, and took up positions by the candle holders. Kelly went outside and allowed his eyes to grow accustomed to the dark. He knew they'd wait for his signal, as they'd done many times before in dozens of courthouses across the State. Their operation was choreographed with military precision, Kelly left nothing to chance.

Kelly knocked on the door, then heard the commotion inside as Merrick and Clive ran along the walls of the building, knocking down candle holders. Kelly pulled out his club and opened the door. The courtroom was in darkness, but he knew the thick black rectangle on the bench was the ballot box. Reaching out for it, a flash of light from the

Sheriff's pistol dispelled Kelly's opinion of the law officer - he *did* pose a threat. Kelly felt the shot sear his earlobe. He wielded his club in a wide arc, connecting with the Sheriff's head. In the gloom, he heard the Sheriff groan. Kelly picked up the ballot box and ran out of the building. Merrick and Clive were already on their horses.

'Persuade them not to follow us,' ordered Kelly.

The two ex soldiers discharged their pistols harmlessly into the walls of the court, then joined Kelly at the gallop.

After a mile they slowed to a trot. Kelly threw the ballot box into a bush. 'The Sheriff's nicked my ear.'

Merrick laughed. 'An old man from Dobbs County has done what British regulars couldn't do in eight years.' Kelly grimaced and didn't reply.

'Where to next, sir?' asked Clive, 'any more ballots for us to attend?'

'No. Dobbs County was the last. We've ridden our luck - the Convention will be weighted with delegates in our favour.' Kelly took off his neck tie and used it to stem the blood that was pouring from his ear. 'We'll head back to Philadelphia. There are some journalists in the city who need attending to.'

CHAPTER FORTY SIX

Pennsylvania Herald
December 1789

D allas was so absorbed with his work, he'd neglected the fire which had diminished to a glowing corner of the hearth. The dying flames made no impact on the cold December air, which advanced unchecked and unrelenting, into all areas of the print room.

The huge demand for news about the Constitutional Convention, and Pennsylvania's own ratification, had meant a third issue of the Herald that week. Dallas was glad of the extra bulletin, as last night's events at Boyd's boarding house - where a mob had smashed windows and called for the anti-federalist delegates inside to be hanged - needed to be reported quickly.

Despite his enthusiasm, Dallas regretted letting his apprentice – and his young nimble fingers - go home early, because the cold numbed his own hands and he fumbled with the type in the composing stick. He dropped a capital 'C' on the floor. As he stooped to retrieve it, the door opened.

There was enough candlelight to illuminate three men. Dallas was alone and it was late, but the men were well dressed and he felt no sense of alarm. He saw one man had a nasty weal on his ear which hadn't healed. Dallas thought he recognised him.

'What can I do for you, gentlemen?' asked Dallas warmly.

The men were stony faced, even hostile, Dallas began to feel uneasy.

'I understand you're not a patriot,' said the man with the scar, who Dallas took to be their leader.

'What do you mean by that?' said Dallas neutrally.

The men approached the editor and stood close to him, the leader spoke. 'You're not even American are you? You're British.'

Dallas sensed the purpose of their visit and determined to defend himself. 'I've been here several years. My wife is American and I intend to apply for citizenship.' Dallas now recognised the men and addressed their leader. 'You pushed a man out of the public gallery of the Convention today, just because he was heckling a federalist speaker. In fact, I've seen you do it many times.'

Kelly didn't answer. Clive glided over to the printing press and examined the type which had already been set. 'He's running last night's fracas at Boyd's boarding house, Colonel.'

Kelly looked Dallas in the eye. 'Now, why would you want to report a silly incident like that?'

Despite his nervousness, Dallas was getting angry. 'Are you saying the intimidation of anti-federalist delegates isn't newsworthy? Their lives were threatened by a mob - they were terrified.' Dallas paused and looked closely at Kelly. 'I wouldn't be surprised if the incident was orchestrated by you and your men here.' Kelly shifted his weight from one foot to the other, and as good as confessed to the editor.

'It was you,' said Dallas. He studied the men. One man continued to circle the printing press, another looked intent on inflicting violence upon him, and their leader, who'd been addressed by one of the others as Colonel, remained passively aggressive.

The editor sensed danger but refused to be intimidated. He spoke as calmly as possible. 'For some weeks I've suspected a plot to rig this ratification - the distribution of the Constitution suppressed, ballot boxes disappearing in the back country, and the weighting of votes. You know by my reckoning, the 24 dissenting delegates got thousands more votes than all 44 of the federalist delegates combined. And I'd be surprised if one in twenty folk in the State had actually read the Constitution.'

Kelly moved towards Dallas and put his arm around him. Merrick shifted his position, pinning the editor between himself and Kelly. Clive continued to circle the printing press. Kelly spoke directly into the editor's ear. 'This is what you're going do for us, Dallas. First, you'll stop printing speeches by dissenting delegates. Then, any anti-federalist letters you get and decide to print, will no longer be anonymous. We want to know who is writing them.'

'It won't look right if you suddenly stop printing all criticism of the Constitution,' interjected Merrick, 'you can still put the odd letter in; we just want to know where these traitors live.'

Dallas had been putting together all the pieces of their sordid campaign in his mind. He ignored Merrick's threat. 'You got to Doctor Taylor as well, didn't you? You had him imprisoned for debt. Other delegates who are critical of the Constitution have also been to see me. Unlike your backers most are poor, and they fear their expenses won't be paid if they don't vote for ratification.' Kelly remained unresponsive. Dallas continued, 'then there's the Amendments Committee, strangely meeting on the Sabbath, when you know that devout delegates from the back country will refuse to attend. I take my hat off to you gentlemen - a well planned military operation. Are these all your own ideas, Colonel? Something tells me you lack the wit for a coup such as this. Who has put you up to it?'

Kelly bridled at this and tightened his grip on Dallas's shoulder. Kelly's tone was chilling, 'no other publication in the city is now reporting criticism of the Constitution, and, from today, neither will the Herald.'

Kelly nodded to Clive, who reached over to the printing press and knocked out the type which had been set. As hundreds of letters cascaded to the floor, Clive kicked them across the room in all directions. Then he knocked a pot of ink over those sheets which had already been prepared.

Dallas flinched and tried to wriggle free, but he was held between Kelly and Merrick. 'You bastards,' he yelled.

After a few seconds, the editor's rage subsided and the ex-soldiers released him. Kelly moved towards the door and spoke with his back to the furious newsman. 'We don't want to come back here, Dallas. I've not let Captain Merrick use his club on this occasion but....'

Dallas interrupted, 'one question, Colonel.' Kelly turned to face him. 'You assume I'm not in favour of the Constitution.'

'Are you?' asked Kelly.

'Yes.'

Kelly smiled. 'Then you'll have no problem complying with my wishes.'

'You don't get it do you,' said Dallas.

'Get what?'

Dallas struggled to keep the passion from his voice. 'Part of what this is all about. The Constitution I mean. The proposed First Amendment guaranteeing the freedom of speech and the freedom of the press. I have to report both sides of the argument, don't you see?'

For the first time Kelly was perplexed. What Dallas said made some sense. 'But it's for the greater good' said the Colonel, 'the end justifies the means.'

Dallas laughed. 'Pleading the greater good is the last refuge of a despot. Your hypocrisy is breathtaking. What you've done, this censorship, vote rigging, hauling critics out of Independence Hall, bribing electors, intimidating delegates, all can be excused for the wider benefit of the people, is that what you're saying?'

'Something like that,' said Kelly, sounding unconvinced.

'This will be a great nation,' declared Dallas, 'this United States will be the greatest nation on earth, the envy of the world, but the country's birth will be forever stained by fraud, violence and criminality.'

Dallas's observations had made an impact on Kelly, but he had his orders from the Commander, which he would carry out to the fullest. 'You are of course entitled to your views, Dallas, but unless you want another visit from us, I suggest you carry out my instructions.'

Dallas nodded. Kelly went out into the frosty street, glad he was a simple soldier.

CHAPTER FORTY SEVEN

Pennsylvania Herald
December 1789

Alexander Dallas had revived the fire and written all night - documenting what the Colonel had said and done. As soon as his apprentice arrived, the type setting would start and the press would roll.

Dallas knew that such widespread corruption in Pennsylvania would be picked up by the New York papers, and then the story would go national. There was no question that the Ratification Convention in Philadelphia would have to be rerun. He also hoped publication of the story would prevent illegality at other state conventions. He was worried his actions would jeopardise the adoption of the Constitution, but it was a risk he had to take. The birth of the United States couldn't take place amidst fraud and criminality, it had to be clean.

The door opened and Dallas was surprised to see the Herald's proprietor, William Spotswood. His employer was expressionless. Spotswood sat down at Dallas's desk.

'Please sit, Alexander.' Spotswood's unusual visit, his demeanour, his manner and his tone, were all ominous. 'You've done a good job here, Alexander. You've been impartial, fair, neutral, and sought the truth, when other publications have feared to do so.'

'You don't know the half of it, Mr Spotswood,' began Dallas, 'late last night, a Colonel Kelly....'

Spotswood raised his hand to silence him. 'It sounds like we've both had busy nights. I was visited in my house, past midnight, by a couple of prominent city elders. They told me that unless 'corrective action' was taken at the Herald, I'd lose hundreds if not thousands of subscribers.'

Dallas tried again. 'But sir, I've been working on a huge story all night, if you'll only...'

'It's no good, Alexander. Of course I'll give you glowing references, and pay you until the end of the month.'

'Sir, you must....' but Dallas knew it was over.

'I want you to leave the building immediately. Take nothing with you. And if you want references, your back pay, and payment for the month, drop this story.'

Dallas had a young wife and three children to support, the threat was not idle. 'But what of the freedom of the press, Mr Spotswood?'

'Someone else's concern. Now please, pick up your things. I'm sorry to say you're fired.'

CHAPTER FORTY EIGHT

Justice Purcell's House
Washington DC
Inauguration Day

Sally woke to find Mackay on his phone. She kissed him and he casually dropped the device onto his belly. Picking it up, she looked at his open email. 'You've had a response then.'

'Yes. From Historic Scotland,' he said.

'Remind me who they are.'

He got out of bed and began to dress. 'They're the government agency that owns Sweetheart Abbey.'

For weeks Sally had been focused on the presidential transition - she'd left Mackay to deal with the gold. The UK was his country anyway, and he knew more about British law than she did. 'Have they agreed to your proposal?' she asked.

'Yep. 50/50. I'll get the legal agreement checked over but it looks solid. All we need to do is tell them where it's buried, and then wait for a big cheque to arrive.'

She laughed. 'If only it were that simple. My government is sure to make a claim.'

'M'Learned friends tell me Uncle Sam will struggle. Treasure trove found on British soil is governed by British law. End of story.'

'I hope you're right. What are we going to tell Calhoun?'

Mackay sighed. 'Nothing at this stage. But if we do get some money, I think we should make an ex gratia payment of some kind. After all, we'd never have got to the Abbey, if it hadn't been for Lieutenant Calhoun's letter to his wife.'

Sally shivered at the thought of the disgraced Professor and was less inclined to be generous. 'Okay. Let's consider it nearer the time.'

Inauguration Day was an important day, with a formal dress code. Sally pulled on her favourite knee length blue dress, and looked approvingly at Mackay's well cut suit.

'Did you get a chance to speak to Ruth or Alex Freeman about the Richmond Papers?' he said.

Sally frowned. Knowing what to do with the Papers was more difficult than knowing what to do with the gold. 'No, I haven't seen either of them since we got back from the UK. They've both been tied up with the transition.'

Sally knew now why Andrews had been desperate to get the Richmond Papers. The Papers threw doubt on the very legitimacy of the United States. She imagined a world where the Constitution hadn't been ratified, and instead, the North America Continent consisted of fifty small disparate states, buttressed by a mighty Canada. But on the other hand, publication of the Papers might lead to a constitutional reset, where insoluble issues like electoral reform and gun control could be addressed.

The problem was that Ruth Callaghan would derive her authority as President, from the very Constitution Sally might jeopardise. Sally knew today, of all days - Inauguration Day - was not the time to saddle the new President with the knowledge that she, and all her predecessors, owed their position to a huge eighteenth century fraud.

'What are we going to do about the Richmond Papers?' asked Mackay, gingerly. He knew she'd wrestled with the dilemma since they'd found them at the Abbey. 'There's a good case for burning them.'

Sally had reached a decision after deliberating for weeks. 'I know I may regret it,' she replied, 'but I'm going to ask my father.'

The purchase of their house in Lafayette Square hadn't yet completed, so they'd been lodging - and sparring - with Sally's father for the last fortnight.

Justice Purcell was at that moment preparing breakfast two floors below them. 'There are some warm bagels there,' said the Judge, as they entered the kitchen.

Purcell was also smartly dressed - he'd be attending the ceremony with the other Supreme Court Justices. Sally made coffee whilst Mackay plastered Cooper's marmalade over the bagels. 'I just don't see the appeal of that stuff,' observed the Judge.

'I bring it with me from the UK,' said Mackay, 'I can't seem to get it here easily.'

'That doesn't surprise me,' said Purcell. The Judge looked him up and down. 'I'm glad to see you've made an effort for the ceremony.'

Mackay ignored the barb. 'I don't think we'll see much from our seats, Anthony. It won't be as good as the view from your position.'

'Given Ruth Callaghan wouldn't be President without me, it's the least I can expect.' Mackay smirked at the Judge's rare display of humour. Sally put two cups of coffee on the table and picked up her bagel. 'You don't eat that marmalade stuff as well, do you, Sally?' asked Purcell.

'If you'd bothered to visit when I was living in the UK, Father, you'd have seen me make it.'

Purcell smiled. 'If I get the oranges, why don't you make some for me?'

She looked at him closely. His attempts at friendliness were rare and often clumsy, but if asking her to make marmalade for him was his way of reaching out, then so be it. 'I'd be delighted to.'

Mackay chipped in. 'Not too sweet please, Sal.'

Sally approached her father and hugged him. 'You're in a remarkably good mood today, any reason?'

The Judge put his chin on her head and gripped her tightly. 'It's just that my only child and her idiot boyfriend are moving within a mile of this very house. I'm pleased you'll be close by.'

Mackay laughed. 'No offence taken, Anthony.'

Purcell continued. 'I'm going to make a real effort to get to know you better,' he gestured to Mackay, 'and this fool. I'll try and make up for the times I wasn't there. And please don't hesitate to ask, if you need my advice with your work in the White House.'

Her father's comment prompted Sally to think of the Richmond Papers. 'There is an issue I'd like your advice on. Tom and I discovered something in Scotland. A secret, hidden for more than two hundred years - I don't know what to do with it.'

She'd piqued Purcell's interest and he moved towards her, speaking in a gentle tone. 'Tell me what it is, and I can ....' He was interrupted by his cell. 'Sorry, I have to take this.'

She could tell from his tone that something had happened. Purcell finished the call and it was clear his unusual spell of gentleness had evaporated.

'What is it, Dad?' she asked softly.

The stress was already etched over his face. 'The Chief Justice has had a minor stroke. He's okay but he'll be in hospital for a few weeks.'

Sally saw at once. 'Then ....'

'Yes, Sally. I'm to administer the Presidential Oath of office.'

'What an honour, Dad.'

But Purcell was in a panic. 'Dear God, where is my robe? Is it clean?'

Purcell left the kitchen and they heard several doors noisily opening and closing upstairs.

Mackay sidled up to her with a mouth full of marmalade bagel. 'Blimey.'

'Yes. I'd keep out of Dad's way for an hour or two.'

'We might get a better view of the ceremony now, Sal.'

She looked at him quizzically. 'What do you mean?'

'The seats allocated to the Chief Justice and his family will now be free.'

'Thomas!'

CHAPTER FORTY NINE

The Capitol
Washington DC
Inauguration Day

It was a bright sunny day, without a cloud, but it was cold, and Mackay was glad of his overcoat. As it turned out their view was good, or at least should have been good. They were seated close to the podium where Ruth would be inaugurated, but directly in front of Mackay, sat a tall Texan, complete with a Stetson.

Mackay reflected on the pageantry of the event. The great and the good of all America were in attendance, and a million folk were crammed into the Mall. The Congressional lunch would follow, then the Inaugural Parade, after which there'd be ten days of balls - eleven official and 121 unofficial. They certainly knew how to celebrate the transfer of power this side of the Pond, he thought.

He compared it with the change over in the UK, where the outgoing Prime Minister was brutally dumped the day after an election. A Transit van would arrive at Downing Street mid morning, and the loser and the loser's possessions would be gone in an instant. The incoming Prime Minister would then have a twenty minute audience with the Queen, before moving in - the whole process completed in less than an hour. Which system was best? There was no denying the Americans put on a good show, but Mackay felt there'd be a similar spectacle in a banana republic.

The murmuring of the crowd escalated as Ruth Callaghan, her husband, her two adult children, and Sally's father appeared. On the podium, MacKay saw that the most senior representative of the outgoing administration was the Vice-President. The President himself had rarely been seen since the Supreme Court ruling, although that morning, he *had* been spotted playing golf at his Florida resort.

'Looks like your Dad found a clean robe,' said Mackay. He saw there were tears in her eyes as Justice Anthony Purcell raised his right

215

hand. Purcell allowed the applause to subside before he addressed Ruth Callaghan, who also raised her right hand.

'Are you prepared to take the oath, Senator?'

'I am.'

'I, Ruth Margaret Callaghan, do solemnly swear.'

'I, Ruth Margaret Callaghan, do solemnly swear.'

'That I will faithfully execute the office of President of the United States.'

'That I will faithfully execute the office of President of the United States.'

'And will to the best of my ability.'

'And will to the best of my ability.'

'Preserve, protect and defend the Constitution of the United States.'

'Preserve, protect and defend the Constitution of the United States.'

'So help you God'

'So help me God'

'Congratulations, Madame President.'

Mackay peered around the Stetson in front of him, and saw Sally's father step aside just as the Marine Band started to play 'Hail to the Chief' - a 21 gun salute sounded in Taft Park. Mackay took Sally's hand and looked at her teary face.

'Well, you got there in the end, Sal. You, Ruth, Alex Freeman. Now is your chance to do something.'

'We will, but somehow...' she tailed off, deep in thought.

He knew what was on her mind. 'You can't get the Richmond Papers out of your head can you? You think this is all false. You think the United States is a fraud.'

'Yes, something like that.'

He gripped her hand tightly and kissed her. 'If the Constitution hadn't been ratified, The Founding Fathers would have worked out some other way to weld this country together, you'll never know, Sal, you've got to move on. They're weighing you down, spoiling your day - let me burn the bloody Papers, then they're gone. I'll take the problem away from you.'

She smiled at him. 'But I'll always know, Tom, I'll always know.'

He sighed. He'd known how she would feel. She had to do the right thing.

Sally's preoccupation with the Richmond Papers meant they'd missed half of Ruth's inaugural address. They caught up with the speech on CNN later that day, as they dressed for dinner. Despite his attempt to 'cut back,' Mackay was disappointed his dinner suit still pinched. Sally looked stunning in her black, Ralph Lauren dress.

The Inaugural Ball was held at the Walter E Washington Convention Centre. Mackay was on his third glass of champagne when the band struck up 'Hail to the Chief' - signalling the arrival of Ruth Callaghan. By the time the President had worked the room, and got to them, Mackay was on his sixth glass.

'Ready to start work tomorrow, Sally?'

Sally smiled, 'yes, and congratulations, Madame President.'

Ruth looked at Mackay. 'You look like you're enjoying yourself, Tom.'

'I never could resist a free drink, Ruth. Well done today, good speech.'

Callaghan smiled and moved on. Former president, Alex Freeman, joined them. 'It's good to have a Democrat in the White House again,' he said.

'Yes, Mr President,' said Sally.

'I'm looking forward to working with you,' said Freeman. Sally was surprised. Freeman continued, 'I was a lawyer if you remember, and I have *had* some experience of government. This business with the Electoral College, the Supreme Court again getting involved in an election and gun control - the Constitution's creaking. Ruth wants me to see if anything can be done. For some reason I'm looked on fondly by both sides of Congress, maybe I can get some sort of bipartisan consensus for reform.'

'We've discovered something historical that should go into the mix,' said Sally. Her excitement was evident; here was the man she could unburden herself to.

'That business with Director Andrews?' asked Freeman.

'Yes,' replied Sally, 'Tom and I have found the....'

'Sorry to interrupt,' said Freeman, 'but the former Vice-President is inbound. I'm going to need his help with some of those Republicans who think Constitutional reform is treason. Excuse me, we'll continue this later.'

Mackay could see Sally was frustrated. Her chance of sharing the burden was, for the moment, gone. 'Don't worry Sal, you can speak to him later.'

'Speak to him about what?' Director Andrews appeared from nowhere. They were astonished. Sally remained silent, but Mackay had enjoyed too much champagne.

'You know what,' said the Briton.

'The Richmond Papers?' asked Andrews quickly.

'Yes,' confirmed Mackay. Sally glared at him fiercely.

'I don't think you were supposed to tell me that, Tom' said Andrews. The Director looked grave. The secret was out, could it be contained? Andrews spoke gently, appealing to her. 'I need you to give them to me, Sally. It's a matter of National Security. We can't have our enemies, both internal and external, thinking the United States was born from fraud and intimidation.'

Sally's problems with the Richmond Papers had just got worse. 'Have you got Le Jeune's copy?' she asked.

Andrews nodded, but his mind was racing. Had she been about to reveal the contents of the Richmond Papers to Alex Freeman? If yes, the problem had to be tied off quickly. If Freeman got to know of the Papers, there was no chance of keeping them secret. Andrews had to act quickly whilst he still could - he'd clashed with Ruth Callaghan before and knew he'd soon be fired.

Putting as much sincerity as he could muster into his voice, he pleaded with her. 'The damage that publication would do is difficult to calculate, Sally. I concede, the Constitution isn't perfect, but it's the

218

foundation of the United States, take it away and the whole house could collapse. It's really difficult to predict where it could all lead. Some of the reports that cross my desk would make your hair stand on end. There are thousands, no, hundreds of thousands, of nationalist extremists in this country who would lose their point of reference. Rioting, insurrection, really, I'm not exaggerating.'

Andrews's comments had made an impact on her. 'All of your points are valid, Director. I've thought of nothing else since we found the damn things.'

Andrews was hopeful. 'Then you'll give them to me?'

'I'm tempted. Tom here thinks we should burn them.'

'That's preferable to publication but it's not ideal. They are a very important part of our history, it really would be best if the Papers were kept safe in the FBI archives.' Andrews paused, 'can I ask you who else knows of their existence?'

'Only us three,' said Mackay.

Andrews's had formed a plan. Now was the time to act. 'Well, Sally, what do you want to do?'

She was deep in thought. Maybe Andrews was right. It was best to keep the Papers hidden. The American people couldn't handle the shock. But who was she to decide. Surely Americans were grown up enough to think for themselves. 'This is too much for me to decide, Director. It's too much for us three. Ruth is having an after-midnight gathering at the White House later. Former President Freeman will be there. I'll seek his counsel and agree to be bound by his advice.'

Andrews grimaced and sighed. 'That's a mistake, Sally. There'll be blood on your hands.'

Mackay lost his temper and pushed the Director. 'Steady on Andrews. You can't lay that on her, I think you should go now.'

Andrews turned and left. He had some urgent calls to make.

CHAPTER FIFTY

Washington DC
Inauguration Day

'I can't see any cabs, Sal.'

'I'm surprised you can see anything, the amount of champagne you've had.'

'What shall we do?'

'We've got about an hour 'til midnight, it's a clear starry evening, I think you could do with some fresh air. I've made a decision over the Richmond papers, and I feel light and unburdened, let's walk.'

Mackay grumbled as she walked off, but he *was* swaying a little. He weighed up the benefit of fresh air versus tripping over and perhaps ripping his suit, but the cab decision was out of his hands, and he caught up with her on Ninth Street.

The air was cold, crisp and clear. They walked in silence, simply enjoying being alive. 'What a beautiful evening,' she said, taking his arm. 'Clean and fresh, ready for a new beginning and a new start.'

Mackay already felt steadier. 'I'll be glad to see the back of Director Andrews, that was an outrageous comment about blood on your hands.'

She frowned. 'Yes, that was unfair. I expect Ruth will fire him next week.'

'What do you think Freeman's advice will be?'

'I know he'll be for publication, he's a libertarian and....'

At the junction with Pennsylvania Avenue, a car suddenly came from nowhere and mounted the sidewalk - heading towards them. The dark SUV was in low gear and the scream of the engine enveloped them. They bolted for the line of trees which bordered the road - their only possible refuge. Sally was in front of Mackay and reached safety before him. Mackay sobered up in an instant. A second later he pivoted around a tree and felt the rush of air, as the car missed him by a couple of inches.

'Bloody idiots,' yelled Mackay, as the car accelerated away.

'Where to now?' asked Travis.

'I don't know, just drive. Get us away from here.' There was silence in the SUV as Calhoun tried to work out what to do next. 'How the hell did you miss them?'

Travis snorted. 'They were lucky those trees were there. I'll get 'em next time.'

Calhoun wasn't so sure there'd be a next time. He called Andrews.

'Well?' said the Director.

'We missed them.'

'Where?' asked Andrews quickly, hoping there'd still be time for another attempt.

'Just before Pennsylvania Avenue. They'll be at the White House by now.'

Andrews sighed. If they were in the White House then Freeman would be told. The secret was out. As a former President, Freeman had lifetime secret service protection, there was no way Calhoun and his idiot sidekick would get past them.

It was time to cut the Professor loose. 'My advice to you, Calhoun, is to get out of the country.'

At the other end of the line, Calhoun was shaken. Whilst Travis would happily knock down a dozen folk a day without giving it a second thought, attempted murder wasn't something the former academic relished.

When the call had come from Andrews an hour earlier, Calhoun had been celebrating in Washington with a million other Democrats, and Travis had been at a rally for the ousted President. Andrews's request had been difficult to resist - Calhoun had come too far to turn back now, and the Director had been very persuasive.

On the phone, Andrews had told Calhoun that a copy of the Richmond Papers had surfaced. This suggested the gold was still missing, and that Sally and Tom had held out on him. James Steele's diary had revealed that both the gold and the Richmond Papers, had been taken by

Prime Minister Palmerston, but now it was clear that for some reason that hadn't happened. Sally and Tom had known this, and hadn't told him - Calhoun was furious.

Andrews had promised to help him get the gold if Calhoun dealt with Sally, but Travis had missed, and now Calhoun was being jettisoned.

Calhoun spoke forcefully down the phone. 'Our deal was for the gold, Andrews. If Prime Minister Palmerston didn't steal it, then where is it?'

'I really don't care, Professor.' Andrews paused, 'look, for what it's worth, Sally didn't mention the whereabouts of the gold to me; she only confirmed she had a copy of the Richmond Papers.'

'If they have James Steele's copy of the Papers, and you have Le Jeune's copy, the gold must still be out there.' Calhoun said this more in hope, than in expectation. He thought it more likely Sally had both James Steele's copy of the Richmond Papers, and the gold.

'That's possible,' said Andrews, 'but you know I'm not interested in the gold. It's both copies of the Richmond Papers I want. I haven't got them, and it's unlikely I'll ever get them. Our deal was the gold for the Papers. You haven't delivered - the deal is off.'

Calhoun played his last card. 'Don't think I'm going to go quietly, Director. Is attempted murder part of the FBI's remit?'

Andrews laughed. 'So you'll add attempted murder to your Mississippi rape charge – need I remind you that's not gone away. Good luck with obtaining evidence linking me with you. Get out of the country, man. I'll be fired soon and my colleagues in Mississippi will come knocking on your door. Go whilst you still can.'

Andrews hung up; glad he'd used a burner phone. How Steele had kept the gold and the Papers away from Prime Minister Palmerston would never be known, but it mattered little to the Director, the secret was out. If Freeman knew of the Papers, Callaghan would soon know. But without the documents themselves, where was the evidence?

Andrews resolved on one last throw of the dice.

CHAPTER FIFTY ONE

Cheyne Walk
London
Christmas Eve, 1868

Steele sat in his winged backed chair in front of the fire, the coal, stacked a foot high, threw off more heat than a furnace. He got up and poured himself another Scotch - it was Christmas Eve, he'd given the servants the night off. Settling back down, and despite the snow falling outside, he wiped the sweat from his brow, and began to snooze.

He hadn't been dozing long before there was a knock at the door. He ignored it but the caller persisted, and there was a second knock. Picking up a lamp to drive the darkness from the hallway, he opened the door and saw a completely white man. The man knocked the snow from his hat and face and, despite the whitening of his hair and beard, Steele recognised him immediately. He deliberated whether to let him in. After a moment he decided it *was* Christmas, and he stood aside.

'You can hang your coat there.'

The man obeyed and followed Steele into the parlour, where Steele drew up a second chair.

'That sure is some fire, Steele.'

'Whisky?'

The man nodded and Steele filled the tumblers.

'Please sit.'

The man took the chair and pushed out his palms towards the warmth of the fire.

'Where are you staying?' asked Steele politely.

'Belsize Park. One of your clergymen up there is a long time friend of our cause. My wife and I are attending Midnight Eucharist at his church, St Peter's it's called.'

Steele shrugged his shoulders. 'I don't know it.'

There was silence, then the man spoke, 'I heard what happened to Le Jeune, he was a good officer.'

Steele frowned. 'That was three years ago. Le Jeune was the last casualty of the war.' Steele looked closely at his guest. 'At the end he'd turned from you and all that you stood for.' Steele paused, 'I gave one of the documents to his family and I have the other copy. You can't have them back so you can start another bloody war, if that's why you're here - it's what Le Jeune wanted.' Davis didn't respond. 'How come you're at liberty anyway? What's happened to your treason trial?'

Davis took a sip of scotch. 'It's not going to happen, there's no appetite for it. I've also heard a rumour that President Johnson will issue a Christmas Day pardon to all Confederates, including me.'

Steele laughed. 'So you get to live when a million others died. Have you no sense of remorse?'

Davis bridled. 'About all of those deaths, of course, I'm not a monster. About our cause, no, now the South labours under the Yankee and Negro yoke, as I predicted it would. Blacks are inferior to whites, today, tomorrow, they always will be. No one will ever change that.'

Steele gulped down some Scotch. 'Well, if you're trying to resurrect the South, you'll have to do it without the documents you entrusted to Le Jeune and me. I promised him to keep them from you and that's what I'll do.'

'Why didn't your Master want them back?' asked Davis. 'The documents could be used as a weapon against the States by the British Government.'

'Palmerston did want them back. After Le Jeune was murdered by your agents, I was in a bit of a trouble. Palmerston threatened to use the incident to fabricate murder charges against me. He would have had me dancing the Hangman's jig unless I did what he wanted. He agreed to sort out the bloody mess in this house with Scotland Yard, if I gave him the documents and the gold.'

'And did you?'

Steele laughed loudly. 'I was about to, but then the wicked old bastard went and died.'

So the British Government didn't get the documents or the gold?' asked Davis excitedly.

'No. As I say, I have one copy - Le Jeune's wife has the other. I also sent her a box of gold.'

'How many boxes are left?' pressed Davis.

Steele looked at the former Confederate President in a new light. Davis seemed more interested in the gold, than the documents. Steele decided to be evasive. 'I'm taking a box to New Zealand with me in the Spring. The other boxes remain buried.'

Davis was irritated. 'You must give them to me. They're not your property. They belong to the South.'

'To the South or to you?' asked Steele slowly.

'Look, Steele. I'm flat broke. We completely rely on the kindness of strangers. I have a wife and four children to support. I've come to England looking for work but no one will touch me here, or in the States, for fear of upsetting the Federal government. I need the money.'

'So if I offered you gold over the documents you'd take gold.'

'Every time,' declared the former President.

'Wow, a million dead, your cause, your principles, your ideals, all have a price Davis - a few boxes of gold.'

'A box then,' pleaded Davis, 'don't you hear me. I don't have a dollar to my name.'

Steele was angry now. 'I tell you what, Mr President,' he said sarcastically, 'you can have that Scotch for free. Now go.'

Davis stood. 'If you don't give me that gold I'll....'

'You'll do what, Jeff, are you threatening me? I know men in this city who'll cut your throat for less than a sovereign. If I send for a runner now, you'll never make it back to Belsize Park for Midnight Eucharist, that's for sure.'

Davis could see the situation was hopeless. 'I can't say it's been a pleasure meeting you again. I can see now I made a mistake in Richmond, four years ago.'

Steele showed him to the door. 'The only mistake you made was thinking that your countrymen, especially in the north, and indeed the world in general, would let you get away with the abhorrence of slavery.'

Davis laughed cruelly. 'Yes. In legal terms slavery is gone, but if you think white supremacy is dead, and there'll be racial harmony in the

States for ever more, you're very much mistaken. I foresee segregation and discrimination in America for centuries.'

'Try not to forget it's Christmas, Jeff. Goodwill to ALL men, that sort of thing'

'But all men aren't equal, Steele.'

Steele had had enough; he shook his head and closed the door on Davis and the snow. Returning to his wing backed chair, he reflected on Davis's departing remarks. He knew from the time he'd spent in America that it was a deeply divided country, but was it so different from the racial prejudice in the British Empire? Were Davis's predictions of centuries of racial disharmony in the States, too pessimistic? Steele finished his Scotch, only time would tell.

CHAPTER FIFTY TWO

Justice Purcell's House
Washington DC
Inauguration Day

'What's the meaning of this outrage, Andrews?' yelled the Judge.

'I'm sorry to disturb you in the middle of the night Justice Purcell, but we need to search your house.'

Sally's father pulled his dressing gown closer around him and continued to block the door. 'What on earth for?'

'Your daughter,' said Andrews calmly, 'she has documents in her possession which threaten the national security of the United States. She has refused to surrender the documents to me, so I have no choice but to search for them.'

'My daughter - a threat to national security, that's ridiculous! She's at the White House at this very moment. What threat? What documents?'

'I'm afraid I can't tell you that Judge. Now, please step aside.'

'I will not.'

Andrews handed Purcell the warrant. Purcell looked at it, and saw it had been signed by a District Court judge whom he had clashed with, and overruled, on many occasions - their mutual dislike had festered since Harvard, and had now led to this warrant. Purcell looked at Andrews. 'There'll be an inquiry into the execution of this search.'

Andrews had an emotionless expression. 'This is your last warning, Judge. Step aside.'

Purcell retreated into the hallway and Andrews waved in two dozen FBI agents. Andrews followed Purcell into the kitchen. Purcell found his cell and called his daughter.

Sally answered after one ring. 'What is it Dad?'

'You should know my house is full of FBI Agents looking for some documents that, according to Director Andrews, are a threat to national security. What on earth is going on Sally?'

'Is Andrews there himself?'

'Yes. He's standing right next to me.'

'Put him on.'

Purcell handed his cell to the Director. 'You won't find the Richmond Papers there,' she said angrily. 'I have them here in my pocket.'

'You're bluffing,' said Andrews, 'they're in this house.'

'Search all you want. I'm at the entrance to the East Wing of the White House. Tom and I are going to hand these damn Papers over to former President Freeman.'

Andrews was alarmed and there was panic in his voice. 'Please don't do that, Sally. Remember what I said.'

Sally was unmoved. 'Why don't you come over here with your men and see if your warrant works in the President's House?'

'Whatever you do, don't give the Papers to Freeman,' pleaded Andrews.

'That's not your call.' She hesitated, 'I hope you had nothing to do with a narrow escape we've just had with an SUV, Director?'

Andrews ignored the question. 'I'm coming to the White House right now.'

'I don't think you're invited.'

Sally hung up.

Andrews headed to his car.

CHAPTER FIFTY THREE

East Wing
The White House
Washington DC
Inauguration Night

The guard checked their invitations and waved them through. On the other side of the security scanner, Mackay took Sally's hand. 'This is serious, Sal, someone's just tried to kill us.'

She nodded. 'We'll never prove it. I'm guessing Andrews was behind it. We'll confront him when he gets here.'

'He's coming here?'

'Yes.'

'What now?'

'That's what he said.'

The guests at the Callaghan's after-midnight party had been given free rein of the East Wing. The attendees were family, the earliest supporters, and close friends, of the new President.

Mackay was worried - their frantic search for Callaghan and Freeman had been unsuccessful. 'We must find them before the FBI gets here,' he said nervously.

'They might stop Andrews at security,' said Sally hopefully, 'he won't have an invitation.'

Mackay wasn't convinced. 'No, but he *is* the Director of the FBI. I can't see them barring the gate to him.'

Sally was apprehensive, and half expected to see Andrews behind every door. 'This is a nightmare,' she said.

'What about the Attorney-General, can't he control Andrews?' said Mackay. 'Will he be here?'

'No. He resigned this morning and Ruth hasn't chosen a successor yet.'

'Bloody Hell.'

In the pantry they passed a Senator from North Carolina, who Sally knew. 'Have you seen the President or Alex Freeman, Senator?'

The Senator detected the urgency in her voice. 'I understand the President is running late - she's been held up at another ball. I thought I saw Alex Freeman in the library.'

'Thank you, Senator.'

In the library, by the fire - above which hung a Gilbert Stuart painting of George Washington - sat former President, Alex Freeman. He was alone and resting, his body language conveyed, 'Do Not Disturb.'

If Freeman was irritated by their approach, he didn't show it - his sixth sense detected a problem. 'What's up, Sally?'

Mackay answered. 'Wade Andrews may have tried to kill us on our way here from the Convention Centre.'

'What?' said Freeman. He looked incredulous, but Sally could see he half believed them.

Mackay continued. 'A black SUV, mounted the sidewalk just before Pennsylvania Avenue and tried to run us down.'

Freeman was stunned. Sally spoke quickly. 'Give him the Richmond Papers, Tom.'

Mackay pulled the Papers from his suit pocket and handed them to Freeman.

Sally spoke. 'One is an affidavit and the other is a letter. Will you please look over them quickly; we believe Director Andrews is on his way to seize them.'

Freeman unfolded the papers and opened his eyes in amazement. He glanced at Washington's portrait above the mantelpiece, and began to read.

CHAPTER FIFTY FOUR

Mount Vernon
Virginia
13 December 1799

It was fortunate that the General's dispatch had reached Kelly in Washington. For months, the Colonel had been working on the relocation of the War Department - constantly travelling between Philadelphia and the new capital. With the move nearing completion, he'd been in Washington, when the General's summons to Mount Vernon had arrived.

The journey was less than twenty miles, but in the snow, sleet, and rain, it seemed double that. Kelly had been to the Palladian style mansion before, and as the rain continued to drive itself directly into his face, he was relieved to see the familiar cupola in the distance. He galloped the last mile, and was soon stood by a roaring fire in the General's study.

The General joined him. Kelly was shocked by his appearance. Whilst his bearing was still erect, and his blue grey eyes alert, he was deathly pale, and struggled to breathe.

The General was only in his mid-sixties, but he shuffled to his Presidential chair like an old man, and sank into it. He gestured that Kelly should also sit.

'Good of you to come and see me at such short notice, Edward.'

'Can I get you something, sir? Forgive me, but you don't look well.'

'Yes. I've caught a chill. The doctors want to take more blood out of me but I'm not so sure, I seem to feel weaker after the procedure.'

Kelly didn't think bloodletting cured anything, but he knew the General believed in the practice and didn't contradict him.

'This chill has reminded me that no one is immortal,' said Washington. 'When I do die, I hope I leave this young United States as a coherent nation, on firm foundations.'

Washington paused, then came to the purpose of Kelly's visit. 'You and I both know that ten years ago the Confederation was failing, and we were on the verge of anarchy. Foreign interventions were likely, and the Revolution was at risk. That is why we had to act, and act we did.'

Kelly nodded in agreement. 'Like you, sir, I believed it was necessary.'

Washington looked at his old comrade closely. In twenty five years, Kelly had never refused one of his orders. Would this be the first time? 'I'd like you to do something for me, Edward.'

Kelly didn't hesitate. 'Anything, sir, you know that.'

'My stepson's children, your children, in turn their children, their descendants, future generations of Americans, they need to know what we did. Centuries from now, when America is a great power and rules the world, I hope historians will judge us kindly, and understand what we did was necessary.'

Kelly was pleased Washington had brought the subject up. Despite holding senior roles during the General's eight year presidency - and meeting alone frequently - they'd never discussed what they'd done to ensure the Constitution was ratified. It was a guilty secret they shared; forbidden, unmentionable, taboo. Kelly had never questioned his orders, but some of the things he'd done with Merrick and Clive had left him uneasy - had unsettled him for a decade and more.

Washington's breathing was laboured, but he continued in the same dispassionate tone for which he was famed. 'In order that we may be judged by posterity, Edward, future Americans will need the facts. I want you to document those facts, here, now, before me, in this study.' Kelly shuffled in his chair uneasily. Washington continued, 'I understand you will be admitting to criminality, some of which I know is serious, but so will I, and you were acting under my orders. The responsibility, the accountability, and if necessary the blame for our actions, is mine, and mine alone. I will of course certify anything which you write.'

Kelly smiled at his old comrade. 'Hand me a quill, sir, and I will draft an affidavit immediately.'

With a tilt of his head, Washington gestured to the writing materials on his desk. 'Some coffee whilst you gather your thoughts, Edward? And some bread and cheese?'

'Thank you, General.'

Washington pulled the servants' bell and a house slave was commissioned to bring refreshments.

'Where shall I start, sir?'

'At the beginning. Set off with Pennsylvania, then proceed in chronological order with the other states.'

Kelly's hand was cold so he warmed it on the coffee cup. He then began to write.

Kelly documented the campaign of bribery, violence, and terror, he'd perpetrated in Pennsylvania. First, he noted the gossip he'd obtained from Benjamin Franklin - about dissident Assemblymen - which Kelly had used to threaten and blackmail. Then he documented how he'd paid a supportive crowd, to cheer the first reading of the Constitution outside Independence Hall.

Next, Kelly wrote about the weight of petitions - demanding a ratification convention - which had landed on the Assembly, most of which had been sent by fictitious people invented by Captain Clive. Kelly then recorded the kidnap of two Assemblymen - forced into the chamber so a resolution could be passed.

Kelly evidenced his misdemeanours in the months prior to the convention itself. There was the interception of State messengers and the burning of copies of the constitution sent to the back country. There was the intimidation of electoral officials and the suppression of votes for anti-federalist delegates.

Kelly stated that it was he who had organised the mob which had smashed windows at Boyd's Boarding House, the same mob which demanded that the dissenting delegates inside be hanged.

Next, Kelly asserted that his lieutenants had thrown citizens out of Independence Hall when they'd heckled Federalist speakers. He also documented how he'd bought the debts of delegates and had them imprisoned when they couldn't pay. He stated that the meeting of the

Amendments Committee on the Sabbath had been his idea, because he knew a dozen delegates from the back country would refuse to attend.

Kelly then turned to the suppression of the Philadelphia press, and wrote how editors - who reported both sides of the debate - were fired.

During the drafting of the affidavit, sometimes Washington stood over Kelly's shoulder and observed what he was writing. When Kelly documented how he'd intimidated Alexander Dallas, the editor of the Pennsylvania Herald, Washington stopped and asked for further clarification. 'You mean you had Alexander Dallas fired? The same Alexander Dallas, who is now effectively governor of Pennsylvania?'

'Yes, General.'

Washington sat down again and had difficulty catching his breath. 'I'm surprised he was against the Constitution.'

Kelly put down the quill and turned to face the former President. 'Dallas wasn't. He was in favour of it. But he also valued the freedom of the press. He said he'd the right, and a duty, to report both sides. What he said had an impact on me at the time.'

There was a touch of apprehension in Washington's voice. 'What sort of impact?'

'You told me, sir, that what we were doing was for the greater good of the people. I believed that then and I believe that now. But Dallas said that pleading the greater good was the last refuge of a despot.'

If Kelly had fired a pistol at Washington from point blank range, there'd have been less impact on him than the use of the word 'despot.' The General recoiled in his chair - which wobbled violently with the sudden movement. After a moment, Washington was motionless, but Kelly saw the look of horror was still fixed on his face.

'Despot,' Washington muttered, almost to himself, 'am I a despot? Is that what I've become? Please no.'

Kelly was taken aback by his Commander's uncharacteristic display of emotion. He desperately thought of something to say to comfort him. 'No despot voluntarily gives up power, as you did three years ago.'

Washington relaxed a little but continued to frown. 'Yes, Edward, there is that.'

Kelly continued to soothe as best he could. 'Anyone who read your Farewell Address, sir, would know no person could be less despotic than you. What you, and the Founding Fathers have created here in America, is the first modern, stable, republican state. You only have to look at the instability of the new French Republic to gauge your achievement here.'

'It is indeed a fragile situation in France,' agreed Washington, 'there has been much bloodshed since they guillotined their King. I fear a coup d'état by some General will lead to decades of tyranny.'

Washington appeared mollified, so Kelly picked up his quill, 'shall I continue, General?'

'Yes, please do. I'll ring for some more coffee.'

Kelly spent the afternoon documenting how he'd influenced the ratification conventions in other states. His methods were similar to those he'd used in Pennsylvania, but the ballots had been closer. In Massachusetts, despite a campaign of bribery over several months, the result had been a slim 187-168. To achieve this slender majority, Kelly had locked nine delegates in a cellar and held the children of another five delegates hostage. Kelly recorded the imprisonment of the nine delegates in the affidavit, but omitted the kidnapping of the children - Washington didn't need to know about that, and would never know.

As darkness fell, and the house slaves began to light candles in the study, Kelly moved his record onto Virginia and New Hampshire, where threatening five swing delegates in each state, had proved crucial. Because New Hampshire was the ninth state to ratify, the threshold had been reached, so adoption of the Constitution was assured.

Despite this, Washington had directed Kelly to continue his efforts in New York, which Kelly did throughout July 1788, but this time using persuasion, rather than strong arm tactics. Kelly had feared the softer approach had failed, and was pleasantly surprised when New York State ratified the Constitution by a mere three votes.

Finally, Kelly noted that by September of 1788, Congress had certified the new Constitution, and by December of that year, the first presidential election had been held. Kelly finished by stating that Washington was inaugurated as the first President of the United States, in April of 1789.

Kelly allowed the ink to dry then handed the pages to Washington. Whilst the General was reading, Kelly took some mouthfuls of bread and cheese.

After a few minutes, Washington placed the last page on his desk and picked up a quill. Kelly could see the affidavit had made Washington uncomfortable. 'You certainly did a thorough job, Edward. I hadn't realised the full extent of it.'

Kelly was glad he'd omitted his most heinous crimes.

'Very well, make a copy, and I'll sign both,' said Washington.

Kelly stood over Washington's shoulder and watched him write on the last page, in his slow deliberate hand.

Mount Vernon, 13 December 1799

In the name of God amen. I George Washington of Mount Vernon – a citizen of the United States, and lately President of the same, do make and declare this Instrument, which has been written by my friend, Colonel Edward Kelly, and every page thereof subscribed, to be a free and honest account of the actions taken by the said Colonel Edward Kelly and his subordinates, in my name, under my orders, and by my command, from 17 September 1787 to 26 July 1788.

In witness of all, and of each things herein contained, I have set my hand and seal, this thirteenth day of December, in the year One Thousand Seven Hundred and Ninety Nine and of the Independence of the United States the twenty fourth.

CHAPTER FIFTY FIVE

The White House
Washington DC
13 December 1800

Kelly had no appointment, but he was known by the White House servants, and shown directly into Adams's study. The President was seated at his desk. Kelly saw that where Washington had been tall and thin, his successor was short, stocky and portly.

Adams didn't know Kelly well, and was surprised to see him. 'To what do I owe this honour, Colonel?'

'Thank you for agreeing to see me at such short notice, Mr President.'

'Please take a seat, Kelly.'

Kelly took the chair that was proffered. It was new. Everything in the room was new. It had taken eight years, but Kelly could see the building really *was* fit for a President.

Adams sensed what he was thinking. 'You approve of the White House?'

'They've done a good job, sir.'

'There are still a few areas to finish, but I'm pleased with it.' Adams paused, wondering where Kelly's political loyalties lay. 'It's a pity I won't be here that long to enjoy it.'

Kelly was impassive and emotionless. 'You think you've lost the election, sir?'

'Almost certainly, it looks likely, Jefferson, will be sitting in this seat next year.'

Kelly debated in his mind whether, out of courtesy, to mention Adams's estranged son who had recently died of alcoholism. He decided against it, and got straight to the purpose of his visit. 'I'm here at the request of General Washington.'

Understandably, Adams looked puzzled. 'But the General's been dead a year.'

Kelly looked closely at Adams. Washington had told Kelly he'd been uncertain which of the Founding Fathers he wanted to entrust his confession to. Unlike his relations with Thomas Jefferson, Washington's bond with Adams had been cordial - Adams was also the sitting President.

'I was at Mount Vernon the day before the General died, Mr President. Together, the General and I documented the activities I undertook, by the General's order, during the turbulent ratification period. I have the documents here in my pocket. He commanded me to wait for a year after his death, before I gave them to you. There are two copies of the affidavit, signed by the General and myself, and witnessed by Colonel Lear. There is also a letter written to you.' Kelly reached into his pocket and pulled out the papers.

Coming from anyone else, Adams would have suspected some sort of hoax, but Kelly was a decorated veteran known for his loyalty and honesty, if not his intelligence. 'Please give them to me, Colonel.'

The affidavit ran to several pages. Adams glanced over it quickly, and immediately understood its unwelcome potency. That Washington would order such measures, surprised, rather than shocked him - Adams thought back to the chaotic Confederation period and wondered what might have been, if his predecessor had not acted. Then he opened the letter which was addressed to him.

Mount Vernon
13 December 1799
Dear Sir,

If you are reading this, I have been dead this past year, and imagine that I am already largely forgotten. I could not though, in all conscience, go to my grave with the knowledge that the campaign which I asked Colonel Kelly to orchestrate would not be recorded for posterity. The campaign, which you could even call a plot, to ensure that the United States was brought into existence, used methods which neither I nor Colonel Kelly are comfortable with.

I hesitate to say the approach we took was justified in the name of the 'greater good,' as Colonel Kelly has reminded me this afternoon that the phrase is often used to defend the actions of despots and tyrants. Be that as it may, I believe that what I instructed Colonel Kelly to do was for the greater good of the American people and our young state. That is my belief, it is Colonel Kelly's belief and I suspect it is your belief, but who are we to conclude that the breaking of many laws can be excused in order to ensure the birth of our integrated cohesive state. Only time will tell, and only history and our descendants can judge, whether our actions were reasonable, because they were certainly not legitimate.

I understand that by confessing my deeds, I expose our nascent republic to our enemies. Our enemies at home who long for the return of the Confederation or even the Crown. And our enemies abroad, the ancient monarchies of Europe who despise and fear our republicanism and all that it stands for. I must therefore leave it to you to judge when to disclose my affidavit. There may never be an appropriate time to reveal my chicanery, but I pray and hope, and know, that this United States will one day be strong enough and mature enough to absorb all truths. That decision though will be yours, or your successors, it is up to you.

I sincerely wish that your Administration of the Government continues to be happy and honourable to yourself and prosperous for the country. Present, if you please, the best respects of Mrs Washington and myself to Mrs. Adams, accept them yourself, and be assured of the high esteem and regard with which I have the honour to be dear sir, your most obedient and very humble servant.

George Washington

Adams sighed and sat back in his chair, casually throwing the letter onto the desk in front of him. With the Federalist Party bitterly divided and relations with the Republicans deeply acrimonious, now was not the time for the publication of Washington's confession. Adams looked across his desk at Kelly, and saw a man who could be relied upon to remain discreet. The physical custody of the papers was more difficult. Who could be trusted?

Adams's eye rested on an inlaid mahogany bookcase which had been installed that morning. He walked over to it and pulled out volume four of Edward Gibbons's 'Decline and Fall of the Roman Empire.'

CHAPTER FIFTY SIX

The White House
Washington DC
Inauguration Night
Present Day

Alex Freeman folded the Richmond Papers, then glanced at the portrait of Washington above the mantelpiece. He stood up and turned towards Sally and Mackay. 'If you two will join me, I propose a toast, to George Washington.' He raised his champagne glass to the picture. 'George Washington.'

'George Washington,' they repeated.

Freeman then lifted his glass towards them. 'I also applaud you. That's some detective work. My compliments to you both.'

They clinked their glasses together. Freeman and Sally took a sip of champagne, Mackay drained his glass. The former President looked up at Washington again. 'It's a sensational discovery, the question is, what to do with it? As Washington himself observes, 'is the United States, strong enough and mature enough to absorb all truths?'

Sally was excited. 'I say it is.'

'I agree,' said Mackay. 'I'm only a Brit and have no standing here, but I don't think it's a question of strength and maturity, now it's a question of necessity. Of course, I've only lived here a couple of years but I've seen some things are crying out for reform. Reforms that won't come whilst you're stuck with your two hundred and thirty year old fixed Constitution which can't be changed. You need to sit down with a blank piece of paper and start again.'

Sally was filled with enthusiasm. 'He's right. This is our opportunity to reset. Ruth and Washington have handed us this opportunity, let's use it.'

Sally's passion was infectious and it had spread to Freeman. He was deep in thought. His mind balancing his natural inclination to reform and improve, with the challenge of combating die hard Republicans who wished they were living in the eighteenth century. But the publication of Washington's confession would at least start a national conversation about the future governance of the country, and could lead to a new dawn for the Republic. 'I'm excited,' he said, 'I really am excited.'

Suddenly there was a commotion in the hallway - Wade Andrews burst in with several FBI officers. Andrews saw Freeman and advanced towards him.

'How did they get in?' asked Sally nervously.

Sensing something untoward, Freeman's Secret Service Agent appeared from nowhere and stood between the former President and the FBI Director. There were a dozen other amazed guests in the library - they left when Andrews shouted, 'clear the room.'

With Freeman's bodyguard blocking the way, Andrews hesitated to approach further. He took a step forward.

'Don't let him come closer, Mike,' ordered Freeman.

The bodyguard put his hand inside his suit, ready to pull his gun. Andrews took a step back. 'Are we really going to have a shootout in the White House Library, Director?' asked Freeman.

Andrews was tense. 'You must give me the affidavit!'

Freeman was surprised. 'You know about it?'

'There are two copies. I have the other one.'

'Have you also read President Washington's letter to President Adams?' asked Freeman.

Now it was Andrews's turn to be shocked, 'there's a letter as well?'

'Yes, 'said Freeman. 'I would read it before you do anything rash here today.'

Andrews wouldn't be deflected. 'The American people aren't ready for that affidavit. It will collapse the country. There'll be rioting and bloodshed. We'll be dealing with insurrections in every state. They'll be especially widespread in the Southern states.'

Freeman frowned. 'You've lost your perspective, Director. You see conspiracy and disorder where there is none and will be none. I trust the American people to deal with all truths.'

241

Sally was angry, 'who are you to decide what the American people are told? Who do you think you are?'

Andrews was resolute. 'I'm the man who sees reports every day that would make your hair stand on end. I'm the man who ensures Americans can sleep soundly in their beds at night. I keep law and order in this land. I must have that affidavit. I will take it and throw it on that fire if necessary, but please know, I can't allow it to be published. The Father of the Country, conspiring in criminality - can't you see what that would do? It strikes at the very DNA of the United States.'

There was a moment's silence. Andrews spoke to Freeman and the threat was clear in his voice. 'Now. Hand it over. And this other letter you refer to.'

'Stand your men down, Director,' said Freeman forcefully.

'This is your last warning, Freeman.'

The Director and the former President stared at each other - like two stags locking horns - with violent intensity. The FBI agents and Freeman's bodyguard moved slowly towards their guns. Sally grabbed Mackay's hand for reassurance.

Suddenly there was a noise from the hallway - in walked Ruth Callaghan with her security detail.

'What is the meaning of this?' demanded the President.

CHAPTER FIFTY SEVEN

The Oval Office
The White House
Inauguration Night

Ruth Callaghan sat behind the Resolute Desk. Her Chief of Staff hovered behind her, former President Alex Freeman was on a sofa in the centre of the room, and Director of the FBI Wade Andrews, stood to her right. Sally and Mackay sat near Freeman.

'Who's going to tell me what's going on here?' asked Callaghan.

'Madam President, if I may ....' began Andrews.

Freeman interrupted. 'Let Sally put you in the picture, Ruth.'

Callaghan smiled at her new Deputy White House Counsel, 'go ahead, Sally.'

'I suppose it began as a family history project. Tom's great.... or was it great great grandfather.... one or the other, I can never remember which.... whatever....called James Steele....was kind of a spy during the Civil War, liaising between the British Government and Jefferson Davis's Confederacy. The day before General Grant captured Richmond, Davis met Steele and a Confederate Officer named Pierre Le Jeune. Davis had in his possession, two copies of an affidavit signed by George Washington, and a letter from Washington to President Adams, which Washington wrote ,the day before he died. Collectively we've been calling these documents, the letter and the two affidavits, the Richmond Papers.'

Sally paused for breath. She could see the others were enthralled. 'Anyway, Davis, charged Colonel Le Jeune with taking these Richmond Papers to London, so he could use them in the future as a weapon against the Union. Le Jeune was also tasked with transporting the Confederate Treasury to the Bank of England for safekeeping. Le Jeune and Steele got the last train out of Richmond and made their way to Florida. As the Confederacy imploded, the bullion they were transporting was gradually depleted to pay troops and line the pockets of fleeing ministers. Tom and I picked up the trail in Florida, and discovered that Steele and Le Jeune took the remains of the Treasury and the Richmond Papers to Nassau. When we were flying back to Philly, we were virtually arrested by Director Andrews at Orlando Airport. That is when we learned the FBI was interested in retrieving the Richmond Papers.'

Andrews was frustrated. 'Now, wait a minute Sally, I didn't arrest you....'

Callaghan interrupted, 'go on, Sally.'

Despite the seriousness of the situation, Mackay was amused. It felt like they were all kids, brought before a headmistress - trying to get to the bottom, of a huge school prank.

Sally took a sip of water, then continued. 'We alerted former President Freeman to our concerns in Philly - at our last fundraiser - before going to Nassau.' Callaghan glanced at Freeman, who nodded his confirmation. Sally continued, 'in Nassau, we discovered that Le Jeune, Steele, the bullion, and the Richmond Papers, were taken aboard a Confederate warship - the CSS Shenandoah - which Le Jeune commandeered. You may remember from your school history that the ship went to Liverpool and surrendered there in 1865 - the last act of the war. What wasn't known, and what wasn't documented, was that the ship carried two extra passengers, who were on a mission for Jeff Davis. We visited Liverpool to find out more, but there was no record of them or the gold arriving in the city. We had reached a dead end, and were on the point of returning to the States, when we received a call from a Professor Doug Calhoun.'

Mackay interrupted, 'looking back, that call looks a bit too coincidental.' He glanced at Andrews, who shifted his eyes away from him.

Sally pressed on. 'I say Professor, but Calhoun had been fired from his university for sexual misconduct. He did have an important clue though. Calhoun's ancestor was an officer on the Shenandoah, who - in a letter to his wife - revealed that the ship had put Le Jeune, Steele, and most of the gold, on an island off the coast of Scotland. We searched the island and found clues, but no gold or the Richmond Papers. We assumed the gold had been deposited in the Bank of England as Davis had instructed, but Tom found no record of this in the Bank's archives. At that point we really thought it was the end of the road, but then Tom had a brainwave.'

Mackay was startled. 'Who am I to push back on the word brainwave, Sal? But yes, I recalled my mother had cousins in New Zealand, a more senior branch of the family, who might still have James Steele's old papers.'

'Which they did,' continued Sally, 'or at least Tom's sole surviving Kiwi cousin did. We met up with him and he gave us Steele's journal.'

'It was sad,' said Mackay, 'the journal told of how one of Davis's rogue agents, murdered Le Jeune in an attempt to get the gold. Then Prime Minister Palmerston, ordered Steele to hand over the gold and the Richmond Papers, in exchange for saving him from the gallows.'

Sally felt almost giddy as she related their tale. 'We thought the gold had been seized by Palmerston. We assumed the British Government had put the Richmond Papers in their state archives. We were sure that was the end of it.'

Mackay saw Andrews was interested and realised the Director was piecing together those parts of the story he didn't already know. Mackay continued, 'Sally and I were in Scotland for Christmas, and, by chance, we were playing an old family board game. We realised the game had been devised by James Steele, and that he'd left a clue embedded in it, signposting the whereabouts of the Richmond Papers and the gold.'

Sally interjected. 'We followed the clue and found the bullion and the Richmond Papers buried in a grave, at a place called Sweetheart Abbey.'

'I'm in discussions with the land owner to have the gold declared as treasure trove,' said Mackay.

Sally was passionate when she spoke. 'Why we're here, today, though, Madam President, is because we discovered the Richmond Papers - which former President Freeman now has in his pocket - contained a letter from George Washington to President Adams, written the day before he died. In that letter, and in an affidavit signed by him, Washington confesses to ordering one of his former officers, a Colonel Edward Kelly, to fix the ratification of the Constitution. Kelly's campaign of intimidation, bribery and violence, took place over nine months across

245

four states, Pennsylvania, New Hampshire, Massachusetts and New York. When you read it, you'll see it's unlikely that the Constitution would have been ratified without Washington's intervention.'

Sally paused and looked at Andrews. 'The Richmond Papers are sensational, and go to the very heart of the founding of our nation. To that extent, I can understand why Director Andrews would go to any lengths to cover up their existence....even murder.'

Callaghan was stunned and glared at Andrews who smirked awkwardly. 'Sally really is living in a fantasy land, Madam President,' said the Director.

'You had nothing to do, with the black SUV that ran us down as we walked here this evening?' asked Mackay fiercely.

Andrews shook his head. 'Of course not, don't be ridiculous.'

The President appeared to accept this and turned back to Sally. 'What I don't understand is how the British got hold of this affidavit in the first place, and how did this James Steele manage to keep the affidavit and the gold, from Prime Minister Palmerston?'

Sally smiled. 'The last bit is easy. We think Palmerston died before he could take the gold and the Richmond Papers, and because Steele worked for him in an unofficial capacity, black ops if you like, no British official had any record of the deal.'

'So Steele kept the gold and the Richmond Papers?' asked Callaghan.

Sally replied, 'exactly.'

The President was thinking aloud. 'So how did the British, get hold of this affidavit and Washington's letter to Adams in the first place?'

Mackay responded this time. 'We're not sure about that. We think they found it when they were in this building in 1814, during the War of 1812, and then held onto it for future use as a weapon. Certainly Lord Palmerston was a Minister in 1814, and largely in office from then right through to 1865, when he was Prime Minister.'

This time Andrews interrupted. 'That's probably right. FBI Director J Edgar Hoover was aware of these Richmond Papers; as were his predecessors, although they'd never read them. Some of the earlier Presidents also knew of Washington's confession and realised the damage it could do. I gather it was a tradition that an outgoing President told his successor about Washington's confession.'

They all looked at Callaghan. 'No one said anything to me.'

'Or me,' added Freeman.

Andrews decided on full disclosure. 'I became aware of Le Jeune's copy of the affidavit, when his sole surviving descendant contacted her Congressman about it. I obtained the affidavit along with Le Jeune's journal. I read the journal and discovered there was a second copy of Washington's confession. I decided in the interests of national security, that the Richmond Papers, as you call them, had to be brought into the FBI's custody. Until this evening, I was unaware of this letter from President Washington to President Adams.'

There was irritation in the President's voice. 'And at what stage were you proposing to tell me about all this?'

Andrews looked at her, his expression was steely, his voice hard. 'I'm sorry, Madam President, I wouldn't have told you. I didn't tell your predecessor, nor would I, or future FBI Directors, have told you or future Presidents. There are some secrets that are best kept from elected officials.'

Callaghan was furious. 'Is that right? You decide what Presidents can and cannot know. You choose what facts are known to the American people. You pick and choose which parts of history to hide or delete.'

Andrews's calmness and resolution contrasted with Callaghan's uncharacteristic emotion. 'It has to be that way, Madam President, you know that. It's for the greater good of the people.'

Callaghan collected herself and stared at him, her eyes blazing. 'It doesn't have to be that way and isn't gonna be that way.' She stood up from behind her desk. 'Director Andrews, I'm relieving you from your post with immediate effect. You are not to return to the Hoover building without supervision, nor are you to contact any other FBI employee.'

Callaghan glanced around the room. 'If he'll accept, former President Freeman will be the interim FBI Director until I nominate a permanent successor.' She looked at Freeman who nodded. 'Do you understand, Andrews?'

Andrews, escorted by a secret service agent, turned to leave, and left the words, 'you're making a big mistake,' hanging in the Oval office's electric atmosphere.

CHAPTER FIFTY EIGHT

Press Briefing Room
The White House
Constitution Day

'The President, of the United States.'

Ruth Callaghan walked into the room and stood behind the lectern. The room was full of journalists and the atmosphere was febrile.

'Thank you all for coming,' she paused and took a moment to scan the room, catching the eye of the reporters she trusted, and ignoring those she disliked.

She took a deep breath and began; 'I've brought you here today, on Constitution Day, to update you and the American people on the work we've been doing since January, on Constitutional reform. This work began soon after the publication of what's become known as the Richmond Papers.'

She paused and cleared her throat. 'Over two hundred and forty years ago, fifty six men committed treason and signed a Declaration of Independence, which asserted that thirteen colonies were now independent sovereign states, no longer subject to the British Crown. But the Founding Fathers soon discovered that the Articles of Confederation, which held these states together, were weak, and that, understandably, each state put its own interests first, to the detriment of the greater good of all.'

Her tempo picked up as she warmed to her theme. 'Internally, rebellions became more frequent, and externally, the British and the Spanish stood ready to intervene. The Founding Fathers saw that a strong Federal government was needed to meet these threats, and we've learnt, via the Richmond Papers, the steps they were prepared to take to achieve this. And so, our Constitution was ratified and this United States was born. And it worked, for a while, for seventy years in fact, until the compromise which they'd reached with slavery broke it, and a million died finding a solution. And that solution has endured, imperfectly, since then, but now we can see that an eighteenth century framework of government isn't fit for the twenty first century. As Supreme Court Justice Ginsburg observed, *'I would not look to the United States Constitution if I were drafting a constitution now.'*

Callaghan's delivery was usually professorial but now it was energetic and pacy. 'Our Constitution has created a system which - with Congress and the Presidency in perpetual deadlock - does not produce functioning government. We have a senate, where senators representing eleven percent of the population can filibuster a bill, and where senators representing sixteen percent of the population, can be in the majority. We have myself, a President, who has been elected by seven million votes less than my opponent. We have a political system awash with money, and a method of campaign contributions that borders on corrupt. Gun violence is endemic, and gun control can't be reformed by a legal framework which enshrined rights, which were important to our forbearers, two hundred and forty years ago.'

She slowed, 'indeed we're often left with a situation where - because no clear intention of a divided Congress can be ascertained - nine Supreme Court Justices undertake judicial legislation, on behalf of three hundred and thirty million people. This Constitution - which was ratified only because of a plot by our most venerated Founding Father - was imperfect at its birth, and, I'm afraid, rotten now. If the American people wish to retain this Constitution, and the system of governance which springs from it, then so be it, but, they must be asked for their consent.'

Callaghan rarely displayed passion but this was an exception. 'Purists will argue the only way to change our Constitution is to use the methods, as laid out by Article 5 of the Constitution itself, to do so. But I would argue that when the delegates gathered in Philadelphia in 1789, they met to consider improvements to the Articles of Confederation, not to devise a brand new Constitution for a federal republic. We now have a sense of why the Convention, and in particular its presiding officer, a certain George Washington, so outrageously and without precedent, exceeded its remit. We are thankful they did so, the alternative was worse. I put it to you now, that the alternative to doing nothing is also worse. If we put our heads in the sand, there is a risk of constitutional collapse, and with it the risk of insurrection or some form of dictatorship, the very tyranny which the Founding Fathers strove so hard to avoid.'

Callaghan stopped and took a sip of water; keen observers would have seen her hand tremble slightly. 'Over the last few months, my team, which has been led by former President Alex Freeman, has been in discussions with state legislatures across the country. And I can tell you now, we have secured undertakings from over forty states - enough to exceed the two thirds required - calling for a Second Constitutional Convention of the United States. The Second Constitutional Convention will be held in Washington, early next year.'

A murmur of excitement rippled through the Press Room. Callaghan waited for it to quieten before continuing. 'Furthermore, and in accordance with the precedent laid down by the Founding Fathers when they exceeded their remit in Philadelphia in 1787, the Second Constitutional Convention of the United States, as its first act, will put in place a national referendum which will ask the American people their view on fifteen measures which I have agreed with the state legislatures. The verdict of the American people on these measures will be final, and these measures will then form the new United States Constitution.'

Her tempo picked up again for her finale. 'Our country is a truly great modern nation - the greatest nation on earth. The world leader. But the world leader needs a world leading system of government and a modern constitution. With the help of the American people, my Administration will deliver such a system.'

Callaghan paused, then smiled and looked around the room. 'Any questions?'

Callaghan pointed to Matt Dickenson from the Washington Post. 'Yes, Matt?'

'What are the fifteen measures, Madam President?'

EPILOGUE

Norlands
South West Scotland
Christmas Day

It was cold, crisp, and bright. The water was like a mirror, and it seemed to be no barrier to walking the mile across the Solway Firth to England. Sally was reading the information board. 'There was a viaduct here once.'

'Yes, not much left of it now. I remember my grandfather telling me, that he cycled across it with my grandmother, on their tandem in the 1930s.'

She smiled, 'how romantic.'

Mackay laughed. 'The council had to pull the viaduct down though.'

'Oh, why?'

'If we drove by road from here, all the way round to the English side, we'd find there a place called Bowness-on-Solway. There are, or were, a disproportionate number of pubs for a village that size.'

She was intrigued and guessed correctly. 'Something to do with different alcohol laws, either side of the border?'

He kissed her. 'My you're a bright girl. In the 1930s, the pubs were open in England on a Sunday but closed in Scotland. Scots from miles around would come here, then stagger back across the viaduct after closing time. Dozens fell off and drowned every year, so they pulled it down.'

She looked across the Solway to England. 'It's an interesting comparison with the States, Scotland and England I mean. A United Kingdom successfully joined without any sort of Constitution, versus a United States, welded together by a piece of paper written in 1789.'

Mackay was reflective. 'I'd never thought of it that way before. A written Constitution does make it easier to keep your States united, but in the absence of one here, it makes it easier for Scottish nationalists to tear our Union apart.'

'I've noticed you guys don't push a sense of Britishness like we push being American. The Stars and Stripes in every classroom, and the Star-Spangled Banner, sung by our school kids every morning.

'They used to do that here, but Empire guilt put an end to it. And so our sense of Britishness has withered.'

A tractor started up in the farm to the east. The noise of the engine startled a flock of geese, which were paddling out of sight to their left - thousands of honking birds took off and blackened the sky. They watched as the mass flew a mile to the west, then settled on mudflats close to the English side.

'That's your entertainment for the day, Ms Purcell.'

She laughed, 'it's very kind of you to put on such a display for me. Are you ready to go home now?'

'Yes. I could do with a drink, hair of the dog. It was good of your Dad, to drive us back from the Steamboat Inn last night.'

Sally shivered. 'A lot has happened since we were last in that pub with Doug Calhoun. I heard charges have been filed against him in Mississippi. He's left the States now, that's for sure.' Sally looked west and saw a faint blur, which she knew to be Hestan Island. 'I hope he's not lurking around here somewhere.'

'I hope not. There's nothing here for him anyway. The lawyers are going to have the fate of the bullion tied up in the courts for years.'

She nodded. 'I told you Uncle Sam would try and get it back.'

They climbed into the car and were at Norlands within twenty minutes.

As they entered the hall, they heard laughter from the library. 'Your father and Bob again,' whispered Mackay.

'They certainly seem to be getting on well,' she said, 'I love seeing Dad so relaxed.'

Some smoked salmon blinis and bucks fizz had survived the family onslaught. Mackay handed Sally a glass from the silver tray, and took one himself. As he did so, a plastic pellet hit his head and he recoiled, spilling half his glass onto the tiled floor.

'Bloody Hell,' he yelled, in the general direction of the landing, but his giggling nephew had already disappeared upstairs. 'Why did they get him that gun?'

Sally smiled, and mopped the orange liquid with a paper serviette.

After Christmas dinner, and following the Queen's speech, they settled down to play the Great Game of Wealth.

Whilst Mackay explained the rules to Bob Steele and Anthony Purcell, Sally reflected on the last time she'd played the game - exactly one year ago. The hidden meaning of the 'Bank of England Prodigy Card' had led them to Sweetheart Abbey, the discovery of the bullion, and ultimately the sensation which was the Richmond Papers.

Looking back, Sally was amazed how George Washington's confession, had initiated a wave of bipartisan fervour for Constitutional reform. She believed the Convention - which was due to start in Washington in the New Year - would be a success.

'Have you got that, Bob?' asked Mackay loudly, trying to make his cousin understand.

'I'm sure I'll pick it up as I go along,' declared the Kiwi optimistically.

'Right. Let's start then,' said Mackay, the frustration clear in his voice.

Towards the end of the game, with only a few cards remaining in each pile, Justice Purcell drew a Prodigy card and read it aloud; 'The First Bill of the Bank of England was minted from gold,' he paused and looked at Sally, 'I take it this is the card that started your discovery?' She nodded. Purcell shifted his gaze to Mackay, then back to Sally. 'I forgot to tell you' continued the Judge, 'I found a mismatch.'

'A mismatch?' said Sally.

'Yes, a mismatch. Flying here on the plane, the wonderful few days I've spent with you all, for once I've had time for leisure reading. Out of interest, I cast my judicial eye over the evidence - Pierre Le Jeune's journal, the letter from Lieutenant Calhoun to his wife, and James Steele's memoir.

'What mismatch, Anthony?' pressed Mackay.

As her father spoke, Sally took the next Prodigy Card from the pile. Justice Purcell continued. 'There's a mismatch in the number of boxes of gold. We assumed ten arrived in Nassau on Le Jeune and Steele's small boat. Ten were supposed to have gone on the Shenandoah. One was taken by the crew when they reached England. Steele sent one box to Le Jeune's family after he was murdered. One box went to New Zealand and bought Bob's family some land. Then you found four boxes in Sweetheart Abbey, so what happened to the other three boxes? Le Jeune's memoir, Calhoun's letter and Steele's journal, aren't consistent, they don't corroborate each other.'

Sally noticed the card she was holding, was, like the Bank of England card, written in James Steele's gold handwriting. She read the card out, her voice trembling, 'where officers or deckhands conceal awesome yellow.'

'We've always assumed the answer to that card was the Golden Hind,' said Mackay's father, 'Sir Frances Drake's ship.'

'It doesn't quite fit though does it, Dad,' observed Mackay's sister, 'none of us have ever been happy with that answer.'

Sally was excited. 'Don't you see? It's another clue. You're right with the Golden Hind, in that awesome yellow must mean gold. But could 'or' also mean 'ore,' she hesitated, 'and could the 'officers or deckhands' refer to the men of the Shenandoah, and....wait a minute....look, look what the first letter of each word spells.'

Mackay formed the new word from each letter out loud, 'W.O.O.D.C.A.Y.'

'Wood Cay,' repeated Justice Purcell, 'or Wood Key, it might mean the key to where the 'wooden' boxes are buried. Wood Cay is that island off Nassau, where the Shenandoah hid to evade Federal warships, I read about it yesterday, in Lieutenant Calhoun's letter to his wife.'

'Well, well,' said Bob, 'James Steele was indeed an amateur cryptographer. So there might be another three boxes out there. How much would that be worth?'

Mackay had already done the sums in his head. 'It's around thirty million dollars.'

There was silence as the players of the Great Game of Wealth absorbed their discovery. The fire was low, so Mackay got up and threw on a log. He turned to look at Sally.

She gazed at him, and smiled before speaking. 'It looks like we're going back to Washington via Nassau then.'

Made in the USA
Middletown, DE
30 May 2022

66410128R00154